NOT A GAME ANYMORE

Sal swallowed the lump in his throat and peered at the swaying tree line. The wind's speed increased. Above them, the sky grew darker.

"We're all alone out here," Richard whispered. "This isn't part of the show. This is real."

Another howl echoed from the trees. It was answered by a third, some distance away. The howls were followed by a series of barking grunts and strange hooting, all from different locations. Neither had heard anything like it. Whatever the animals were, it sounded almost as if they were communicating. Then something crashed through the foliage, heading toward the beach.

Sal grabbed Richard's arm. "You're right! What do we do?"

"Run, you dumbass!"

"Where? They're in the jungle—between us and the camp."

"Down the beach, toward the sea. If they're animals, maybe they're afraid of the water."

As they turned to run, a figure emerged from the jungle.

Sal paused. "What the hell is that?"

The creature opened its mouth and roared....

BRIAN
KEENE

CASTAWAYS

LEISURE BOOKS   NEW YORK CITY

This book is dedicated to the memories of Richard Laymon,
Dan "UK" Thomas, and Bruce "Boo" Smith.
We miss you guys...

A LEISURE BOOK®

February 2009

Published by

Dorchester Publishing Co., Inc.
200 Madison Avenue
New York, NY 10016

ISBN 10: 0-8439-6089-2
ISBN 13: 978-0-8439-6089-1
E-ISBN: 1-4285-0600-4

The name "Leisure Books" and the stylized "L" with design are trademarks of Dorchester Publishing Co., Inc.

Printed in the United States of America.

10 9 8 7 6 5 4 3 2 1

Visit us on the web at www.dorchesterpub.com.

ACKNOWLEDGMENTS

As always, thanks to: my family; everyone at Leisure Books; my pre-readers—Tod Clark, Kelli Dunlap, and Mark 'Dezm' Sylva; and to my loyal readers and the members of the F.U.K.U.

And thanks to the following people for various reasons: Valarie Botchlet, Joe Branson, Jesse Carroll, Richard Chizmar, Richard Christy, Geoff Cooper, Brian Freeman, Bob Ford, Mark Hickerson, Michael T. Huyck, Christopher Golden, J. F. Gonzalez, Sal Governale, Jack Haringa, Joe Hill, Scott Ian, Michael Laimo, Ann Laymon, Kelly Laymon, Tim Lebbon, Edward Lee, Bentley Little, Nick Mamatas, Joe Maynard, Regina Mitchell, James A. Moore, Michael Oliveri, Gene O'Neill, Jason Parkin, Tom Piccirilli, Brandon Ramsey, Larry Roberts, Stuart Schiff, David J. Schow, Bryan Smith, Eric Sneddon, Nate Southard, Shane Ryan Staley, Dave Thomas, John Urbancik, Bev Vincent, and Roberta Walsh.

CASTAWAYS

CHAPTER ONE

Becka knew she was going to drown. Gasping, she filled her lungs as another massive wave forced her below the churning turquoise waters. As she plunged downward, all sound ceased, except her heartbeat pounding in her ears. The saltwater irritated her eyes. The light dimmed. Her muscles ached and her lungs burned as she sank lower. Despite the pain, she kicked and thrashed. Bubbles ringed her body like a halo. Becka's headache, which had tormented her for the last few days, throbbed in steady time with her pulse. She'd spent the last two weeks with very little food or water. Now exhaustion, dehydration, and hunger were taking their toll on her.

She should have never applied for *Castaways*. Watching it on TV every week was very different from actually competing in the show. Watching it didn't require pain or sacrifice or pushing your body to its limits.

What was she doing here, drowning in the waters off an uninhabited South Pacific island? Was being on television or a chance at the million-dollar prize

BRIAN KEENE

worth all this? It was insane. She couldn't do this. She'd applied on a whim, never believing she'd actually make the final cut. She'd filled out the online application, but so had a million and a half other people. There was no way she should have been picked. Yet here she was, one of the twenty who'd been selected—a twenty-two-year-old Penn State graduate who still lived with her parents because she couldn't find a job. A month ago, she'd been at home, attending employment fairs and desperately trying to find herself. Find *anything*. Now she was here, in the most beautiful place she'd ever seen, and Becka was so tired and demoralized that she couldn't even enjoy it.

She was tempted to just close her eyes, exhale, and slowly drift to the bottom of the sea. The other people on the island craved fame or notoriety or wealth. Let them have it. She didn't want those anymore. Maybe she had at one point, even if it was just a whim. Otherwise she wouldn't be here. Now all Becka wanted was oblivion—the blessed bliss of unconsciousness. The smothering kiss of death. A very long sleep.

The water felt like a blanket, snuggly and comforting.

Becka closed her eyes and let the blanket engulf her.

. . . *sleep*.

No, fuck that.

Her depressed futility gave way to a sense of frustration and competitiveness. Screw it. She hadn't come all this way just to give up now. She was in this to win. No matter how much she hurt, there was no retreat, no surrender. Not yet. Her family and some of her friends would understand if she quit, but they weren't the only people Becka had to worry about. There were others—the countless, faceless millions on the Internet, eager to log on and share their opinions and critiques on countless trivial pop culture icons, including her. A month ago, she'd been nobody, with a grand total of eight subscribers to her blog. After this aired, her face and name would be recognized by everyone in America who owned a television or read the newspapers. She was a reality television star—or would be, once this aired.

In just a short time, Becka had learned what other public figures before her had known, as well—fame or infamy (because the two were often synonymous) sucked in equal measure. You craved them until you got them, and then you didn't want them anymore.

And she didn't even have them yet.

But there was no going back.

Spurred by anger, Becka gritted her teeth and kicked hard for the surface. A vibrant rainbow of tropical fish darted around her, chased by a grayish white sea snake with prominent dark bands encircling its body. Becka paused. Eyeing the serpent's paddle-shaped tail, she tried to remember if this particular type of sea snake was venomous. Before her arrival, she'd studied the Pacific Islands as best she could, memorizing the flora and fauna. Despite all her preparation, she couldn't recall whether this one was poisonous. Becka gave the sea snake a wide berth, just to be safe. Ignoring her, the serpent continued pursuing the fish. A stingray glided by, oblivious to both Becka and the other marine life, or perhaps indifferent. She stared at it, carefully avoiding the barbed tail.

The aching in her oxygen-starved lungs grew stronger. Above her, Becka saw the wiggling legs of the other castaways. She swam toward them. Her head broke the surface. Coughing, she spat saltwater and gasped for air. Her throat was sore. The sun was blinding. Waves buffeted her about. Another big one almost sank her, but she fought to stay afloat. Blinking the water from her eyes, she glanced around.

A television camera stared back at her.

Ignore it, she thought. *It doesn't exist. Remember that. I'm supposed to pretend it isn't there.*

Becka treaded water next to a small boat. On board were four men—a camera operator, a sound engineer, a field producer, and a pilot—all network employees. As Becka coughed, they merely glanced at her, impassive. They didn't speak or even nod in acknowledgment. Becka drifted away from the craft, debating whether she should break the rules and ask for assistance. Contestants weren't supposed to talk to or interact with the crew unless it was a dire emergency—or unless the crew initiated the contact.

"Think they'll give us a ride?"

Jerry treaded water beside her, droplets rolling off his shaved head and chest. Like Becka, he was in his early twenties and in impressive physical shape. He was cute, and she'd noticed him checking her out several times since they'd arrived on the island two weeks ago. She didn't know much about him—just that he owned a video store in Santa Monica, California. Under different circumstances, Becka might have considered getting to know him better, but

4

there was no time for that out here. It was every man or woman for themselves. Confiding in the wrong person or trusting someone just a little too much led to disaster. After twelve seasons of *Castaways*, even a novice knew that.

"Give us a ride?" She struggled to catch her breath. "You know the rules. Initiating contact with the crew means immediate disqualification from the—"

Jerry held his hands up. "I know, I know. Jesus, Becka, I was just kidding."

Another wave crashed over them. Becka fought to keep from swallowing more water. This wave was smaller than the last, and she managed to stay afloat. The two of them bobbed up on its crest and then back down again as it rolled past.

Three times a week, Becka and the other castaways had to compete against one another in a series of contests and challenges. Sometimes they were physical. Other times the puzzles focused on intelligence and wits, or trivia based on the region where the current game was being played. The winner of the challenge gained temporary access to the circle of protection and was safe until the next challenge. The other castaways would then select someone to exile—meaning the chosen person was ejected from the game. Any contestant was eligible for exile, with the exception of whoever had won the circle of protection.

For today's challenge, they'd been brought offshore by boat and then told that they had to race to shore. Now that Becka had surfaced, the other castaways were swimming away again, leaving just her, Jerry, and the camera crew on the small boat.

Becka frowned. "Shouldn't you be trying to finish the race?"

"It doesn't matter now." Jerry shrugged. "Stefan already won this round."

"Shit."

"Yeah. Pompous Brit bastard. Jeff and Richard were right on his ass the whole way. All three made it to shore at the same time, but Stefan crossed the finish line first. He's got his place in the circle of protection now, so somebody else will have to go home tonight."

"Who?"

"I don't know. Any ideas who you'd like to see gone?"

Becka's response was cut off by another bout of coughing.

"You okay?"

Jerry sounded genuinely concerned. Becka eyed him carefully.

"I don't like the water."

She immediately regretted revealing her weakness to him. Now, if he wanted to, Jerry could exploit it to advance his own standing in the game.

"This?" He grinned, dog-paddling. "This is nothing. Just some minor swells."

"I thought there was a storm coming. That's what one of the crew—Mark, the guy with the mullet—said earlier."

"Maybe." Jerry glanced up at the sky. "But the sun is out and there ain't a cloud in the sky. These aren't storm waves. The sea is choppy, sure, but it's nothing to worry about. I surf waves bigger than this all the time back in Santa Monica. Hang on to me and I'll get us both to shore."

"I'll be okay. It's just . . . I had a bad experience in a swimming pool when I was little. My brother pushed me in the deep end when I was like four years old. The water scares me a little bit, but I'll make it."

The boat's engine throttled up, and the small craft raced ahead. The camera crew's lenses were now trained on Pauline and Roberta. Coughing, Becka watched the two women swimming toward shore and felt a twinge of jealousy. Even Roberta, a middle-aged librarian, was doing better than she was.

"Come on," Jerry insisted. "Let me give you a lift."

Becka hesitated, still not trusting him.

Jerry's grin vanished. "Look, that million dollars isn't going to do you much good if you drown before reaching the island. You're coughing and hacking and obviously worn out. Use your head. The challenge is over, anyway. Stefan already won."

"Yeah," she said. "I guess."

He held out his arm. Becka paused, then took it. His muscles were hard as stone beneath his slippery skin. She shivered and felt a warmness in her belly. If Jerry noticed, he didn't comment on it. Instead, he propelled them forward with strong, confident strokes. They rose and fell on the crests of the waves. Seabirds circled overhead, riding the breeze and squawking incessantly.

The boat slowed, engine idling softly, as it reached Roberta and Pauline. The two women were quite a pair. Roberta, fifty-four, was a librarian at the Ulster County Community College in Poughkeepsie, New York. Pauline, forty-one, was a dancer, model, and former NFL cheerleader from Tampa. Roberta was kind, soft-spoken, and sedate. Pauline was gregarious, manic, and possibly the biggest airhead on the planet—at least, that was what her fellow castaways believed. Still, despite their differences, the two had formed an alliance within their first day on the island. They swam next to Troy, a skinny, tattooed, foul-mouthed auto mechanic from Seattle.

Jerry didn't speak as he guided them toward the beach.

"Are you okay?" Becka asked. "Am I too heavy?"

"No, you're fine. Light as a feather."

She blushed. "That's because we've had nothing to eat at base camp except rice and fish for the last five days."

"Yeah," Jerry agreed. "Lucky for us that Raul and Ryan have been so good at catching fish."

"Lucky for them, too. Keeps them from getting exiled."

"Even so, I'd kill for a pizza right about now."

Becka started to pull away from him. "I think I'm okay now. I've got my breath back, and I don't feel like I'm going to pass out anymore."

"Well, maybe you'd better hold on to me a little longer, just to be safe. You can let go when we reach the boat. That way, they don't capture this on camera. Wouldn't want your boyfriend back home to see this when it airs and get jealous."

"I don't have a boyfriend."

"Really?"

"You sound surprised."

"I am," he admitted. "I figured you'd be fighting guys off with a stick."

Becka blushed again. Before she could respond, they neared the camera boat. One of the crew members had noticed their approach and was beginning to swing the camera back around on them. Becka felt a twinge of regret as she let go of Jerry's arm and began to swim on her own. They drew alongside Roberta, Pauline, and Troy. The rest of the castaways were already on the beach.

"Hey." Roberta waved her hand in greeting. "Looks like Stefan won again."

"We saw," Jerry said. "Which sort of screws up our whole plan. Anyone have any ideas on who to exile from the island instead?"

"We were talking about Jeff," Roberta said. "Thoughts?"

Jerry nodded. "Good choice. He's physically fit, and kicking ass in the challenges. He's definitely a threat."

"But he's so nice," Pauline said, treading water. "Can't we pick someone else? I hate voting to exile the nice guys."

The cameraman leaned over the side of the boat, focusing on their conversation.

"Nice?" Troy smirked. "You mean you think he's hot. Ain't that right?"

Pauline shrugged. "Sure. What's wrong with that?"

"Nothing," Troy said, "except that Jeff's got you and every other chick on this fucking island not voting to exile him because he's a goddamned pretty boy."

"Don't forget Ryan," Becka teased. "He thinks Jeff's pretty cute, too."

Troy poked his cheek out with his tongue and mimed fellatio.

Jerry rolled his eyes. "With your sparkling personality, Troy, I bet you never get exiled."

"Fuck you, baldy."

"Great retort, tough guy."

Scowling, Troy swam ahead of them, muttering a string of curses that grew louder when a strong wave knocked his battered Seahawks cap off his head. Arms flailing, he surged after it. The hat drifted back to Pauline, who plucked it from the water and waved it over her head. Her breasts bounced up and down as she did, and the camera zoomed in on them.

Becka frowned, noticing the leering expression on the crew's faces. No doubt this footage would make it through the editing process and end up on the air.

Pauline held the hat out to Troy.

"Thanks." He reached for it.

Laughing, she jerked the hat back and swam away.

"Hey," Troy shouted. "You're playing with your fucking life, sweetheart!"

He chased after Pauline, and the camera crew followed them, forgetting about the others to remain focused on Pauline's attributes. Somehow her ass stayed above the surface as she swam, and her thong bikini, threadbare from all this time spent outdoors, left little to the imagination. It certainly kept the interest of the four men on the boat. Becka was certain that Pauline was aware of it. So far, her strategy for winning had been to use her sexuality—flirting with the men and playing the helpless damsel in distress, or worse, sucking up to the other women when the men weren't around.

"She's certainly got no problem staying afloat," Becka said. "Wonder how much she paid for those things?"

Jerry laughed. "Remember, all of America might hear you say that."

"No, they won't. The camera crew went chasing off after her."

But even if they didn't hear me, Becka thought, *Roberta did. She and Pauline are pretty tight. If she tells Pauline what I said, and Pauline gets offended, it could be me who gets exiled tonight. Shit! What was I thinking?*

Roberta swam ahead. Frowning, Jerry watched her go. Becka noticed the worried lines on his face.

"What's wrong?"

"We may have just screwed up really bad."

"Why?"

"Pauline and Roberta are part of Stefan's clique. So is Jeff. And we just told them we thought Jeff was a threat and that maybe we should vote to exile him tonight."

"Yes, but they were the ones who brought him up in the first place."

"True. But why? Why would they do that, unless maybe they were testing us? Find out our plans and then report them back to the rest of their alliance."

"Shit."

"Yeah."

A helicopter roared overhead, filming aerial footage of the race. Becka watched it swoop toward land.

11

Over the last two weeks, she'd come to hate the island, but despite the treacherous living conditions, she was still impressed and awed by its beauty. It loomed before them, a foreboding but picturesque mass of rocky hills, dark forest and thick jungle. Towering volcanic mountains descended into blue-green bays and white sandy beaches covered with seashells. Far above the mountain peaks were a few thin clouds, but otherwise the sky was clear. If there was a storm on the way, as Becka had been told, then it was still a long way off.

They swam for shore and caught up with Roberta. Becka continued staring at the island. Jerry and Roberta followed her gaze.

"Pretty, isn't it?" Roberta asked.

Becka nodded, watching the sunlight glint off the highest peaks.

"We don't have anything like it back in Poughkeepsie," Roberta said. "Even if I don't win, it doesn't matter to me anymore. Just seeing this place—just being here—has been worth it. Never in a million years would I have ever thought I'd get to do something like this."

"It looks like something out of *Jurassic Park*," Becka said, eyeing the lush, green tropical foliage.

"Yeah." Jerry flicked water from his eyes. "But on this island, it's not the raptors you have to watch out for. It's our fellow castaways. They're the predators. Everybody's out to get paid. That's why we should form an alliance. What do you say? I'll watch your backs and you guys watch mine. Deal?"

Roberta shrugged. "I've already got an alliance with Pauline, so you'd have to bring her in."

"Do you trust her?"

"Sure," Roberta said. "I mean, she's sort of flighty, but I don't think she's deceitful."

"What about Stefan and Jeff and Raul? Aren't you loyal to them?"

"It's a game, right?"

"Okay," Jerry said. "I'd be up for that. How about you, Becka?"

Becka tried to catch her breath. Exhaustion was creeping back into her muscles.

"Let's focus on getting to shore first."

They reached shallow water and found their footing. Then they waded toward the beach and joined the rest of the contestants, who were killing time while the crew put makeup on the show's host, Roland Thompson. Becka sprawled in the white sand next to Shonette, a twenty-five-year-old single mother of two from Detroit, Michigan, and Ryan, a strikingly handsome, twenty-one-year-old hairstylist from Los Angeles. Jerry joined them after a moment, sitting cross-legged next to Becka. She wondered if he was being friendly, or just waiting for her decision on forming an alliance.

Farther up the beach, Roberta joined Pauline in a game of keep away with Troy's hat. The feisty mechanic was frothing now, letting loose with one string of curse words after another. A few feet away, Sal, a stockbroker from Long Island, and Richard, a drummer from a small town in Kansas, were deeply involved in a hushed conversation. Becka wondered if they were scheming about tonight's choice for exile. Both men were in their thirties, and unlike the other contestants, they seemed to have formed a real friendship during their time on the island, rather than just an acquaintance of convenience.

Beyond them were Stefan, Jeff, and Raul. Stefan was originally Welsh, but had moved to the United States several years ago and now worked as a music producer in Nashville. Jeff was an adventure tour guide from Estes Park, Colorado. Along with Jerry, the two were the most physically fit contestants, and therefore among the most formidable in the challenges. Raul, who hailed from Philadelphia, worked in a machine shop.

And finally, standing apart from the rest of the group was Matthew, a lanky, dirty twenty-eight-year-old from the small town of Red Lion, Pennsylvania. The laconic loner didn't interact much with the other castaways, and his rat-faced features seemed frozen in a perpetual scowl. In Becka's opinion, the only reason he hadn't been exiled yet was because he was so uninvolved with the other players that he was often forgotten when it came time to vote. Currently, he was drawing stick figures in the sand with a six-foot length of bamboo. He'd used the implement as a walking stick since their second day on the island, sharpening one end against the rocks to form a makeshift spear. He took it with him everywhere, even slept with it. Becka had to give him credit, though. Matthew's spear had come in handy a few times. He'd used it to catch fish in some of the island's shallower pools.

Missing was a girl named Sheila, who had forfeited her position in the game the day before due to a medical emergency. She'd fallen out of a tree while trying to pick coconuts and had broken her leg.

Unable to compete, she'd decided to quit and was now back on the ship with the other contestants who'd already been exiled. Becka grew maudlin, remembering Sheila. She'd liked her, and although they weren't friends, the two had gotten along well.

All the contestants did their best to ignore the cameras flitting among them, filming their every word and action. More crew members worked on Roland Thompson's hair and clothing, making sure the host looked his best before going back on camera again. He sat removed from the contestants, occupying a small pavilion above the high-tide line. As a longtime *Castaways* viewer, Becka was secretly disappointed with Roland. On television, he was charming and witty and handsome. Here, in reality, he was haggard, cranky, and usually sipping a gin and tonic. He stank of cologne, cigar smoke, and sweat. When he was actually on the island, he spent much of his off-camera time hitting on Pauline.

The beach was noisy. Snatches of conversation blended with the shrieks of seabirds as they circled overhead or darted across the sand looking for crabs. The waves crashed against the shore. Farther inland, the treetops rustled in the breeze.

As Becka watched, Troy succeeded in reclaiming his hat and gave a victorious, profanity-laden cheer. Pauline began stretching, bending over to touch her toes and then reaching for the sky. She brushed grains of sand from her coffee-colored skin. Becka frowned. Her own skin was blotchy and peeling from overexposure to the elements, while Pauline's stayed smooth and unblemished. As Pauline's acrobatics continued, Raul, Sal, and Richard openly leered at her, while Jeff and Stefan cast furtive glances in her direction. Troy seemed oblivious. Ryan was checking out Jeff, rather than Pauline. And Matthew . . .

Matthew was also staring at Pauline, but his expression was one of contempt.

Despite the warm sun on her skin, Becka shivered. She glanced at Jerry to see if he was also captivated by Pauline's aerobics, then wondered why she cared. Even so, she felt relieved when he turned his attention to her and smiled.

"When this airs," he said, "I'll be amazed if Troy gets any screen time."

"Why?"

"Because they'll have to bleep everything he says. Dude swears more than a sailor."

Becka, Ryan, and Shonette laughed. Noticing them, Troy walked over and joined the group. He plopped down onto the sand and scowled. Becka studied the tattoos covering his forearms, back, and chest. Most of them were basic black, and the ink had faded in spots.

"What's wrong?" Shonette asked him. "You got your hat back."

"I need a fucking cigarette," Troy said. "Thirty days of this shit without a fucking smoke? What the hell was I thinking, man?"

Jerry brushed white sand from his forearms. "Why didn't you just bring some cigarettes as your one luxury item?"

"Because the fuckers at the network made me pick between my hat and my smokes."

"But a hat is clothing," Becka said.

"They didn't see it that way, and I don't go anywhere without my fucking hat."

"Why not?" Jerry asked.

"Because it's my lucky fucking hat!" Troy's tone was incredulous, as if Jerry should have already known that. "I've traveled all over the fucking place, and this hat is the only thing that's been with me each and every time."

"You're from Seattle, right?" Becka asked.

"Yeah. But I moved around a lot. I was born in New York. Brackard's Point, armpit of the fucking world. Me and my older brother, Sherm, ran away from home when I was fourteen. Our parents didn't give a fuck. We went from New York to Florida, and stayed there for a while. Then we lived in fucking Texas. Then Wisconsin, which was even worse than fucking Texas. Eventually, we ended up in Seattle. Been there ever since. My hat stayed with me the whole fucking time."

"It's funny," Jerry said. "Seeing as how you've lived in Seattle for so long, I would think you'd be craving a Starbucks caramel macchiato rather than cigarettes."

Troy scowled. "And you'd be wrong. I hate that fucking shit. Starbucks tastes like hot cat piss. Whatever happened to just plain old coffee? Black, no flavors or fancy names that sound like French and Italian run through a fucking meat grinder? This country is going down the fucking tubes. Not every person from Seattle is a Starbucks-loving asshole. I hate Starbucks. Give me fucking Folgers any day of the week. If I want vanilla, I'll eat some fucking ice cream. You know what I'm saying?"

"I guess so." Jerry shrugged. "I kind of like their iced cappuccinos."

"So," Becka said, trying to change the subject, "I bet your brother will be pretty excited to see you on TV, then?"

Troy lowered his head and stared at the sand. "Not really. Dumbass got in trouble a few years back and had to bail. Moved his ass to Pennsylvania and got shot during a fucking bank robbery."

"I'm sorry."

"Don't be. It was his fault. Stupid son of a bitch. He was always doing crazy shit like that. You should have seen what he got up to in Seattle."

Sensing that Troy's mood had soured even more than normal, Becka tried to distract him again by returning to the original subject. "You could have hidden some cigarettes underneath your hat."

"Nah," Troy said. "Wouldn't have worked. They checked us all pretty good. What'd you bring as your luxury item?"

Becka blushed. "My diary."

"No shit? That's cool."

"I've been keeping them since I was a little girl."

Troy turned to Jerry, Ryan, and Shonette. "What'd you guys bring?"

Before they could answer, Stuart, one of the field producers, grabbed a battery-powered megaphone and shouted directions.

"Okay, everyone, if you could please gather together here, we're ready."

The contestants made their way to a large makeshift stage that the construction crew had built before filming commenced. The stage was lined with bamboo torches and authentic native masks and carvings. Above it, out of sight of the cameras, were rows of lights, microphones, and other equipment. The group gathered on the stage after each contest and when they voted on who to exile from the game. In the center of the stage was an ornate white circle, painted directly onto the planks—the Circle of Protection. When it was time to vote, whoever had won the previous contest stood in the center of the circle, granting them immunity from exile. The contestant who was exiled had to leave the island immediately and join the game's other losers on the network's ship, a large freighter floating off shore that housed the camera and sound people, helicopter pilots, medical personnel, the director, Roland, and all the show's other crew members.

When they were all onstage, arranged in a semicircle, Stuart flashed a cue, and Roland Thompson strolled across the sand toward them. A camera filmed his approach. He was dressed in a safari outfit, and when he smiled, his capped teeth gleamed in the sunlight. There were dark sweat stains beneath his armpits, but Becka knew now that the producers would edit those out before the show aired.

"Prissy fucker," Troy muttered. "I'd like to see *him* spend a night in this fucking place."

Becka and Jerry stifled their laughter.

"Hello, everyone." Roland's deep baritone boomed across the stage. "And congratulations to Stefan, who won today's challenge."

"Thank you." Stefan smiled, flashing his own perfectly capped teeth. "I never had any doubt."

"As you know," Roland continued, "the last

castaway to leave this island will go home with one million dollars. You are now one step closer to that prize, Stefan. Tonight, weather permitting, you will stand in the Circle of Protection, and one of your fellow castaways will go home. The rest of you have until sundown to figure out who that will be. Head on back to base camp, and we'll see you tonight."

Roland began to turn around, but Richard raised his hand. The host called on him, visibly annoyed.

He probably can't wait to get back to the ship, Becka thought. *Sit in the air-conditioning with his feet up and have a drink. Or take a shower. God, what I wouldn't give for a hot shower.*

"I noticed that you said 'weather permitting,'" Richard said. "Any word on the storm? There was a rumor going around that a cyclone might be coming."

Roland glanced at Stuart, motioning for him to join them. The assistant producer stepped forward and cleared his throat. The cameraman and sound engineer turned off their equipment.

"There is indeed a tropical storm warning," Stuart confirmed. "But as far as we know, it's not going to amount to much, at least not here. It's currently tracking farther north. We've got a staff meteorologist back on board the ship keeping an eye on things, and he'll let all of us know if things change. They've named the storm Ivan, if that matters to any of you."

"So what if it does hit?" Shonette asked. "That mean you're gonna pull us off the island until it passes?"

Stuart smiled. "As I said, we're keeping a watch

on things, and if the situation changes, we'll let you know. Now head on back to base camp. We'll have more information for you tonight, after exile."

They filed off the stage and began walking along the beach, heading toward their camp. Becka noticed that everyone had split off into subgroups. Sal and Richard walked together, laughing at some private joke. Stefan, Jeff, Raul, Pauline, and Roberta celebrated Stefan's victory as a group. So much for Roberta and Pauline switching alliances. Jerry had been right to worry. Becka glanced from side to side. Ryan, Jerry, Shonette, and Troy walked next to her.

Our own little cabal, she thought.

Jerry must have been thinking the same thing.

"That's trouble." He nodded at the group in front of them. "Stefan and the rest of the big dogs. Unless we come together, they can start picking us off one by one. There's five of them and five of us. If we make an alliance and get Sal and Richard to vote with us, we can come out on top."

"Count me in," Ryan agreed. "I say we exile Jeff."

"I thought you had the hots for him," Becka said.

Ryan shrugged. "Sure, he's cute and all, but this is a million dollars we're talking about."

The others laughed.

"I'm in, too," Shonette whispered. "And I bet you can convince Roberta to switch sides."

"Yeah," Jerry said, "we talked to her earlier. She wouldn't commit to anything, though. In fact, I'm a little worried that she might rat us out to Stefan and the others."

"She wouldn't do that," Shonette said. "Pauline might, but not Roberta."

"We'll see." Jerry turned to Troy. "How about you?"

Troy shrugged. "Fuck it."

"Is that a yes?"

Troy shrugged again. "It ain't a fucking no, dude. Yes, I'm in."

The cameras filmed it all.

"Aren't you forgetting someone?" Ryan asked.

Jerry frowned. "Who?"

Ryan glanced back over their shoulders. Matthew trailed after the group, slinking along behind the camera crew.

"Yeah," Jerry said. "I guess I did forget about him, after all. Kind of easy to do. He never says anything."

"He's flying under the radar," Shonette said. "Hoping that if he doesn't get noticed, he won't get exiled from the game."

Troy snorted. "He's a fucking weirdo. Always watching people. Like a snake. Dude never fucking blinks."

Becka turned, and sure enough, Matthew was staring at them. His expression was sullen.

She moved a little closer to Jerry, feeling Matthew's eyes crawl over her exposed skin.

They continued along the beach, unaware that other eyes were watching them from beneath the jungle's greenery, as well.

CHAPTER TWO

The males of the tribe crouched, hidden within the foliage, watching the intruders as they walked along the beach. The tribe's females and few young were hidden in the caves, where they'd been since the strangers first arrived. Both had to be guarded. With each passing year, the females bore less young, and many of the newborns were severely deformed and unfit to live.

The tribe did not like the newcomers. They were noisy and destructive, and had chased away much of the island's wildlife. Their unfamiliar scent wafted through the jungle, souring everything it came in contact with.

The tribe had watched them from the shadows since their arrival, studying and learning, unsure whether the intruders were predators or prey. At first, the tribe members were afraid. Like them, the newcomers walked on two legs, but they were clearly not the same. There were far more differences than similarities. The intruders' bodies were mostly hairless, except for a few of the males who had a sparse covering of hair on their chests and backs—but nothing like the thick, curly hair covering the males of the tribe. The hairless ones' heads were bigger, but their brows weren't quite as sloped as the island's inhabitants. Their feet weren't as broad, nor were their lower jaws. While the tribe members could crack a coconut with their teeth, the strangers had to use rocks to penetrate the hull. They were much taller, and their language was different. Most bizarrely, they covered their bodies in a colorful, unknown material—not animal skins, or at least, not the hide of anything that lived on the island. They used strange and frightening tools, the purpose of which the tribe couldn't discern.

Perhaps the new arrivals were distant cousins—a missing tribe from far-off shores. The tribe members knew that other islands existed somewhere beyond the vast waters that surrounded them. Occasionally, debris washed up on the beach—items native to the island. And their legends told of a race of hairless visitors who had arrived on the island many generations ago, crossing the water on long, hollowed-out trees. The strangers had spoken an odd language. They carried shiny sticks that were harder and sharper than stone, and had spears that belched smoke and flame. Eventually the tribe's ancestors determined the newcomers were a threat and had slain them all. From that point on, whenever strangers arrived on the island, they were met in the same manner, until eventually the others stopped coming.

Now a similar decision faced this new generation of tribe members.

After a week of observation, their fears and

misgivings had given way to cautious urgency. The tribe was overcome with conflicting desires. Clearly, the strangers were a threat to the island's ecosystem. Their continued presence was throwing everything off balance. If the tribe did not act, and soon, its entire existence could be in jeopardy.

The time for watching was over. It was time to act.

Leaving a few sentries behind to keep track of the intruders, the tribe withdrew to the island's center. In a deep, hidden valley they used for important gatherings, the males hooted and grunted among themselves in their guttural language. Finally the elder stood and hissed for attention. The others fell silent, eyeing him with respect. His body was covered in thick, silver hair, and long, ragged scars from old battles crisscrossed his massive arms and chest. Despite his age, the chieftain was still strong and had almost all his teeth. He was a formidable opponent, and the few younger males who had dared to challenge him for leadership had been torn apart at his hands.

Growling, the elder pronounced judgment.

Meat was scarce. For generations, the tribe had supplemented their diet of fruit, bark, and plants with birds, turtles, snakes, insects, spiders, crabs, and whatever sea creatures happened to wash up onshore. There had once been wild pigs on the island, or so they'd been told, but none of those living had ever seen one, or knew what they tasted like. For reference, they only had the pictures, drawn on the cave walls by their ancestors.

The males among the hairless newcomers would

be caught, killed, and eaten. Perhaps they would taste like pig. Perhaps not. In either case, they would fill bellies. The tribe had long kept the practice of eating their own dead, when sickness, injury, or old age took them. This would not be so different. In fact, the new arrivals might taste better. They appeared well fed, for the most part. Many of them had succulent layers of fat around their abdomens.

The females would be taken to the caves as breeders. If they could not bear children, or if the fruit of their wombs was defective, then they would be eaten, too, along with the deformed infants.

The wind blew in from the sea, and the treetops rustled and swayed.

The elder raised his tiny head and sniffed the air. The breeze ruffled his hair. He knew from experience that a storm was coming—more proof that the intruders had upset the natural balance.

They would act tonight, under cover of the darkness and the weather. They would be swift and merciless. And then they would feast.

On the island, the night had teeth.

CHAPTER THREE

The contestants made their way back to the base camp, followed by camera operators and sound technicians. They reached a point along the beach where a narrow trail cut into the jungle, and they turned toward it. The path was only wide enough for three people to walk side by side at a time, and Becka noticed that everyone continued to stick to their various cliques. One crew member took the lead, walking backward and filming the procession. Becka was surprised he didn't trip.

Sal and Richard walked slightly ahead of the others. Becka couldn't hear their conversation, but both men were snickering. She wondered what they were talking about. Stefan, Jeff, Raul, Pauline, and Roberta strolled along behind them, but Roberta was just a few steps behind the others. Becka wondered if maybe Jerry and Shonette were right. Maybe Roberta could be swayed over to their side, after all.

A few more crew members—Mark, Jesse, and Stuart—followed Stefan's group, recording their conversation. Ryan and Shonette were in front of

Jerry and Becka. Troy stumbled behind them, slapping at mosquitoes.

Becka glanced over her shoulder. Matthew trudged along silently with his spear, keeping several yards' distance between himself and the rest of the group. He stared straight ahead, as if trying to bore a hole between Troy's shoulder blades with his eyes. His face was expressionless. Another cameraman brought up the rear.

The network's construction crew had built the path. It was outlined with lime, so the contestants could see it at night. (For safety reasons, midnight strolls through the jungle were discouraged, unless, of course, it was for something that would bring in ratings.) Bamboo handrails were positioned at swampy or hilly spots. But despite the conveniences, the dense tropical undergrowth crowded the path on both sides. As they walked, Becka noticed how still the jungle was. Normally, the terrain was alive with insects and birds. The trees and sky were usually filled with parrots, albatrosses, honeyeaters, frigates, gulls, and boobies. At times, their noise was almost deafening. Now there was only silence.

Jerry paused, staring into the dense jungle. Becka and Troy stopped with him.

"What is it?" Becka asked. "Is something wrong?"

"I don't know. Hear that? It's quiet. No birds, nothing. Just silence."

"I was just thinking the same thing. Maybe the helicopter scared them all away?"

"Maybe," Jerry agreed.

Troy slapped another mosquito. "Or maybe these fucking bugs got them all. Swear to Christ,

I'm down a fucking pint of blood. I don't weigh but a buck-oh-five to begin with. By the time this is over, I'll be nothing but fucking bones."

Grinning, Becka and Jerry started forward again.

"So, do you have a girlfriend?" Becka immediately regretted asking.

"No," Jerry replied. "But I'm always on the lookout. I figure that once I win the million dollars, finding a girlfriend will be a little easier."

"That's why you wanted an alliance," she teased, "so you could win."

Jerry feigned surprise. "Well, why else would we form an alliance?"

"I don't know. It would be nice to have someone to trust."

"Yes, it would," Jerry agreed. "But an alliance doesn't mean you'd be able to trust me. What if we play the game all the way to the end and avoid getting exiled, and then it comes down to you or me? What then?"

Becka grinned. "Then I'd have to kick your butt and win the million. But don't worry, I'd give you a loan."

"Thanks."

Ahead of them, Shonette let out a frightened squeal. All the contestants stopped walking. Ryan and Shonette stared at the ground. Shonette stumbled backward, pointing.

"What the hell is that?"

Mark and Jesse jostled past the others. Mark trained his camera on the disturbance and Jesse leaned closer with his microphone.

The group gathered around them. Only Matthew

remained in the background, leaning on his spear and looking disinterested. Troy pressed up behind Becka, craning his neck to see, and accidentally shoved her forward. She recoiled in disgust.

In the center of the path was a small, wormlike creature, as thick as a pencil and about eight inches long. It was so small that Becka was amazed Shonette had noticed it at all. The creature was gray and pink in color, with ugly splotches along its length. The thing's head was not offset from its body, and Becka couldn't tell which end was which. She peered closer and saw two tiny black dots on one end—the creature's eyes. The worm wiggled back and forth. Becka thought back to the research she'd done on the region before leaving home, but didn't recognize the wriggling creature.

"What the hell is it?" Shonette asked again.

"Disgusting," Ryan said. "That's what it is."

"It's a fucking worm," Troy said. "What's the big deal? Step on it. Or better yet, eat the fucker."

"Oh, man," Raul moaned. "You'd eat a worm, dog?"

Pauline scowled, hands on hips. "That's gross."

Troy shrugged. "Hey, we're all sick of eating rice, right?"

"I think I'll stick with rice," Roberta said. "It doesn't move when you eat it."

"I'd eat a worm," Richard said, in his slow Kansas-drawl. "I used to eat possums and squirrels and groundhogs. A worm ain't much different. I bet it tastes just like chicken. Maybe put a little barbeque sauce on it."

Sal nudged him. "You'd eat shit if somebody paid you five bucks to do it."

"Yeah," Richard agreed. "You got five bucks on you?"

"It's not a worm," Stefan said. "Unlike some of you, I prepared for this contest by familiarizing myself with our locale. I did my homework."

Troy yawned. "Well, aren't you just fucking special?"

"I'll certainly outlast you, you foul-mouthed little troglodyte."

Troy turned to Richard. "What'd he just call me?"

Richard shrugged. "I'm not sure. Nothing good."

"No," Jerry whispered in agreement, "it wasn't."

Becka considered telling Stefan that she'd done her homework as well, but decided to keep quiet. There was no sense in drawing attention to herself. Otherwise, she might be the next one exiled.

"Anyway," Stefan said, "this isn't a worm. It's called a blind snake."

"A snake?" Roberta knelt for a closer look. "But it's so small."

"Well, this one is rather large, all things considered. Probably an adult. They rarely exceed twelve inches in length, if I remember correctly."

"Is it poisonous?" Jeff asked.

"Not at all. They're timid creatures. Harmless, unless you're an ant or a termite, like our friend Troy here."

"Fuck you, motherfucker."

"No, thank you. You're a bit too greasy for my tastes."

31

"You think you're better than me, Stefan? Is that it?"

Stefan rolled his eyes. "Heavens no. I'm sure you make valuable contributions to society."

"I bend wrenches for a living. Maybe I'll take one upside your head when we get home."

"You'll get there before me. I *will* be the last person left on this island."

"Not if we cook you and eat you first, you yuppie fuck."

Ignoring him, Stefan turned his attention back to the blind snake. "Interestingly enough, they're an all-female species."

Ryan peered at the snake. "What does that mean?"

"It means that they lay eggs without the benefit of a male snake to fertilize them."

"Where's the fun in that?" Pauline asked.

The men laughed obligingly at Pauline's joke, and Becka gritted her teeth to keep from responding. A dozen different sarcastic replies came to mind. She glanced at Shonette, who rolled her eyes.

The group began to split up again. Stefan, Jeff, Raul, Pauline, and Roberta walked on, along with half the crew. Jerry pulled Sal and Richard aside, and watched until the others had disappeared around a turn in the path. Then he gathered Sal, Richard, Troy, Shonette, and Ryan together. Mark and Jesse remained behind as well, filming their discussion.

Becka tugged on Jerry's shoulder. He leaned close.

"What about Matthew?" she whispered.

Jerry glanced over at the loner. Matthew stood apart from the group, staring off into the jungle. Jerry sighed.

"Matthew, you want to join us for a second?"

Shrugging, he stepped forward.

"Here's the thing," Jerry said. "Stefan, Jeff, Raul, Pauline, and Roberta have a pretty strong alliance. We think we may be able to pull Roberta, but the others are sticking together. Stefan and Jeff need to go. They present a physical threat in the challenges."

Troy interrupted. "Not to mention Stefan is an asshole."

"Yes," Jerry agreed. "There's that, too. And after what just happened, I think it's a good bet that he's gunning for you tonight. Let's make sure he doesn't get the opportunity."

"How?" Richard asked.

"Me, Becka, Shonette, Ryan, and Troy were talking. There's five people in their alliance. We were thinking maybe you guys would want to join us. You, too, Matthew, if you like. We don't know for sure who they're going to vote for tonight, of course. It'll probably be whoever Stefan says. Like I said, I'm guessing Troy."

"I heard them talking earlier," Sal said. "It *is* Troy."

"That motherfucker!" Troy yanked his hat from his head and threw it on the ground. "So he was planning this shit even before he talked smack just now?"

Sal nodded. "Looks that way."

"Stefan's untouchable," Jerry said. "He's got the circle of protection—for now, at least. But if you guys join up with us, we could exile Jeff tonight. That would leave Stefan's alliance weaker. Then we could start picking them off one by one. We could take out Stefan next week."

"Unless he wins another challenge," Richard said.

"If he does," Shonette replied, "then we exile Pauline or Raul."

"Exactly," Jerry said. "If we can't get to Stefan, we can at least take out his supporters. Leave him vulnerable. That's gonna fuck with his head, and then he'll start slipping up."

Sal frowned. "Okay, but what happens once we've exiled all of them? You realize we'll have to turn on each other then, right?"

"Well," Jerry said, "it *is* a game, right? No hard feelings at that point. Agreed?"

Sal and Richard glanced at each other, then back to Jerry.

"Fuck it," Sal said. "I'm in."

Richard nodded. "Yeah, let's do it."

Jerry turned to the others. "You guys still up for this?"

Troy picked up his hat, brushed off the dirt, and plopped it back on his head.

"Fuck that fucking fuck. Let's exile his ass, and all his little fucking cronies, too."

Ryan laughed. "I'm with Troy."

"Let's do it," Shonette said.

They all turned to Becka.

"Okay," she said. "Sounds like a plan, I guess."

"Matthew?" Jerry smiled. "Will you help us?"

"Sure." His voice was a sullen monotone. "For now. But this doesn't make us friends. Like you said, it's a game. Stefan and Jeff are the most immediate threats. Taking them out will level the playing field."

"The enemy of my enemy is my friend?"

Matthew's smile was tight-lipped. "Something like that."

"Gotta admit," Jerry said, "you didn't strike me as the type of guy who reads Sun Tzu's *The Art of War*."

Matthew's smile vanished. "That's because you don't know anything about me. None of you do."

He raised his bamboo spear, pushed past the group, and trudged away. They watched him go, shaking their heads.

"Nice guy," Ryan whispered.

Troy began slapping mosquitoes again. "Dude's an asshole, if you ask me. Not as much as Stefan, maybe, but still . . ."

"Well," Jerry said, "as long as he keeps his word with us and helps take down their alliance, I don't care what he does. We can exile him after we finish with the others."

Tired, hungry, thirsty, and pestered by mosquitoes, they plodded along the trail, making their way back to the base camp.

As she walked, Becka got that weird feeling of being watched again. She tried to ignore it. Although she'd never admit it to the other contestants, the island was pretty spooky at night, and even during the day, if she happened to be off by herself. As a result, she tried to stay close to the others—or at least near the base camp. Maybe it was just her imagination, or perhaps it was the island's local lore. Upon their arrival, Roland had filled them in on its history. Tradition held that the island was haunted. The region had been populated for over seven thousand years, but in all that time, the island had remained uninhabited because the natives from the surrounding islands avoided it at all costs. Legends were passed on from each generation to the next that many of the caves scattered across the island were actually mouths leading into the underworld. A tribe of small, inhuman creatures were said to emerge from these caves to rape or devour anything in their path. Unlike the Indonesian folktales of the little people of Flores—cave-dwelling South Seas leprechauns who accepted gourds full of food that the Floresians set out for them as offerings—the diminutive creatures on this island were said to be savage and demonic.

Over the years, various traders, explorers, and adventurers from as far away as Europe and America had vanished in the region. There was also the legend of the *Martinique*, a merchant vessel that had anchored on the island in the early 1900s. The crew had supposedly stayed one night on the beach and then fled, swearing never to return. And a Japanese squadron had disappeared in the vicinity during World War II. According to several television documentaries, they crashed on or near the island and were never heard from again. Supposedly their spirits still haunted the jungle.

Becka knew that Roland had told them this as part of the show—a bit of local color to enthrall the viewers—but that didn't make her feel any better late at night when she was lying in the darkness, listening to the jungle.

And it didn't make her feel better now.

Jerry tapped her shoulder. "Earth to Becka. Penny for your thoughts?"

"Sorry. I was just thinking about our first day here—all the stuff Roland told us."

"I liked that part," Jerry said. "The celebration they threw for us onboard the freighter? That was cool."

Becka nodded, remembering. Before they'd been transported to the island, the network had treated them to a welcoming party on the ship. Natives from neighboring islands were brought in to share their culture and traditions. There was a great feast and live music, and the contestants were treated to displays of dancing, tattooing, wood carving, and other regional pastimes. She'd especially been enamored of the women's colorful tribal garb.

"Yeah," she said, not telling Jerry that hadn't been what she was thinking about, "it was pretty cool, wasn't it?"

"It was," Jerry agreed. "Even if I don't win, I'll never forget that. I mean, how often do you get to experience something like that? We're very lucky to have been picked. Good thing we fit the stereotypes."

"What do you mean?"

"Oh, come on. Think about it. You've seen past seasons, haven't you? Each of us is here because we fit a certain profile the producers were looking for. We've got a black guy, a black girl, an older woman, a hick, a handsome stud, the bad boy, a yuppie, a gay guy, a hot chick, and you—the pretty, nice girl next door."

Becka blushed. "And you're the handsome stud?"

"Me?" Now it was Jerry's turn to blush. "No, I'm just the regular dude."

"Goddamn," Troy muttered behind them. "I really need a fucking smoke. You two are so fucking sweet, you're gonna send me into a diabetic coma."

They turned to glare at him, but then realized that Troy was laughing. He winked conspiratorially and after a moment, they laughed, too. The noise disturbed a roosting parrot, who voiced its displeasure.

They walked on.

Once more, Becka felt eyes on her, but when she glanced around, it was just the camera, filming everything they did.

Chapter Four

The base camp offered few luxuries. Rustic and simple, it consisted of a large structure built of bamboo, rocks, and leaves—basically a roof held up by poles, with walls manufactured from branches and palm fronds. It had two open-air doors. There was a similar construction that served as a latrine, a hole in the ground to catch rainwater, and a fire pit made of stones. The contestants had built it all themselves during their first few days on the island. When not competing in contests, exploring their surroundings, or lying on the beach, they spent their time at the camp, as did the camera crew.

But while the castaways had to remain on the island, the crew was allowed to return to the relative comforts aboard the ship when off duty. They worked in eight-hour shifts, covering the contestants twenty-four hours a day, even when the castaways were sleeping. There were nine, three-person camera crews, consisting of a "shooter," sound technician, and field producer. Three of the crews were on the island at a time, along with at least two emergency medical technicians. There were also crew members the contestants never saw or had little interaction with—construction workers and various people from the production office. The audience would never realize these people had been involved with the production, because the producers did such a good job of presenting the *Castaway* contestants as being on a remote island by themselves.

The network helicopter shuttled the crew members back and forth. When not working, they had a wide variety of amenities aboard the freighter, ranging from video games and first-run movies to a swimming pool and full-service spa. While they dined on lobster, steak, and pasta each night in the ship's galley, those left on the island made do with rice—the only food provided by the show's producers. While the crew slept in comfortable, two-person cabins, the contestants huddled together, shivering in the darkness. The ship was equipped with a state-of-the-art communications center and wireless internet, so that network employees could stay in touch with their loved ones. It also had a laundry, medical staff, counselor, and even a nondenominational clergyman who held services every Sunday.

The contestants who had already been exiled from the game were also allowed to enjoy these luxuries—a small comfort after losing their chance at a million dollars.

Mark Hickerson, Jesse Carroll, and Stuart Schiff were all reality television veterans, and they'd each been with *Castaways* since its first season. Mark, who hailed from Tennessee and whose blond hair frequently took first place in mullet contests, was a shooter, or camera operator. Jesse, the sound engineer, was from Florida. He played guitar in a band and enjoyed collecting rare books in his spare time. Stuart split his time between his hometown of Binghamton, New York, and Los Angeles, and had worked his way up the ranks over the past few seasons to become a field producer. Network gossip pegged him as the next big thing—the future wunderkind of reality programming and becoming executive producer of his own show. All agreed that he'd more than earned the opportunity.

While the other crew members hovered around the contestants, filming their every action and word, the three men huddled together in the undergrowth near a small, weatherproofed storage shed used by the crew to house tools and equipment. The shed was close to the base camp, but hidden in the trees so that it didn't appear in any footage, thus ruining the viewer's illusion.

Stuart was involved in a conversation with the ship via satellite phone. Mark and Jesse occupied themselves by discussing the technical aspects of other reality shows and how they compared to *Castaways*.

"You ever watch the one where they compete to see who can lose the most weight?" Mark spoke quietly so as not to disrupt Stuart.

"Yeah," Jesse said. "The season finale was fucking painful, man. It should have been the biggest show of the season, but it was shit. Whoever the network has producing that show should be getting water-boarded at Guantanamo Bay right now and never be allowed to work in television again."

"Why's that?"

"Well, it's the season finale, right? And they announce the winner. They do it live, just like us. And when the big moment comes, instead of showing the winner's face, they pull back and do a wide pan of the audience. The poor guy who won is crying and showing all this emotion, and instead of zooming in on that, they cut to the host."

Mark shook his head. "That's pretty bad."

Jesse was about to respond when Stuart clipped his satellite phone back onto his belt and looked at them. His expression was worried.

"What's wrong?" Jesse asked.

"The meteorologist says the storm might change course, after all."

Mark and Jesse glanced at each other and simultaneously said, "Shit."

"Yeah," Stuart agreed. "And speaking of which, I really wish you hadn't let that slip to the contestants earlier, Mark."

"What else did they say?" Mark asked, ignoring the reprimand.

Stuart shrugged. "A lot of technical stuff about thermal currents interacting with the various jet streams and how that might produce hurricane-force winds."

"Just to be clear," Jesse said, "we're talking about a cyclone here, right?"

"Right. Its name is Ivan—I think that means 'a real pain in the ass.'"

Jesse frowned. "Not to put too fine of a point on this, but cyclones are air currents with a swirling pattern, right? Like what took Dorothy to Oz?"

"On land," Stuart said. "But this is on the water."

"Well, then why would they call it a cyclone? It's the air masses themselves, not the water currents and such, right? Seems to me like they'd call this Hurricane Ivan or Typhoon Ivan. Tropical Cyclone Ivan just doesn't have a ring to it."

"They should call it Bob," Mark suggested. "That's always a good name. If I ever get another dog, I'm gonna name him Bob. It sounds friendly."

Stuart rubbed his temples and sighed. "We're getting a little off track here, guys. I don't know why they call it what they do. I'm not a weatherman. All I know is what they tell me."

"Sorry," Mark apologized.

"Yeah," Jesse said. "Sorry about that, man. So what's the network want us to do?"

"Well, they're still not sure if the storm itself is gonna hit us or not. It may just skirt us and head farther north. It's moving quick and defying all their computer models. But at the very least, we'll have some killer winds tonight. Because of that, the pilots are refusing to fly, unless there's a medical emergency on the island or something like that. So the producers have decided to hold off on tonight's exile vote. We'll do it tomorrow night, once Ivan has passed on. The last chopper is leaving in twenty minutes."

"Well," Mark said, "let's get going, then, so we don't miss it."

"Yeah," Jesse agreed. "At least we won't have to be stuck here tonight."

"That's where you're wrong. Even though they're recalling all nonessential personnel back to the freighter, the producers want a skeleton crew to stay behind with the contestants."

43

Mark flinched. "They're leaving the castaways here?"

"Yep."

"Is that even legal?"

Stuart nodded. "Apparently, the network lawyers seem to think so. And you've got to admit, if the storm *does* hit here, it will make for some great drama. Somebody needs to capture that footage—and the castaways' reactions to it all. That's why they want a skeleton crew on hand."

"How many?" Jesse asked.

Stuart held up three fingers. "Field producer, shooter, and sound tech. They're even sending the EMTs back to the freighter."

"One crew for everything," Jesse said. "That's a tall order."

Mark sighed. "Poor bastards."

Stuart didn't respond.

"Wait." Jesse groaned. "Let me guess. That skeleton crew is us?"

"Bingo."

"But our shift is over this afternoon, Stuart."

"Yeah, but they're evacuating everyone now, and since we're already here at base camp, we drew the unlucky straws. I'm letting everyone else go, but you guys need to stay with me. I need professionals—people I trust to get the job done. And don't start quoting union regulations at me, either. You guys know basic first-aid, in case things get hairy. Plus, you've both been with the show long enough to know the drill. This is what you signed on for."

"Screw that," Mark said. "Getting bit by a snake

or stung by a scorpion is one thing. Sitting around waiting for a cyclone to hit is a whole other ball of wax."

"We'll be fine," Stuart insisted. "Believe me, I don't like it any more than you guys. But it is what it is. I know I can trust you both to get the job done. You're the most competent crew members we have. I'll make sure you guys get taken care of—some kind of recognition for your dedication above and beyond the call of duty and all that shit."

Jesse rotated his finger in a circle. "Whoopee."

Scowling, Mark stuck a twig in his mouth and stared at the horizon.

"And besides," Stuart said, "maybe Pauline will sleep in the nude again tonight. You guys weren't on duty last time she did that."

Both men grinned. They'd seen the raw footage of Pauline in the buff. It was a popular choice in the editing room onboard the ship.

"So when do we inform them?" Mark cocked his thumb over his shoulder at the contestants.

"Now. And make sure you film it, because their reactions should make for great footage. We'll send the rest of the crew back to the landing zone, so they can evacuate. Then we've got some other scheduled shoots while there's still daylight and before the weather gets bad. We need to do some one-on-one interviews with Matthew, Roberta, and Stefan. We need to get some stock footage of Matthew and Roberta, because what we have so far isn't that useful. Also, I'm noticing some sparks between Jerry and Becka."

"Yeah," Jesse said, "I picked up on that, too, during today's challenge. They were pretty cozy on the swim back to shore. Took their time together."

"Might be worth keeping an eye on that. And, of course, the ongoing conflict between Troy and Stefan should be focused on, as well. With an extra day before exile, that should lead to some interesting opportunities. Make sure we film it."

Mark spit out his twig and hefted the equipment. "How in the hell are we gonna capture all that with only one camera?"

"We'll have to pick and choose, of course. I've got a spare handheld stowed with my gear. We'll make due. In fact, I'll stay here while you guys conduct the interviews with Roberta, Stefan, and Matthew. Just in case something big happens."

Mark shrugged. "You're the boss."

Stuart stood. "Let's go tell them the good news."

"How do you think they're gonna take it?"

"Everything will be fine," Stuart said. "They'll be okay with it. After all, this is showbiz! They want to be famous? This is a part of it. The show must go on."

"Fuck that shit," Troy shouted. "You've got to be fucking kidding me. There ain't no fucking way I'm staying on this fucking island in the middle of a fucking hurricane. Fuck that."

"Jesus," Raul muttered. "The air's gone blue, dog."

Jeff nodded. "He curses more than the guy on *Deadwood*, doesn't he?"

"And I'll tell you something else," Troy continued, ignoring the comments. "You're postponing the next exile vote until after Ivan passes, right? I say the hell with that. I want to know right fucking now if I'm getting fucking exiled or not before I agree to fucking stay here during a goddamned storm."

Richard nodded. "Yeah, that sounds about right. I'm with him. I've lived through tornadoes in Kansas. I don't really want to do it again."

While Mark and Jesse captured their reactions, Stuart held up his hands for silence.

"Obviously," he said, "we can't force you to remain behind. If you are that concerned, you are certainly welcome to evacuate with the rest of the crew. But understand, according to the contract you signed, if you choose to do so, you are forfeiting the game."

"What?" Troy was exasperated. "What the fuck are you talking about?"

"If you leave the island for any reason—be it by personal choice, medical emergency, death at home, whatever—that counts as a forfeiture. You agreed to that when you signed up, Troy. You too, Richard."

Richard shook his head.

"It's just like what happened with Sheila," Stuart pointed out. "She broke her leg and was unable to play anymore. Legally, we could have allowed her to keep playing, but she chose not to—wisely, I might add. So she forfeited. You can do the same thing, if you want."

Troy opened his mouth to curse some more, but Stefan interrupted him.

"Go ahead and leave, you bloody gearhead. Go back to Seattle with your tail between your legs and bend wrenches for the rest of your life. Live up to your potential as a loser and let us big dogs compete without the constant annoyance of your presence."

"Yeah," Jeff chimed in, "in fact, I'm willing to carry you down to the helicopter if you can't make it. What do you say, Troy?"

Mark zoomed in on Troy, capturing his expression.

"Fuck you, pretty boy. I'll outlast a metrosexual fuckwit like you any day of the fucking week— storm or no storm. You and your English buddy."

"I've told you before," Stefan said, "I'm not English. I'm Welsh."

"Whatever. We still kicked your ass during the Revolutionary War, bitch."

Raul, Stefan, and Jeff feigned shock, but before they could respond, Stuart appealed for silence again.

"So all of you are staying, correct?"

The contestants nodded and shrugged.

"Okay. Then on behalf of the producers, the network, and Roland, I'm glad to hear it. And keep in mind, they don't even know for sure if the storm will hit us directly. Ivan may turn out to be much ado about nothing. It might just be some winds and rain. Mark, Jesse, and I will be here with you. I've also got a satellite phone. We'll be in constant contact with the ship, should an emergency arise."

"Do all three of you have one?" Richard asked.

"No," Stuart said, "just me."

"Well, I know who I'm sticking close to then."

Sal elbowed him in the ribs. "You can stick close to me tonight."

"You guys are something else," Ryan said, shaking his head. "I mean, seriously, you make *me* look straight, and I fit every gay stereotype there is."

"You can stay close, too."

Ryan grinned. "You're not my type, Sal."

"Okay," Stuart said, "if there are no further questions, we need to do a few more one-on-ones. Matthew, you're up first. Please follow Mark and Jesse. And let me remind the rest of you—the interviews are totally confidential and off-limits, so please, no eavesdropping or being sneaky. Find something else to occupy yourselves until we're done. Stefan, we'll need you when they're finished with Matthew. It should be about forty-five minutes or so. No more than an hour, I'm sure."

"Fine," Stefan agreed. "I'll stick close to camp."

"And then we'll get to you, Roberta," Stuart said. "But it will be a while, so feel free to do something else until then."

She nodded.

Matthew stepped forward, spear in hand, and followed Mark and Jesse into the undergrowth. The rest of the group dissolved again into their various cliques and alliances. Sal and Richard gathered their crude fishing implements—netting, a few sharpened sticks they used as both spears and poles, and some hooks they'd won during a challenge—and headed for the beach. Stefan's group settled in around the campfire, stirring the coals and building it up again. As Sal and Richard departed the camp, Stefan called out to them.

"Where are you gents going?"

"Fishing," Sal told him.

"Bollocks. Do you really think that's wise, what with the possibility of inclement weather and all?"

Sal shrugged. "Storm or no storm, we've still got to eat. I don't know about you all, but I'm frigging sick of rice. We'll be back before the rain starts."

"Be careful of the tide," Jeff warned. "It might be rising already. Don't want you guys getting washed away."

"We'll be fine," Richard assured him.

After they were gone, Jerry pulled Becka, Shonette, Troy, and Ryan aside. Sensing something good, Stuart followed them, backup camera in hand.

"Okay," Jerry said. "This storm bought us some unexpected time, but we need to take advantage of it. Who wants to work on Roberta? How about you, Becka?"

Becka hesitated. "I don't know, guys. I'm not very good at all this duplicity and sneakiness."

"You can do it," Jerry said. "It's just like playing chess."

"I suck at chess. My brother used to beat me all the time."

"Do we even need Roberta?" Ryan asked. "I mean, we've got seven of us in our alliance. We control the vote, so what's the point of swaying her?"

"Insurance," Jerry said. "Let's be honest—if Stefan's group approaches one of us, can we really be sure someone from our alliance won't switch sides?"

"I fucking won't," Troy spat. "Fuck that limey cocksucker."

"No," Jerry agreed, "I don't think you would, Troy, but we can't say that for certain about everyone else. Richard and Sal, for example. So adding Roberta would just give us extra insurance. Plus, it might be good to have a spy in Stefan's group. So who wants to talk to her?"

"I can give it a try," Shonette volunteered. "It's my turn to get fruit, anyway. How about me and Ryan ask her to go with us and help us out? And then we'll talk to her about Stefan while we're away from camp."

"That might work," Jerry agreed. "But the others might wonder why me or Becka or Troy didn't go help you instead. Or, they might want to tag along with you. We'll have to distract them."

Ryan frowned. "How?"

"I'm not sure yet," Jerry admitted. "We'll just play it by ear. If we get the chance, we can—"

He stopped, glancing at Troy, who was twitching and playing with his hat.

"What's wrong?" Jerry asked.

"I told you before. I need some fucking nicotine, man. Just ignore me. I'll be okay."

"Have you tried chewing on twigs or something?" Becka asked.

"Twigs? Ain't no nicotine in twigs, Becka."

"Maybe you should eat something," Shonette suggested. "That's what I did when I quit. I gained like fifteen pounds."

"I would, but all we've got is that fucking rice and fruit and shit. I'm sick of that stuff. Maybe I'll take a nap."

"Go ahead," Jerry said. "If you do, maybe Stefan will leave at least one of his group here to keep an

51

eye on you. That would help with keeping them away from Shonette and Ryan while they try to get Roberta to switch sides."

Troy grinned. "Shit, if sleeping will do that, then I'm your man, dude. Fuck it."

"Okay," Jerry whispered. "Let's do it."

Becka, Shonette, Ryan, and Jerry returned to the campfire while Troy made a big production of getting some sleep. Stuart followed along, hovering at the edge of the group, filming everything. When Troy was sure that Stefan and the others had noticed him, he crawled into the lean-to and lay down on a bed of leaves.

"What's up, guys?" Raul waved his hand, offering them a seat.

"Not much," Jerry said. "We were just talking about the storm. Pretty freaky, isn't it?"

"Yeah," Pauline said. "We were just saying the same thing. Something like this has never happened on *Castaways* before. I mean, people have been bitten by snakes and stuff, and Sheila broke her leg. And that one season, the camp flooded and that guy got pneumonia, but there's never been anything like this."

Raul glanced up at the sky. "It doesn't look like rain. You ask me, they're exaggerating it so that they can get a reaction out of us."

"Maybe," Ryan agreed, "but the wind has definitely picked up. You can feel it. And look at the tree-tops."

They did, and saw the trees swaying back and forth in the breeze. The sky was noticeably free of birds.

"We should have more firewood on hand," Jerry suggested. "Just in case, you know? Maybe we can put it in the shelter so it doesn't get wet."

"That's an excellent idea," Stefan agreed. "You gents should get started while there's still daylight."

"You want to help?" Jerry asked.

Stefan smiled. "I would, but you heard Stuart. I'm afraid that I've got an interview scheduled for later."

Jerry turned to the others. "Jeff, Raul, Pauline? Care to give us a hand?"

Jeff and Raul stood up and brushed themselves off. Pauline hesitated, but then reconsidered and stood as well.

She smiled coyly. "Guess I wouldn't want to lie around camp when there's an exile coming up."

"No," Shonette agreed. "Probably shouldn't."

Stefan, Jeff, Raul, and Pauline glanced knowingly at Troy's prone form inside the open shelter.

"Roberta," Ryan said, "Shonette and I were going to go get fruit before the weather gets bad? You want to come along?"

"Sure."

Stefan frowned, but said nothing. Jerry held his breath. If Stefan voiced his suspicions or directed Roberta to stay with him—or with Pauline and the others—their newly formed alliance was screwed.

Instead, Stef's frown slowly transformed into a broad smile.

"I'll stay here and—what's the euphemism you Yanks use? Hold down the fort?"

Jerry shrugged. "Suit yourself, man."

"Cheers."

They split up, leaving Stefan alone by the fire. Soft snoring drifted from the shelter, and Troy's fellow conspirators wondered if he was faking or really asleep. Shonette, Ryan, and Roberta started down the trail while Becka, Jerry, Jeff, Raul, and Pauline headed into the jungle around the camp's perimeter.

Stuart watched them leave, breaking his silence just long enough to remind them all to avoid the interview area. Then he began filming again. He debated internally which group to follow, and decided to stick with his instincts and stay in camp. The possibility of a confrontation between Troy and Stefan was too strong to ignore, and with the two of them alone together, things could quickly come to a head. Stefan would probably avoid taunting Troy without the others present. He needed an audience. But Troy . . .

Troy was the wild card.

Stuart gripped the camera and waited for all hell to break loose.

And eventually it did.

CHAPTER FIVE

Mark led the way through the jungle, followed by Jesse and then Matthew. They walked along a small service trail used primarily by the show's crew members, rather than the contestants. It wasn't as heavily traveled as the main path, nor did it appear on camera. As a result, it was choked in places with vines, logs, tree limbs and roots, and harder to navigate than the main path. They trudged along, panting for breath. Low-hanging branches smacked their skin. All three men had dark circles under their shirtsleeves. Both Mark and Jesse had turned their equipment off during the trek. The air was damp and heavy. Sweat ran down their foreheads and into their eyes. Mark's blond mullet lay flat and lifeless, plastered to his head. Mosquitoes darted around them in clouds. Both men slapped incessantly at the buzzing insects.

"This sucks," Mark said. "I wish that storm would hurry up and hit us, if only to cool things down a bit."

"It would get rid of the bugs, too." Jesse glanced behind him at Matthew. "How you holding up?"

"Fine."

Jesse turned around and focused on the trail. He reflected again on how weird Matthew was. Most of the crew had commented on it over the last few weeks. None of them was sure how Matthew had passed the application process, let alone the extensive array of psychological, physical, and personality tests the network required of all potential contestants. He certainly wasn't photogenic or interesting. Nor was he funny or charismatic. One crew member had compared him to wallpaper; he was just *there*. But while Matthew's behavior wasn't overly eccentric or confrontational, the guy gave off odd vibes. Maybe that was why the producers had picked him.

Jesse glanced backward again. Matthew stared at him, unblinking. Jesse smiled, trying to appear polite and nonpartial.

"Sure is hot, isn't it?"

Matthew winked. "I've been in worse."

Matthew did not seem to be bothered by the oppressive, cloying heat or the annoying bugs. He didn't complain or sweat or breathe hard. He simply walked along behind them in silence, using his bamboo spear as a staff.

Jesse turned around again, as Mark pushed a low tree branch out of the way and hummed Molly Hatchet's "Flirting with Disaster" under his breath. The thin branch snapped backward and smacked Jesse in the face. Crying out, he touched his cheek. It felt hot. He looked at his fingers and was relieved to see there was no blood.

"What happened?" Mark asked.

"You nearly put my eye out with that branch, man! Watch where you're going."

"Jesus, I'm sorry."

"It frigging hurts."

"You've got a welt. I'm really sorry about . . ."

Mark trailed off, noticing that Matthew was smirking.

"What's up?" he asked the contestant. "You think this is funny?"

Matthew shrugged, but didn't reply. His smile vanished again, and his expression became stone.

"Come on," Jesse said. "I'll be okay. Let's just get this over with so we can be done with it and move on to more important things."

He heard the contempt in his own voice, but was no longer concerned whether Matthew picked up on it. It was too hot to care.

Mark walked on and commenced with his humming. Jesse followed him. He'd gone about five steps when something sharp and pointed pressed against his lower back, right between his spine and left kidney.

"That's far enough," Matthew said. "Move and you'll be pissing into a bag for the rest of your life."

Confused and angry, Jesse started to spin around. The pain and pressure in his back increased. The point—it had to be Matthew's bamboo spear— pierced his flesh. Jesse gasped, wincing in pain.

"I mean it," Matthew said. "Don't you fucking move."

Mark turned. "What's going on?"

He froze, staring at them. Had circumstances been different, Jesse might have been amused by the expression on his friend's face. Mark's jaw grew slack. He gaped, mouth open like a cartoon character. Whatever was happening, it was enough to shock the usually unflappable Mark. Seeing that, Jesse felt the first twinge of real fear. Dropping his equipment, he put his hands up in the air.

"Quit messing around, now," he said. "You don—"

Matthew prodded him with the spear again. The pain grew worse. Jesse moaned.

"Shut up, and stand real still. Mark, you turn on that fucking camera and start filming."

Mark licked his lips and started to speak, but Matthew jabbed Jesse again. This time, the pain was enough to make him cry out.

"Do it. I won't tell you again."

Hands trembling, Mark fumbled with the camera.

"T-take it easy," he stammered. "You're the boss. What's the p-plan?"

Matthew put a hand on Jesse's shoulder and forced him down. "Kneel."

Jesse obeyed. His eyes locked with Mark's. Pebbles and branches dug into his knees and mosquitoes whirled around his face, but he ignored them all. He tried to pray and realized that he'd forgotten how.

Please, he thought. *Please . . . please . . . please.*

The pressure in his back vanished. Jesse sighed. He sensed movement behind him and saw Mark flinch. A second later, Matthew grabbed a fistful of his hair and yanked his head back. Before Jesse could resist, the point of the spear returned. This time it was pressed against his neck. Jesse's breath caught in his throat.

"Now," Matthew said, "I want you both to listen to me very carefully. I've been working on this piece of bamboo since the night we arrived. It is very, very sharp. Yes, I'd prefer a knife or a handgun, but since we weren't allowed to bring those along as our luxury items, this will have to do—and it can, if you force me to use it. Believe it."

"What do you want?" Jesse wheezed. "Is this about winning?"

Matthew laughed. "No, this is about something more important."

"What?" The pain in his throat grew worse.

"Mark is going to film me, and you're going to play the part of the good little hostage. If either one of you does anything stupid—anything at all—I will shove this thing into your throat and bleed you like a stuck pig. It means nothing to me. I slaughtered pigs back home when I was a boy, and I've got no qualms about doing it now. Do you both understand?"

"Y-yes," Mark whispered. His eyes were wet.

Jesse started to respond, but found that talking made the spear point sink deeper into his skin. He tried to stay as motionless as possible.

"Tell me when you're ready," Matthew said.

Mark nodded. "Y-you can go ahead. Just stay cool, okay?"

"Don't you have to give me a countdown or something?"

"I-I can if you want me to."

"I'd like that. Keeps things professional. And

Mark, you'd better be filming. No fucking around here. Not unless you want to help paint this jungle red."

Jesse closed his eyes and tried to keep from shaking. He listened to Mark count down from three and heard the fear in his friend's voice.

"Two . . . one . . ."

"Hello, America." Matthew's voice was calm and measured. "Your regularly scheduled broadcast of mind-numbing shit has been interrupted tonight by the Sons of the Constitution."

Jesse shuddered. Like most Americans, he was familiar with the name, and it filled him with dread. The Sons of the Constitution was a militant group dedicated to bringing about a second American revolution and overthrowing the current political system through a campaign of bombings, assassinations, and other terrorist acts. They'd been active in the '90s and had since slipped from the public radar, replaced with the more current specter of Islamic radicals and other religious fanatics. Their most notorious acts were the bombing of the FBI's database and crime lab buildings in Quantico, and the assassination of several political and corporate figures.

"For too long now," Matthew continued, "you have sat back and done nothing while our country has been taken over by corporations and special interest groups. You've cheered for the Republicans and Democrats like they were your favorite football team, blindly echoing their talking points without daring to think for yourself, swallowing whatever propaganda the corporate-funded media groups fed you.

Our reporters no longer report the news. They simply parrot whatever the government tells them. The war, our economy, our social mores—all of these are reported on as a series of press releases, read to us by empty-headed, good-looking news readers.

"Our young men and women are dying in far-off lands. Our jobs are going overseas. Our country is being overrun by foreigners who don't respect our culture or language or ideals. Our courts are a joke. Our children are illiterate. Our economy is in the gutter, and while most of us work two or three shit jobs to feed our families, a select and powerful few carve this country up a little bit more among themselves, and get rich from our sorrow.

"Political correctness is the new racism. Our culture and beliefs are under attack. A war has been waged against them for decades now. It was slow and insidious, and you did not care because you were taught not to. You were kept silent—fat and pacified—on a diet of movies and television and pop music. Instead of showing you footage from Iraq or our inner city neighborhoods, the media shows you pop starlets and celebrity marriages. Instead of voting in our elections, you vote for reality-show contestants. You can't name the Bill of Rights, but you can name all of the members of the latest boy band. You demonize us for our tactics, but then allow your children to idolize musicians who glamorize drug dealing and murder and promiscuity. You watch the Grammy Awards and the Oscars and the Golden Globes but don't take an interest in your government."

Matthew paused and took a deep breath. Jesse

opened his eyes. The pressure on his neck increased slightly and the point sank deeper, almost piercing the flesh. When Matthew spoke again, his voice was louder, his pace more frantic.

"Wake up, America! The world thinks you are a joke. God has abandoned you, and who can blame him. You are spoon-fed daily government-approved sound bites from CNN and Fox News, and think yourself informed, but you are not. The media is nothing but their mouthpiece.

"Your rights are being eradicated daily by the FBI, CIA, Department of Homeland Security, Wall Street, the oil companies, and Hollywood—and you don't care. You can no longer be bothered to get out of your chair and run out into the street and protest. Where is that radical spirit this country was founded on? Where is that urgency for change that defined a generation in the sixties? Why are you so content to allow your civil rights to be trampled on? Why do you let them treat your children and your elders this way? Are you really so jaded that you no longer mind your bondage? Why do you allow them to strip you of your inalienable human rights? Where is your anger? Where is your outrage? Why have you not marched on Washington with torches and pitchforks and dragged these criminals out into the street? Why have you not hanged them for their crimes?

"It's because you're asleep. Indifferent. Depressed. You swallow your antidepressants and turn the television up louder and shrug, because you've been conditioned to believe that you can't do anything about it. You can't change anything."

His voice grew softer again, but still forceful.

"Well, we can. We can and we will. We are the Sons of the Constitution. They say we are criminals and terrorists, but that is simply more propaganda. The truth is that we are freedom fighters—fighting for your freedom and ours and our children's. Our political system is in shambles. The two parties are the same coin. We will enact change by whatever means necessary, and we will not stop until things are different. This is your wake-up call, America. You want reality television? Well, by God, we will show you reality. We will show you how the world really is. This is your fault."

Jesse felt Matthew shift his weight. The bamboo was pressed harder against his neck. He started to speak, but then there was a sharp, burning sensation, and suddenly, his neck and chest felt hot. The pain vanished. He heard a hissing, sputtering sound, like a leaky garden hose. Something wet trickled down his arm and soaked his shirt. His eyes darted to the right, and he saw blood splattered all over a fern.

Blood. His blood.

Jesse tried to scream, but found he couldn't breathe.

The jungle grew blurry and red.

"Jesse!"

Mark lowered the camera and ran to his friend. Jesse slumped over onto the trail, blood jetting from the deep, ragged wound in his throat. It pulsed in time with his heart, and bubbles formed around the gash each time Jesse tried to breathe.

"Jesse, hang on, man . . ."

Straddling Jesse's body, Matthew thrust the spear at Mark. Blood dripped from the tip. Mark backed away.

"Freeze."

Mark stopped, his face aghast.

"Keep filming," Matthew ordered. "I'm not done yet. You keep filming, or I'll kill you, too."

Mark paused. His gaze flickered from the spear to Jesse to Matthew. Then he dropped the camera, turned, and fled.

"Help," he shouted. "He's fucking crazy! Somebody help."

Behind him, he heard Matthew curse. Footsteps pounded along the trail as the crazed man gave chase.

"Get back here. You're only making it worse. Don't make me chase you."

"Go to hell!"

Mark ran harder, his hair flapping in the breeze. Sweat stung his eyes, but he didn't blink. His lungs burned, but he dared not stop. He felt his pulse pounding in his throat. Too late, he remembered his pocketknife, folded up and resting against his right thigh inside his jeans pocket. There was no time to stop and pull it out now. Matthew charged along behind him, but Mark didn't dare turn around.

Something punched him hard in the middle of his back. It felt like he'd been kicked by a mule. Suddenly, it hurt to breathe. Behind him, he heard Matthew grunt, as if straining from some task. The pain in his midsection grew worse. Mark glanced down and saw something protruding from his chest, just beneath the fabric of his T-shirt. He tasted blood in his mouth.

Matthew pushed the spear the rest of the way through, then yanked it back out and impaled the cameraman again. Mark gritted his teeth against the pain and tried to turn around to confront his attacker. He couldn't. He felt weak, and his legs and head didn't want to work. He opened his mouth to scream, but all that came out was a sigh. Blood dribbled down his chin. He felt pressure on his back a third time, but now there was no pain. Struggling, he managed to raise his head enough to see the sky peeking through the treetops. The deep blue had given way to foreboding gray.

Got to get back to the ship, he thought, *before the storm comes. It's gonna be bad.*

Mark reached for his camera, intent on getting a shot of the incoming storm. When he couldn't feel it nearby, he wondered where it was.

Then he knew no more.

CHAPTER SIX

Pauline stretched, thrusting her ample breasts forward. Her nipples stuck out. The breeze ruffled her hair. She preened and pouted, alternately displaying her rump and bosom, and complaining that her back hurt and her arms were tired. Jeff and Raul doted on her, administering back rubs and offering to carry her share of the firewood. Their fellow contestants weren't as sympathetic. Jerry and Becka stuck with the threesome for a while, making small talk and feigning polite interest, but slowly they lagged behind, eventually separating from the other three.

"Oh," Becka whined when they were out of earshot, pretending to faint, "my poor little arms and legs hurt. Jerry, will you carry me back to camp?"

Chuckling, he shook his head. "Unbelievable, huh?"

"It makes me sick, how the rest of the guys buy into her act. Well, except Ryan, of course."

"And Troy. And Matthew."

Becka frowned. "Troy's smarter than he looks. Matthew really creeps me out, though."

"Yeah," Jerry agreed. "I think he's asexual or something. That's probably why Pauline can't play him."

"And what about you?"

"What do you mean? I'm not asexual."

"No," Becka laughed. "I mean, why don't Pauline's charms work on you?"

"That's easy. It's because I'm here to win. I'm not here to get famous or spin my appearance into an acting gig, or to hook up with people or make new friends. I'm on this show because I want to win a million dollars. Is she good-looking? Sure. I'm not gonna pretend she isn't. But I keep my eyes off her and on the prize instead. I'm here for the money. Aren't you?"

"I don't know. I guess so. At first, anyway. I thought it would be fun."

"Having second thoughts?"

"Maybe. I don't know. I think I'm just homesick."

"You said you brought a diary as your luxury item. Does it help?"

"Not really. I've been so tired since we got here, I haven't really kept up with it. There's only three entries so far."

"Well, you'll be around for a while yet, at least. I'm sure you'll have time to write more."

Becka smiled. "I hope so. As long as I outlast Pauline, that's all that matters to me at this point."

"You will. Just don't count on beating me."

She slapped at him playfully, and he caught her hand in his. Becka felt a tingle course through her body. Jerry's hands were firm and strong, yet his skin was smooth and soft, just like his eyes.

They stayed like that for a moment without speaking, just holding hands and staring into each other's eyes. Then Jerry broke contact and glanced away. He cleared his throat and shuffled his feet.

"It's sort of weird, not having the cameras following us around for once."

"Yeah," Jerry agreed. "It is. When we first got here, I had a hard time getting used to them. Now that they're gone, it's even stranger. I keep wanting to play to the camera, but it's not there."

"Good. I could use a break."

"Yeah, me too."

"So, what would you do with the money if you won? If you don't mind me asking? Not that I'm being nosy or anything."

"No, not at all. You'll probably think it's stupid, though. I mean, it's nothing grand or noble. I don't want to give it all to charity or help my sick mother or anything like that."

"Try me."

"Okay. Well, I work in a video store, right? Nothing glamorous and it doesn't seem to impress women, but I like it. But video stores are a thing of the past—a real dying breed. They've got to compete with movies online, Netflix and big discount stores marking DVDs down so low that it's cheaper to buy them than rent them. So I've been thinking about alternatives lately. The writing's on the wall. Sooner or later, I'll be out of a job."

"So what are you thinking about?"

"What I always wanted to do was open my own comic-book store." He paused, and wagged his finger at her. "I know what you're thinking right now just by the expression on your face. It's the same thing everybody thinks. You mention a comic-book store and they immediately think of some small dive in a strip mall with a bunch of smelly geeks playing *Warhammer* and the fat guy from *The Simpsons* sneering behind the counter. Am I right?"

"Pretty much," Becka admitted. "My brother was into comics and gaming, and the few times I went to the store with him, those were my impressions."

"But they're not all like that. The stereotype is a misconception. What I want to do is make a chain of comic-book stores for the next generation."

"Like a boutique?"

"Close." Jerry winked. "I'm thinking more along the lines of a café. Put them near college campuses and places like that. Rather than focusing on single-issue comics and boxes of back issues, I'd stock graphic novels, coffee, and pastries. Play good music in the background and offer free Wi-Fi. People can sit around my comic shop just like they would a Starbucks or Borders. It would be clean, well lit, comfortable, and free of all those stereotypes that keep people like you out of the store."

Becka pursed her lips. "I can't believe I'm saying this, but that's not bad. That's not a bad idea at all."

"I know. Thanks. And that's what I intend to do with the money when I win."

"You mean *if* you win."

"Listen to you, all cocky now."

"So is that what you're into? Comics and stuff?"

"Well, I'm not rabid about them, but yeah, I dig reading them sometimes."

Becka wondered if he was downplaying his

enjoyment of comics just to make some sort of impression on her. Not that she would have cared anyway, but it seemed to her that if Jerry was interested in opening a comic book shop, he'd have more than just a passing interest in them. She kept this to herself, however, so as not to embarrass him.

"Do you have any other hobbies?"

Jerry hesitated. "Promise you won't make fun of me?"

Becka nodded.

"I'm an amateur cryptozoologist."

"A what?"

"Cryptozoology. It's the study of unknown animals and creatures. Every year, they find new birds and fish and animals we didn't know about before— or thought were extinct. Like the coelacanth. It's a fish that was supposed to have died out with the dinosaurs, but they found them living off the coast of Africa. And a few years ago, some French scientists discovered a species of shrimp that was supposed to have been extinct for like sixty million years. They found it in this part of the world, believe it or not."

"A prehistoric shrimp?"

"I know. Sounds stupid."

"No, it doesn't," Becka said. "It's kind of cool. Did you go to college for this?"

"No." Jerry glanced at the ground. "But I wanted to be Loren Coleman when I grew up. Hell, I still do."

"Who's Loren Coleman?"

"He's like the godfather of this type of research—a very great man. Him and Ivan T. Sanderson and Charles Fort. Heroes of mine."

"So why didn't you go to college for it?"

"It's not really an accepted science. But I've read a lot of books and do a lot of research online."

"Have you ever found anything?"

"Not yet. Tramped around in the woods of Oregon for two weeks, looking for hominids, but all I caught was a cold."

"Hominids?" Becka giggled. "You mean Bigfoot? Or is it Bigfeet, if we're talking plural?"

Jerry's ears turned red. "Laugh if you want, but it's perfectly reasonable to think that there might be an as-yet-unidentified species of ape wandering the remote regions of North America. It's not like they're aliens or something."

Becka touched his arm. "I'm sorry. I'm not making fun of you. Honest."

"You must think I'm a real geek. Comic books and Sasquatch hunting. Jesus . . ."

"Not at all. I think it's cool. Certainly different from the guys back home. All they care about is NASCAR and football and deer hunting. You're unique. And you know what you want to do with your life. You're not studying to be a doctor or a lawyer or something just because that's what your parents wanted you to do. I like that."

Jerry met her eyes. "Yeah?"

"Yeah."

Grinning, he bent over and picked up a length of deadwood. Then he stuck out his arms.

"Come on, give me a hand. I'll carry. You load me up."

Becka began gathering dry branches and limbs and stacked them in Jerry's outstretched arms. Above them, the leaves rustled in the wind.

"The wind's getting stronger," Jerry observed. "Look at those trees bend."

"The bugs aren't as bad either. Have you noticed? I haven't swatted at a mosquito in ten or fifteen minutes. That's what happens back home, right before a thunderstorm."

They heard a distant drone of the helicopter. It grew louder as it approached their location, and then they glimpsed it soaring overhead, flying the last of the crew back to the freighter to wait out the storm.

"Well," Jerry said. "That's it. We're stuck here now."

"Do you really think it's going to be bad?"

"I don't know. I mean, legally, I guess there's a precedent for leaving us here. Like Stuart said, we signed a contract. And I guarantee you, the drama will be good for ratings. But if it were really bad, I think the network would be more responsible and evacuate us along with everybody else. Plus, Stuart and those other guys didn't seem too worried. They were going about the interviews and stuff like it was just another day."

Becka didn't respond. Frowning, she picked up more firewood and added it to Jerry's bundle.

"You okay?" he asked.

"Sure. Why?"

"Because you're biting your lip."

"I'm sorry. I've done that since I was a little girl. Every time I get scared."

"You don't have to be scared. Seriously. I'll take care of you."

"I just . . ." Sighing, Becka sat down on a rock. "I don't know what I'm doing here. I mean, why did I think I could do this? I can't. I'm lonely and scared and so frigging tired. God, listen to me. Now I sound like Pauline."

Jerry dropped the firewood and sat down next to her. He placed a tentative arm around her shoulder. Becka stiffened, but then relaxed. When she didn't protest, he squeezed gently.

"You want the truth?"

Wiping her eyes, Becka nodded.

"I'm tired, too. I've done okay in the challenges so far, but it's tough, keeping up with Stefan, Jeff, Raul, and Ryan. Those guys are pretty fit. Between the bugs and the jungle sounds and the heat, I sleep like shit in that shelter. Not to mention Troy's snoring."

He tilted his head back and imitated the foul-mouthed mechanic's nocturnal noises—a cross between a snuffling pig and a lawn mower. Becka giggled, then laughed. Jerry dropped his arm, but she didn't move away.

"That's exactly how he sounds," she said. "I tried rolling up leaves and sticking them in my ears so I wouldn't hear him, but they kept falling out."

"He wakes me up at least four or five times a night," Jerry agreed. "By the time the sun comes up, I'm beat. And our lack of food is contributing to it, as well. That's why I did so bad in the challenge this morning. But I'll be damned if I'm going to quit. I meant what I said earlier."

"I wish I had your strength," Becka said. "Your resolve."

"You do. I can see it inside you."

"I don't feel very strong."

"But you are. I think that before this thing is over, you'll find out just how much."

"I hope so."

Jerry nudged her. "I know so. And I'll help you out. We're in this together now, remember?"

"You promise?"

"I promise."

"And what about when it's over, and we're off the island and back home again. What then?"

Jerry stood up and began gathering the firewood again. "Let's just concentrate on winning first. We'll worry about what happens later . . . later."

"I guess you're right. A lot could happen between now and then."

Jerry nodded, grunting as he lifted a particularly large branch.

She watched him work and marveled at how much her attitude toward him had changed—and how quickly. Earlier today, she'd been cautious of him, not trusting any of her fellow contestants. Now he was the closest thing she had to a friend here on the island.

Becka got to her feet and winced. Her tailbone hurt. She rubbed it.

"You okay?"

"Sure," Becka said. "My rump hurts. That's all."

Jerry laughed.

"What's so funny?"

"Rump. Not a word you hear very often. You struck me as more of a 'butt' kind of girl."

"And you struck me as an ass."

"Hey!"

Giggling, she walked over to help him. Becka noticed an olive-colored tree snake slithering past them. She eyed the serpent's slender body, relatively large head and eyes, and conspicuous dorsal stripe. She was fairly certain it wasn't poisonous, but waited until it had disappeared into the undergrowth before picking up the dead branches.

"Come on," Jerry urged. "We'd better catch up with the others. We don't want to piss them off."

Becka shivered.

"The temperature's dropping," she said.

"Yeah." Jerry glanced up at the sky again. "Won't be long now. Tropical Cyclone Ivan is on his way."

His words seemed to hang in the air like heavy storm clouds.

CHAPTER SEVEN

"Hey." With a big grin, Richard held up a thrashing fish. Its lips puckered and its gills flexed as it gasped in the suffocating air. "This one's got a real nice mouth on it. Reminds me of this one girl back home."

"Why don't you stick your dick in it?" Sal's voice carried over the crashing waves.

"Maybe I will."

"I dare you."

"How much will you give me if I do?"

"I don't have to pay you to do it. You're so horny, you'd fuck the crack of dawn."

"Who's Dawn? Is she pretty?"

"You'd fuck a garden hose if there was enough pressure behind it."

Richard appeared doubtful. "I don't know if I could fit inside a garden hose. I'm pretty big."

"I bet that fish would be the best-looking piece of ass you've ever had."

"Maybe. It's definitely prettier than my prom date."

Laughing, Richard tossed the wriggling fish into

a crude basket that the castaways had woven together from reeds and branches. Then he wiped his hands on his lime-green shorts. The fish flopped on top of the rest of their catch—four other fish of varying sizes. Seabirds circled ravenously overhead, daring to dart lower each time any of the men walked away from the basket, and then squawking angrily when Sal or Richard returned.

"I never fucked a fish before. I wonder how it would feel."

Sal strolled across the wet sand toward him. The surf lapped at his bare feet. Since their arrival on the beach, the tide had crept steadily closer, rising as the sky grew darker and the winds increased.

"You say that like you've fucked other animals."

Richard shrugged.

"Oh my God." Sal snickered. "You have, you sick fuck! What was it?"

"When I was about fourteen, I fucked a chicken. All my friends did. One after another. It was sort of a dare."

"You fucked a chicken?"

"Sure."

"Why?"

"We were bored."

"You couldn't find anything better to do than to have sex with a chicken?"

Richard shrugged again. "It was Kansas, after all."

"You are one sick puppy, my friend."

"Oh, like you never fucked something disgusting?"

"Well," Sal admitted, "I fucked a fat chick once. I was shit-faced at the time. It was back in the eighties, after the KISS *Asylum* tour. Does that count?"

"I don't know. How big was she?"

"Well over three hundred pounds. I had to roll her around in flour just to find the wet spot."

"I'd say that qualifies."

"Maybe so," Sal said, "but at least I've never fucked a chicken."

"I may have admitted to fucking a chicken, but I'd never admit to seeing KISS on their *Asylum* tour."

"What, you don't like KISS?"

"They're okay, but that era was terrible. Give me the band in full makeup any day."

"You don't know what you're talking about. When they got rid of the theatrics, they were able to just focus on the music. That was a great era."

"I don't know about that."

"Just because you play drums, that doesn't make you an expert, Richard."

"I'm enough of an expert not to fuck a fat girl after the show."

They fell silent for a moment, each lost in his own thoughts.

"I wonder how a fish would feel," Richard asked again. "Probably cold and slimy."

"Go ahead and try it," Sal said. "Seriously, I won't tell anybody. You're stuck on this island without any pussy—who could blame you?"

"That's not exactly true. We've got pussy here."

"Not any that you're getting."

"I think Pauline's pretty hot."

"She is," Sal agreed, "and she's way out of our fucking league, dude. So was Sheila and that other chick we exiled a few days ago."

"Why is that?" Richard asked. "Have you ever noticed that on every season of *Castaways*, the hot girls get exiled first? I always said that if I ever made it onto the show, I wouldn't do that, and yet I helped get rid of her. Why?"

"I don't know. But I did, too, so we're just as guilty as those previous contestants. And now all the nice-looking ones are gone. Except Pauline. But she's in tight with Stefan's group. That's why Jerry's plan better work, or our asses are next, right after they exile Troy."

"Do you really think we should join forces with Jerry?"

Sal shrugged. "I don't see why not. It makes sense for now. Maybe when it's just Pauline left out of their group, we can offer her immunity in exchange for some of that ass. I mean, she likes sticking her tits in everyone else's face. Why not stick them in mine for a while?"

"You wouldn't really do her."

"Are you crazy? Try me. I'd do her in a heartbeat."

"No," Richard insisted. "You wouldn't. Not with the cameras around all the time. You've got a wife and kids back home. There's no way you'd let them see that on television. You'd end up divorced."

"Shit. I don't get laid at home either. I might as well take advantage of it here if the opportunity presents itself."

"What about Shonette? Would you do her?"

"Yeah, in a pinch. She's not all that, but she's better than your fish. Becka, too."

"Becka's cute," Richard agreed, "but I think she likes Jerry."

"Even if she didn't like him, she wouldn't do you, man. She'd sooner fuck that worm snake we found today. You're better off sticking to the fish."

Richard laughed, then shivered as a particularly fierce gust of wind blasted across the beach. The skin on his arms prickled.

"It's getting pretty chilly," he said. "Maybe we should head back to camp."

Sal glanced up at the foreboding sky. It was growing darker by the minute. The sun had almost completely vanished behind a mass of thick, roiling clouds.

"If it's gonna rain," he muttered, "then I wish it would start already."

"I can't believe how cold it's getting."

"It's not," Sal said. "We've just gotten so used to the heat that as soon as the temperature drops a little bit, it feels like we're in Antarctica or something."

Richard gathered their equipment—netting, lines, and hooks that they'd won during a challenge, and two bamboo spears they'd fashioned in camp—while Sal continued studying the sky.

"Come on," he urged. "Let's head back."

Nodding, Sal picked up the bundle of fish. "Don't forget about your girlfriends."

"Hey, listen." Richard glanced around, making sure they were alone. The beach was deserted. "You're not going to tell anybody about the chicken, are you?"

"That depends. How much is it worth to you?"

"Oh, come on, Sal. That's not right."

"You shouldn't have said anything. You're just lucky we don't have a camera crew following us around."

"Well, even so, I'd appreciate it if you kept it between us."

"I will—for half your prize money if you win."

"Half?"

"Half."

"How about I just wait till we get back to camp, and then look in the camera and tell America all about the fat chick you banged."

"I've changed my mind," Sal said. "The chicken will be our little secret."

They walked along the beach, heading back toward the island's interior. They didn't hurry, but they didn't lag either. Neither man wanted to get caught in the jungle during the storm. As they crossed the beach, their discussion changed from women and fish to music. Both of them were metalheads, but while Sal was a fervent KISS fan, Richard was into more esoteric bands like Iced Earth and Death. He was telling Sal about his current favorite group, Coheed and Cambria, when something in the sand caught his attention. He paused, cupping his hand over his eyes, and stared.

"What's wrong?" Sal asked.

"Look over there."

A few yards away from them were a series of footprints. They led from the jungle to the beach, stopped, and then went inland again in a U-shaped pattern.

"Big deal," Sal said. "They're ours."

"No, they're not." Richard pointed. "Ours are over there. See? That's where we came down, over near the path."

"Then they're our tracks from yesterday."

"They can't be. The tide would have washed those away last night. These are fresh. It looks like whoever made them sneaked onto the beach while we were fishing, stood here looking at us, then went back into the jungle."

"Maybe Mark or Stuart shot some footage of us."

Richard didn't respond. He continued staring, fascinated by the tracks.

"I'm telling you," Sal said, growing impatient, "they're our footprints."

Richard put down the fishing equipment and stepped closer, studying the tracks. They were human in shape, but child sized. The five toes were longer than a human's, and the heel seemed rounder. At the tip of each toe there was a long impression that designated a claw or talon. He reached out and ran his hand over them. The wet sand shifted and collapsed, partially filling the depressions.

"This isn't us," Richard insisted. "I'm pretty sure of it."

"Maybe it's one of the girls, then. Roberta has small feet."

"She hasn't been down here since she got that bad sunburn. And look at them. They look more like a monkey's prints than they do a person's."

"There aren't any monkeys on this island," Sal said. "They're not indignant."

Richard chuckled. "You mean indigenous."

"Whatever. There aren't any monkeys here. If there were, you'd probably try to fuck them."

Richard ignored the taunt. "Maybe it's some other kind of animal. I guess that could be possible. There's been a lot of rain lately. Some wild animal could have left them, and then the prints got distorted or something."

Sal knelt next to his friend and studied the tracks closer. "Except there aren't any wild animals on the island. Just snakes and turtles and stuff. And these definitely aren't turtle tracks."

"So now you agree with me?"

"I didn't say that. I just said there aren't any wild animals on the island that could make tracks like this. The only thing that was ever here were wild pigs, left over from shipwrecks, and Roland said they died off years ago."

"Well, then what are they if it wasn't us and it wasn't an animal?"

"I think that's obvious. The producers faked it."

"That's no special effect!" Richard jabbed a finger at the prints.

"Sure it is." Sal's knees popped as he stood again. "This has got to be part of the show. Think about it, Richard. When we first got here, Roland told us that bullshit story about how the natives in this region thought this island was haunted by a bunch of little hairy people. So now they scare us with some phony footprints and film our reactions. It makes for great drama back home. They probably had one of the crew strap on some fake feet and stomp around out here, like one of those Bigfoot hoaxes. Then they just waited for us to go fishing, and now we'll look like douche bags on national television. I'm telling you, the whole thing is a hoax. This is just some new twist on the game. Anything for ratings."

A savage, screaming howl erupted from deep within the jungle.

"Then what the hell was *that*?" Richard leaped to his feet.

Sal was startled, but kept his voice calm. "They're just fucking with us, man."

"You forgot something."

"What?"

"There's nobody filming us. Mark and Stuart are the only ones left on the island with cameras, and they're back at camp interviewing Roberta, Stefan, and that weird guy. So if they were playing a joke, wouldn't they want to capture our reactions like you said?"

Sal swallowed the lump in his throat and peered at the swaying tree line. The wind's speed increased. Above them, the sky grew darker.

"We're all alone out here," Richard whispered. "This isn't part of the show. This is real."

Another howl echoed from the trees. It was answered by a third, some distance away. The howls were followed by a series of barking grunts and strange hooting, all from different locations. Neither had ever heard anything like it. Whatever the animals were, it sounded almost as if they were communicating. Then, something crashed through the foliage, heading toward the beach. A thicket of reeds swayed violently as something barged through them.

Sal grabbed Richard's arm. "You're right! What do we do?"

"Run, you dumbass!"

"Where? They're in the jungle—between us and the camp."

"Down the beach, toward the sea. If they're animals, maybe they're afraid of the water."

As they turned to run, a figure emerged from the jungle. It was short and squat, standing barely four feet high. Because of the distance, they couldn't make out any details, but it appeared to be naked and covered in long brown hair. It had a tiny head but large mouth.

Sal paused. "What the hell is that?"

The creature opened its mouth and roared.

"Holy shit," Richard gasped.

Sal fled. Richard followed, glancing over his shoulder as more of the creatures leapt from the foliage and gave chase. One of them looked horribly deformed. Its bulbous head seemed overly large, like a melon. A few others had obvious deformities, as well. Their angry cries echoed across the beach. Whatever the things were, they weren't human. Nothing about them resembled humanity. And when they caught up with Richard and Sal, the two men didn't resemble anything human, either. The two men were reduced to nothing more than steaming, bloody piles of torn meat and offal—limbs severed, organs splattered, blood drained out and swallowed by the sand.

When it was over and the prey had been butchered, the creatures carried the meat back into the jungle. A few small crabs emerged from the sand and battled for the remaining scraps. Then the rising tide washed the blood and hair and flecks of skin away, and the beach was quiet again.

CHAPTER EIGHT

"Dude, get off your lazy ass. I ain't lugging these fucking rocks all by myself!"

Grunting, Troy lurched toward the shelter, carrying a large, heavy stone. Unable to sleep, he'd gotten up after the other contestants had left and began building a crude barrier around the shelter to prevent water from flooding the interior if the storm grew too bad. Stuart followed along, filming Troy's efforts, while Stefan sprawled next to the fire pit with his eyes closed.

"Tell me something, Troy. Is it really bloody necessary for you to punctuate your every utterance with a curse word?"

"Damn straight it is. That's how I talk. Want to make something of it? Am I offending your delicate fucking sensibilities?"

"I'm sure your mother is quite proud."

"Hey, *don't* talk about my fucking mother."

"Please be quiet." Frowning, Stefan waved him away. "Can't you see that I'm preoccupied?"

Struggling with his burden, Troy stopped and readjusted his grip on the stone.

"Oh, yeah," he snorted. "With what?"

"I'm thinking. You should try it sometime. It's quite liberating."

"I *am* thinking. Thinking about my fucking foot in your ass."

Stefan rolled over onto his stomach. Dirt and leaves clung to his back. He rested his chin in his hands and smiled at Troy.

"Such insolence. Is that any way to speak to the one person on this island who can get you a cigarette?"

"You got some?"

"No, I quit years ago—nasty habit. But I know somebody who does."

"Don't bullshit me, man."

"I swear. Someone on this island has cigarettes."

"Who? The crew? They're not allowed to give us any. I tried already. Fuckers filmed me begging for one."

"I should like to see that footage. But to answer your question, no, it's not the crew. One of our fellow castaways brought cigarettes as their luxury item and they've been using the campfire to light them when everyone else is sleeping. They've limited their smoking to one per day, so the pack will last."

"Get the fuck out of here."

"I'm serious."

"Who?"

Stefan paused. "The nigger. Raul."

Troy dropped the stone. It thudded to the ground, narrowly avoiding his toes, and rolled a few feet away, coming to rest against a tree trunk. He didn't notice. His attention was focused on Stefan.

"You realize what you just said on national television? Did you forget that you're being filmed?"

"And what of it?" Stefan shrugged. "I'm not here to win the hearts and minds of America. I'm here to play a game. And the network will edit that part out anyway."

"You're a real piece of fucking work, man."

Stefan smiled. "How so?"

"Not only are you a lazy motherfucker, you're a racist, too. I thought you and Raul were tight, but all along, you've just been playing him, haven't you? I bet he wouldn't like it if he heard you calling him that. Some fucking friend you are."

"Bollocks. I'm not here to make friends, Troy. I am here to win a game."

"Yeah? Well, we'll see what Raul has to say about that when he gets back. You ain't gonna win shit when everyone turns against you. Fucking asshole."

Stefan ignored the threat. "Raul brought along a pack of cigarettes as his luxury item. He doesn't think any of the others know about it, but I do. It's doubtful that he'd give you one, let alone admit he has them in his possession. Make a deal with me, and I'll obtain one for you."

"What kind of deal?"

"You have to give me your word that you won't vote against me, should you be given the opportunity."

"How could I? We all know you and your fucking cronies are aiming for me during the next exile vote."

"Perhaps." Stefan paused. "Or perhaps that's just

what we want everyone to believe, so that we can catch someone else unaware and exile them instead. After all, you're not much of a threat, all things considered."

Frowning, Troy turned away and kicked the ground. Then he whirled on Stefan, fists clenched. Calmly, Stefan rose to his feet. Stuart zoomed in closer with the camera and tried to stay out of the way.

"You know," Troy spat, pointing a dirty finger-nail at Stefan, "back in Seattle, we get guys like you in the shop all the fucking time. They bring their BMW in for an oil change and expect to have it done in five fucking minutes. Want us to drop whatever we're doing and focus only on *their* car."

"Actually, I drive a Lexus. The engineering on the more recent BMWs is vastly overrated."

"You're wrong. And that ain't my point!"

"Well, then, please do make your point."

"A few months ago, a guy like you came in with a blown head gasket. *A blown fucking head gasket.* He didn't think that's what it was. He wanted me to fix it right away, and when I told him I couldn't— that he needed a whole new head gasket—this stupid fucker got all prissy with me. He insisted that it could be fixed without that. Said all he needed was a fucking tune-up. Dude knew absolute shit about engines. When I told him again that there was no fucking way, he wanted to know why not. Know what I told him?"

"Something profound, I'm sure."

"Damn straight. I told him, 'that fucking fucker is fucking fucked.'"

"And your point is?"

"So are you, you Lexus-driving piece of shit."

Stefan's smile faltered, then returned. "Is that a threat?"

"It is what it is."

Stefan's smile vanished. His face grew red. He stood slowly and took a step toward Troy. The mechanic did not back down.

"You want some?" Troy balled his hands into fists. "Bring it, bitch."

"I shall." Stefan inched closer. "You need to be taught some manners, you bloody little troll."

"Not by you, shithead. And not today."

"Oh, yes? Do you think so? Then you are mistaken, my friend. I outmatch you in a battle of wits, and I can certainly best you in a physical matchup as well. School is now in session. Consider this your first lesson."

Yawning, Troy readjusted his hat. "You want to talk all day, or are we gonna throw down?"

The two men drew to within inches of one another. Stefan glared, puffing up his chest. Troy grinned. Stuart held his breath.

"Pussy."

"It shall be my pleasure to wipe that grin off your homely face."

Stuart braced his feet and zoomed closer, nervously trying to stay out of the way of both men's fists. A fight was imminent. He licked his lips in anticipation. Not once did the thought of intervening cross his mind. This was ratings gold in the making.

Stefan leaned forward, his nose almost touching Troy's. "I'm going to enjoy this."

"Whatever."

"We'll see how you feel once I've knocked that hat from your head."

Troy shrugged. "Put up or shut up. Daylight's fucking wasting."

The vegetation on the edge of the camp rustled, and Raul, Pauline, Jeff, Becka, and Jerry emerged from the jungle. Everyone except Pauline was carrying an armload of tinder.

"We've got firewood. Should be enough to get us through the night, provided the storm doesn't . . ." Raul trailed off, staring at Stefan and Troy in confusion.

Stuart panned over to catch the group's expressions and then pulled back, trying to capture the entire group, along with Stefan and Troy.

"What's going on?" Jeff asked. "Everything okay?"

Stefan glanced at the others. Troy continued staring at him, unblinking.

"Nothing," Stefan said. "Troy and I were just discussing the impending storm. Isn't that correct, Troy?"

"Whatever you say, dickhead. Whatever you say." Snickering, he shook his head and turned to the others. "Need a hand stacking that wood?"

"Sure," Jeff said. "Feel free."

Stefan leaned forward and whispered in Troy's ear. "You'd do well to keep in mind what I said, if you want that cigarette."

Ignoring him, Troy relieved Becka of her burden and carried the firewood over to the pit.

"Thanks." Her shoulders sagged.

"Don't mention it."

Stefan announced, "I'm off for a slash."

"What's that mean?" Raul asked.

"As you Yanks put it, I have to take a piss."

He disappeared into the undergrowth around the camp.

"I thought you were taking a nap," Jerry said to Troy. "Change your mind?"

Troy adopted an English accent. "And miss out on this stimulating fucking conversation with my fellow contestant? No way. Cheerio, old chap."

"That's the worst fake accent I've ever heard," Pauline teased. "You sound like Dick Van Dyke in *Mary Poppins*."

Troy winked at her. "Well, maybe when this show is over, I'll get a job as a fucking chimney sweep."

"If you win, I'll let you sweep *my* chimney."

Becka and Jerry glanced at each other. Becka rolled her eyes.

"Careful what you wish for," Troy joked. "You just might get it."

Stefan returned from the undergrowth and sat back down around the fire pit. Pauline sat next to him. Becka chose a seat on the other side of the fire pit. Troy collapsed next to her, sighing. Raul, Jeff, and Jerry unloaded their firewood and then joined them. Stuart hovered in the background, filming.

"Well," Becka whispered to Troy, "I don't know what's going on, but you certainly seem to be in a better mood."

Troy glanced up at the darkening sky. "What can I say? I love this weather. It suits my fucking mood."

Raul nodded toward the jungle. "I wish Richard and Sal would get back with dinner. I'm starved."

"I'm sure they'll be back soon," Jerry said. "Hopefully, Ryan, Shonette, and Roberta won't be far behind."

Still filming, Stuart noticed that the group had once again forgotten about Matthew. Although he didn't mention it aloud, he hoped Mark and Jesse would return soon. There was no doubt now that Ivan would impact their location. He didn't like the idea of them being out in the jungle when the storm finally hit. With the weather worsening, the interviews with Stefan and Roberta would have to be rescheduled, but that was okay, as long as everyone was safe and accounted for.

Raul started to speak, but thunder rumbled in the distance and he fell silent. The jungle turned dark. The breeze increased, hissing through the trees.

"Oh shit," Troy cursed. "I didn't finish building the barrier. Hope we don't get flooded out."

"Here it comes," Jeff said. "Say hello to Ivan."

It began to rain.

CHAPTER NINE

"Oh shit." Ryan gaped at the tumultuous sky. "It's starting already. We'd better head back before it gets worse."

"A little rain ain't gonna hurt us," Shonette said. "In fact, some of those men back at camp could use a shower." She fanned her nose.

Ryan's nervous laughter echoed through the trees. "Yeah, but this is more than just 'a little rain.' This is a hurricane."

"Cyclone," she corrected.

"Whatever."

"It ain't even started yet. This is just the beginning."

"The calm before the storm?"

Shonette nodded. "Something like that."

Ryan picked some more plump berries, placing them on a wide, sturdy piece of tree bark that served as a makeshift basket. Pausing, he brushed a twig from his blond-brown hair and frowned, looking again at the sky.

"You're right, though," Shonette said. "Ivan is coming in a lot quicker than they said it would."

Ryan was about to respond when Roberta stepped out of the foliage.

"Found some good ones," she announced, holding up two large coconuts. "These are a lot bigger than the ones at the grocery store back home."

"Bigger than Pauline's coconuts, too," Shonette said.

All three laughed.

Shonette pointed at the coconuts. "Those will go good with the fish—if Richard and Sal catch any, that is."

"Doesn't matter to me," Roberta said. "I'm pretty much a vegetarian for health reasons."

"But I saw you eat fish before."

"Sometimes I do. I just hope we don't have to eat maggots at some point, like they did in previous seasons. Only way I can do that is if they're fried in olive oil because I'm watching my trans fats."

Shonette shivered. "If they make us eat maggots or fish eyes or any of that nasty stuff, it's game over for me."

Roberta noticed that rather than joining the conversation, Ryan kept looking at the sky.

"What's wrong with him?" she asked.

"He's afraid he's gonna melt," Shonette told her. "Afraid the storm might blow his skinny self away."

A blast of thunder rocked the sky. All three of them jumped. Startled, Ryan dropped his berries.

"Great." He knelt, retrieving the spilled fruit. "Instead of winning, I'll be famous for being the first-reality show contestant to die during filming."

"No," Shonette said. "You're right. We should get going."

"That thunder change your mind?"

She nodded, grinning sheepishly. "Can't win a million dollars if a tree falls on us or if lightning comes down and strikes us all dead."

"I bet you wouldn't admit that if the cameras were here," Roberta teased.

"No," Shonette said, "I wouldn't. But they ain't, so yeah, I'm a little spooked. Let's head back. If the others want more fruit, they can go look for it themselves."

"It's kind of weird, isn't it?" Roberta asked. "Having the cameras follow us around everywhere?"

"I've gotten used to it," Ryan said. "Sometimes I forget that they're there."

They started down the trail, walking single file. Shonette was in the lead, followed by Ryan. Roberta brought up the rear. The rain hissed through the trees, pattering against the leafy canopy above them. The trees bent and swayed as the wind increased. A limb crashed to the ground behind them. They threaded their way through a fallen tangle of vines, pressing slowly onward and becoming more and more soaked as the rain fell harder.

"This sucks." Shonette wiped water from her eyes. "All this just to get some dinner."

"Yeah," Roberta agreed, "but it beats having to lug back firewood. We'll let Stefan and the other men do that."

"Excuse me?" Ryan pointed to himself. "Man right here."

"Sorry," Roberta apologized. "Present company excepted."

"All I know," Shonette said, "is that I'd let Raul

do a lot more than lug my firewood. That man is Fine with a capital F."

"Jerry isn't bad either," Roberta said. "And he's so nice. Too bad he's young enough to be my son."

Ryan blinked raindrops from his eyes. "I think he's got a crush on Becka."

"True that," Shonette said. "Any fool can see it."

"Well," Ryan said, "you both know who I think is the supreme hottie."

"Jeff," Shonette and Roberta said in unison.

Grinning, Ryan nodded enthusiastically.

"You should go for it," Shonette said. "Make a play for him."

"No," Ryan said. "He's hopelessly straight. Never stops talking about his wife and kids back home."

Roberta stepped over a fallen tree limb. "Poor Ryan. Came to the tropics on a wonderful vacation and can't get laid."

Ryan frowned. "I wouldn't exactly call this a vacation."

"Maybe," Roberta said, "but still . . ."

"That Troy guy is cute, too," Ryan admitted, "but in a bad boy, psycho kind of way."

"Psycho?" Roberta pushed her wet hair out of her eyes. "I think Matthew qualifies for that."

"Oh, definitely," Ryan agreed. "He gives everyone the creeps—even the crew. You have to wonder how he ever made the final cut. The *Castaways* application form on the website says that contestants must be in excellent physical and mental health, and he must have undergone the same evaluation we did. So how did he pass?"

"Easy," Shonette said. "The examination was in

Los Angeles, and the medical personnel were selected by the producers. He could have easily faked it."

"And besides," Roberta said, "the application also says that contestants will be selected based on their ability to be outgoing, adventurous, adaptable to new environments, and that they must have interesting lifestyles, backgrounds, and personalities. I don't fit any of those criteria."

"Sure you do," Ryan said.

"No, I don't. I'm a librarian, for crying out loud!"

Shonette stopped so suddenly in the middle of the trail that Ryan almost ran into her before stumbling to a halt.

Roberta paused behind them. "What's wrong?"

Shonette held a finger to her lips.

All three grew silent, listening. Shonette tilted her head and cocked an ear. The wind howled through the trees, rustling the leaves. In the distance, they heard the surf crashing against the beach. Then, much closer, just off the path, came a droning buzz, almost lost beneath the storm's growing cacophony.

"What is that?" Shonette stepped off the trail, lashing at the foliage with a stick. Ryan and Roberta glanced at each other, shrugged, then followed her. Roberta's nose wrinkled as she sniffed the air.

"Do you guys smell that?"

"All I smell is the storm," Ryan said. "You know, that electric smell?"

"Not that. Something else."

"What?"

Roberta shrugged. "I don't know. It's sort of familiar, but I can't place it."

Shonette pushed farther into the undergrowth,

and they reluctantly followed her. The buzzing sound grew louder. A stand of fern fronds parted, revealing a splash of red. Then more. Crimson spattered the leaves and the ground. A sour stench, faint but noticeable despite the rain, hung over the area.

"Oh Jesus," Shonette gasped.

Richard's swim trunks lay at the base of a tree. All three contestants recognized the lime-green garment immediately. The shorts were torn and bloody. Flies crawled over the shredded cloth, ignoring the inclement weather. Another squirming mass of flies scurried over something nearby. Shonette poked at it with her stick and the insects took flight, revealing part of a human hand. It had been severed at the wrist and cut in half. Only the ring and pinkie fingers remained, along with a ragged flap of palm. Sinew and bone jutted from the meat.

Cringing, Shonette recoiled in disgust. Ryan turned away and collapsed to his knees, dropping his berries again. He vomited onto the spilled fruit. Roberta closed her eyes and kept her breath measured and controlled, inhaling through her nose and exhaling through her mouth.

"That smell," she wheezed. "What's that smell?"

Ryan tried to answer, but his stomach convulsed and he threw up again.

"Blood," Shonette gasped. "It's the blood."

Backing away from the grisly discovery, Roberta shook her head. "No, it's not the blood. It's something else. Sour and musty. Like wet fur. I'm allergic to dogs, and this smells like that. And my allergies are acting up all of the sudden. I'm supposed to take antihistamines and use nasal spray, but I don't. I use a lot of Kleenex. Or a sleeve. I'm not particular; I could use anybody's sleeve."

"Calm down," Ryan gasped, and then bent back over as another convulsion shot through him.

Shonette didn't respond. She continued to gape at the gory scene.

"It's Richard's," she said. "I'd recognize those ugly green swim trunks anywhere. We've got to get back. Got to tell somebody! He's dead."

"We don't know that," Roberta wheezed. "There's no body."

"There's a goddamn hand. Part of one, at least."

"But we don't know that it's his hand, and we don't know that he's dead."

Groaning, Ryan clambered to his feet. "Does it matter? We still have to tell the producers. If he's hurt, they have to send help."

"How?" Roberta pointed at the sky. "They can't travel in this. They grounded all flights and boat operations."

The musky, cloying stench grew stronger. All three of them noticed it now. Roberta flung a hand over her mouth and sneezed. Her eyes began to water. Overhead, thunder boomed.

"Oh God . . ." Shonette's attention was still focused on the severed hand. "What could have done this?"

As if in answer, something growled in the jungle. It was close, judging by the sound of it. An answering cry erupted from nearby.

"Go!" Ryan shouted. "Let's get the fuck out of here."

Before they could flee, the bushes in front of

them and on either side rustled. A second later, five shadowy figures emerged. They rushed through the rain toward the three hapless victims, and their features grew clearer as they bore down on them. They were about four feet tall and covered in brown hair. Their heads were small, but their jaws seemed oversized and jutted from their faces like stone outcroppings. The creatures had long fingers with curved, black talons.

"Monkeys!" Ryan pointed, screaming.

But he was wrong.

He turned to run but slipped in the mud. One of the brown-haired creatures flung itself at him, knocking him to the ground. The air rushed out of Ryan's lungs. The furry thing straddled his chest and bared its yellow-white teeth. Its breath was like an open sewer. It was naked, except for the thick hair covering its short form, and its thin, soiled penis and testicles rubbed against his abdomen. Despite his fear, Ryan noticed that the creature had no tail. Sucking in a lungful of air, Ryan started to shout for help. Then his attacker swiped at his face with one clawed hand and ripped Ryan's cheek open. It seized the loose flap of skin and tore it free, exposing pink meat and teeth on the right side of Ryan's face, from his lower jaw to his scalp. His shriek became a wet warble. The monster lowered its snout and snuffled the wound, licking the raw tissue. Ryan squirmed beneath it, kicking and thrashing but unable to dislodge the beast.

Two more of the creatures tackled Shonette, flinging her to the jungle floor. She landed in a thicket of ferns, near the severed hand. Shonette screamed. Crawling on all fours, she tried to scramble away, but one of the attackers seized her long hair and jerked her back. It grunted with a sound that clearly indicated delight, and laughed as she screamed louder.

Another monster advanced on Roberta. It held its arms out wide, as if to embrace the terrified woman. To her surprise, it was grinning. Her allergic reaction grew worse in this close proximity. The thing crept closer. A liver-colored tongue slipped from between the beast's lips, as if tasting the air. Droplets of water dripped from its bushy fur. Roberta uttered a half scream, half sneeze. In response, the creature opened its broad mouth and hissed. Then it groped itself between the legs. Roberta's eyes flickered downward. The thing had an erection. Two kiwi-sized testicles dangled below the engorged organ, swaying with each step.

She glanced back up again. The creature's grin grew wider—

—and vanished a second later when she kicked it in the nuts.

Roberta felt the monster's testicles flatten beneath her toes, felt the hot, foul air rush from its lungs, heard its startled howl of pain and rage, but there was no time to relish the victory. She turned and fled back down the path. Her eyes watered uncontrollably and snot dripped from her nose, running down her upper lip. Her lungs burned as she gasped for breath. She prayed her throat wouldn't close up as it had in the past during her most severe allergic reactions.

She heard the sounds of pursuit behind her and

swerved off the trail, plunging headfirst into the jungle. A shrill, mournful cry rang out. It sounded like a cross between a human and a hyena. Heedless of the grasping vines and prickly thorns that tore her skin, Roberta charged through the undergrowth, seeking to lose her pursuers. She concentrated on her breathing and tried to ignore the crashing sounds throughout the jungle—snapping tree limbs, rustling ferns, padded feet running along in time with the rain. She thought of her husband, Stephen, and her best friend, Sherry. Her thoughts turned to her three cats: Nike, Tinkerbelle, and Jack Byron. In many ways, they were like her children. She had to make it out of here alive. Who would take care of them if she didn't?

Roberta risked a glance over her shoulder, and saw two brown forms darting between the trees. She quickened her pace, ignoring the pain in her chest. She considered climbing a tree, but she was deathly afraid of heights. Instead, she plowed straight ahead, half blinded by the rain. With some distance between herself and the creatures, her allergy symptoms lessened, but now her breathing was impeded by sheer terror.

As she fled, she wondered where the others were. She was supposed to be getting interviewed by Mark and Jesse soon. They should have finished up with that weirdo, Matthew, by now. Surely they'd be looking for her soon.

Wouldn't they?

Gasping for breath, she stumbled onward.

CHAPTER TEN

Matthew stood in a broad clearing along the utility path. All around him, trees bent against the wind, threatening to snap, but he did not seek shelter. His arms were outstretched and his face upturned. He smiled at the storm, and when a bolt of lightning split the clouds asunder, he imagined that the sky smiled back at him. For a moment, the jungle looked stark, like a black-and-white photo negative, flash frozen in time. Then his eyesight returned to normal. When the thunder followed the lightning a moment later, he felt it rumble in his chest. The wind howled through the jungle, sounding very much like a speeding train. Fat raindrops pelted his face like pellets from the BB gun the neighborhood bully had shot him with when they were kids. Matthew welcomed the shower. The baptismal metaphor was not lost on him.

Here, on this primal, remote island, he'd redis-covered a part of himself that he'd never known was lost. He'd been happy all along that he was able to fool the network screeners and pass his background check, physical exam, and mental evaluation, but now he was ecstatic. This was so worth it.

He was reinvigorated. Recharged. Gone was the old Matthew, the guy who'd plotted and schemed and complained, who'd issued missives and propaganda and calls for action on various blogs and message boards but had never actually shed blood for the cause. That had changed. Blood had been shed—and then some. Not only could he die for the cause; he could kill for it, too. He was someone different now. A loaded gun, ready to fire. A kettle set to boil. With each drop, the rain washed away the old Matthew, scrubbing him layer by layer, stripping off the fat and getting down to the meat of things. He was Matthew version 2.0, and he had never felt more alive.

He glanced behind him as another bolt of lightning slashed the sky. Mark's and Jesse's bodies still lay where he'd hidden them, just off the path. Matthew grinned.

It was a good start.

Two down. Many to go.

The original idea—infiltrating a network reality show and then using it as an opportunity to further the cause and disseminate the truth—had been Matthew's. He'd expected his cell leader to laugh at him, but instead, he'd offered to help Matthew take it up the chain of command. When they'd approached Barnes, the Sons of the Constitution's leader, with the proposal, Matthew had assumed he would assign it to someone else, another member of the brotherhood more suited for such a mission— or else Barnes would disregard it totally. After all, Matthew was a nobody—a mere foot soldier for the revolution, one of dozens scattered throughout various cells whose duties involved using the Internet to spread discontent regarding the current state of American affairs to the nation's sleepy, disaffected millions, thus gaining new recruits or at the very least, sympathizers to the cause. And although he was good at it, that was the extent of his abilities. He wasn't a demolitions expert or proficient with firearms. As far as his neighbors were concerned, Matthew was a faceless nobody. When he wasn't hiding his tracks online, he was careful to fit in with what society deemed as normal. The organization made a big point of insisting that members not draw attention to themselves. Matthew went to work, paid his taxes and utility bills on time, drove the speed limit, and kept his head down. He was nobody, just another drone slaving—or pretending to slave—for The Man. He had no illusions. He wasn't a hero. He wouldn't be infamous. He was just a means to an end. A cog in a much bigger machine. His mission wouldn't save the world. It would only help further the cause. Saving the world was for greater men than he.

So it came as a surprise when Barnes not only agreed, but also decided that Matthew himself would undertake the assignment.

"Make us proud," Barnes had told him, squeezing his shoulder. "Do right by the movement and your country. We can strike a major blow here. A real turning point. Don't fuck this up."

Matthew had assured him that he wouldn't, trying to project confidence and strength. Inside, he'd felt anything but self-assured. He'd been terrified, worried that he'd fail, or worse, chicken out when the time arrived. But those fears had vanished the moment he'd jammed that bamboo spear into Jesse's throat. In that second, his doubts were replaced by a sense of righteous excitement. Matthew had marveled over how it felt—the shaft sliding into the soft, semiresistant flesh, the warmth spilling from the wound, the smell of Jesse's blood and urine and feces as he died. Matthew had enjoyed it. The murder had felt right. Felt . . . *good*. Following it with Mark's murder had felt even better. Neither man was guiltless. Both were parts of the corporate machine. They willingly participated in the numbing of America in exchange for a paycheck, and thus, they were acceptable targets. They were a beginning to something great. Something huge. Something that would change the world forever.

This was something different from assassinating political leaders or—the organization's greatest effort—blowing up the FBI's database in Quantico, Virginia. This mission struck at the heart of the problem—those who lied to the American public. Those who kept them asleep. Take out the propaganda, wake up the populace, and things would change. That was where people like Timothy McVeigh had fucked up in the past. McVeigh would have been branded a hero had he parked his truck bomb in front of an Internal Revenue Service building. Instead, he'd blown up a day-care center.

You had to pick your targets wisely. Most of America loathed reality television, even though they tuned in to watch it every week. Like the old song said, free their minds, and the rest would follow.

He shivered, more from excitement than the dropping temperature.

Another blast of thunder shook him from his thoughts, and for just a moment, Matthew felt the fear and doubts creep back in. Maybe Barnes and the others were wrong. Maybe not all the contestants and crew needed to die. They couldn't all be collaborators, could they? Maybe some of them just didn't know any better. After all, he'd been like them once upon a time. He'd believed what the nightly news told him, trusted in his government and law enforcement, paid his taxes, and went to sleep at night thinking everything would be all right. He'd grown up to believe everything his parents and teachers and church told him. If his parents hadn't been killed in that car wreck, maybe he'd still be that way—oblivious to the real world. He'd gone out to find himself and found the truth instead. Maybe some of the other contestants hadn't had that opportunity to learn. Becka, for example. He'd watched her constantly, fascinated and attracted to her like no other girl he'd ever met. She had a wholesome quality to her, yet she wasn't a Goody Two-shoes. She seemed innocent but wary. She was the kind of girl he'd always fantasized about. Maybe she could be spared or converted.

No. A point needed to be made, and he was the one to make it. Even if he'd wanted to, there was no going back now. There were two dead bodies behind him, and before he was done, there would be many more.

Matthew stretched one more time, cracked his joints, then bent over and retrieved Mark's camera.

During his time on the island, he had carefully watched the cameramen, studying how they operated the equipment. After killing Mark, he'd experimented with the camera until he was confident he knew how to work it. After all, the entire plan hinged on getting this footage into the hands of the public, so that the Sons of the Constitution's message and reach would be known. Matthew knew that the network freighter had a communications center with Internet access. Once he'd finished here on the island, he was supposed to upload the files to one of the group's servers. Once they'd been edited and polished, they'd be uploaded to the Internet for all to see. Hopefully, that would coincide with the media frenzy that would erupt once news of the massacre was leaked.

Matthew had no illusions. This mission would undoubtedly end with his death. Realistically, there were no other options. There was nowhere on the island or the ship where he could hide without eventually being found. When the end came, it would not be pleasant or without violence. The storm had been a godsend. It gave him better control of the situation, a chance to eliminate more people in relative secrecy. The rest of the crew wouldn't return until the storm was over. When they did, he'd be ready for them. All he had to do was take care of things here, then keep enough hostages to guarantee him safe passage to the ship, and hang on to them long enough to send the videos. Then . . .

Well, in between now and then, he'd have some fun. After all, there was no reason why he had to kill them all immediately. Especially Becka and

109

Pauline. Once he'd finished with the others, he'd pay some extra attention to them.

With his free hand, Matthew rubbed his erection through his shorts. His eyes shone with anticipation. He picked up the bloodied spear. Bits of hair and tissue clung to the tip. In addition to the weapon, he now had a pocketknife, which he'd found after searching through the dead men's pockets. Wondering why Mark hadn't tried to use it on him, Matthew had tossed aside everything else—money, keys, their wallets and pictures of their loved ones. Curiously, Jesse had carried a guitar pick in his pocket. Matthew had tossed that aside as well.

Hefting the camera over his shoulder, he walked through the jungle, listening to the rain drum against the leaves. His thoughts were on Becka and all the things he wanted to do with her before he killed her. With Pauline, he'd probably be quick. A fast, brutal fuck and then cut her throat, or maybe cut out her breast implants first.

But with Becka, he intended to take his time. He'd save her for last.

Matthew cleared his mind, remembering that he had a job to do before he could enjoy any final reward. He walked on through the jungle, heading for camp, his senses alert and his thoughts focused. At one point, he felt eyes on him, but when he glanced around, there was no one in sight. Ignoring the sensation, he continued. There was a lot to do and not much time to complete it.

Above him, the storm unleashed its fury.

He knew how it felt.

CHAPTER ELEVEN

Reaching its full strength and ferocity, Ivan raged over the island, carving a wide swath of destruction in its path. It swallowed the last vestiges of daylight and the area around the base camp grew pitch black. The last, persistent flames of the campfire flickered under the assault from the rain, and then were extinguished. The smoldering wood hissed and sputtered under the constant barrage of water. The glowing coals faded. Within a few minutes, the temperature had dropped considerably. A fierce gust of wind tossed the campfire's wet ashes into the air and sent them smacking into the contestants like chalky mud. A few drier ashes, that had somehow miraculously escaped the drenching downpour, swirled about like a miniature tornado. The gale also littered debris around the camp: broken tree limbs, leaves, bird feathers and carcasses, sand, a dead turtle, and trash left behind by the absent crew members. The storm uprooted a particularly large tree, its trunk several feet thick, and sent it crashing into the latrine. The structure crumbled beneath the weight. Water coursed through the camp in small, twisting streams, carrying away some of the lighter flotsam and jetsam. Troy's partially finished rock wall helped divert the floods from the shelter, but the water carved shallow trenches throughout the rest of the camp, eroding the ground.

Stuart and the contestants huddled together inside the shelter, clinging desperately to one another and shivering. Some sat in silence. A few of them prayed. A few more wept. The gale ripped off part of the shelter's roof, and it fluttered away on the wind. The walls were leaning and swaying perilously. Despite the damage, the construction held and the shelter remained standing, although precariously. Stuart considered congratulating the frightened contestants on their engineering abilities, but talking was useless. The howling wind drowned out all other sound. Rain streamed through the holes in the roof, exposing the cowering players to a steady soaking. Even though he was wet and miserable, Stuart thought that was better than being exposed to the savage downpour outside.

When the storm first hit, he'd suggested that they all take shelter inside the small weatherproof storage shed, but that plan had been stymied when a tree fell on top of it, smashing the roof and one wall. They'd opted for the camp shelter instead.

He looked around the shelter's interior. Becka was huddled between Jerry and Troy, gripping both their hands tightly. Neither man seemed to mind. Indeed, they barely seemed to notice; their attention was preoccupied with the terrifying storm. Troy's teeth were chattering, and he looked even more miserable and pissed off than usual. Water streamed off the mechanic's beloved hat. Becka mouthed the Lord's Prayer silently, and although he couldn't hear her, Stuart read her lips. Pauline clung to Jeff, and unlike Jerry and Troy, Jeff definitely seemed to notice. He kept risking glances at Pauline's cleavage and "accidentally" groping quick feels around her bikini line. Then, with each blast of thunder or lightning strike, the startled man would jump, jerking away from her. This was the first time Stuart had seen him displaying anything other than confidence and strength. Stefan sat on the other side of Pauline, kneading his temples with his fingertips. His eyes were closed. Raul crouched in the corner, trying to avoid the rain streaming through the holes in the roof.

Palm fronds from the roof tore loose in the wind and fell on top of Stuart. He uttered a small, surprised cry, and then disengaged himself from them, throwing the wet leaves to the muddy floor. The others glanced at him—all except Stefan, whose eyes were still closed—but they said nothing. They, too, saw the futility in trying to speak.

Stuart fumbled for his satellite phone and brought it out. He was surprised to see that he still had a signal, despite the ferocity of the storm. He considered calling the freighter, but decided against it. They might be able to hear him, but he wouldn't be able to hear their replies. Not only that, but what could he report? That they were wet and cold and this sucked? Nobody was injured. Everyone was safe.

At least he hoped so. He was concerned that Sal and Richard weren't back yet, and extremely worried about Mark and Jesse. The two should have wrapped up their interview with Matthew and been back hours ago. Sal and Richard and the others might be wandering around out in the storm, but the two crew members had worked on *Castaways* for a long time, and both Mark and Jesse were smart enough to head back to camp as soon as the weather had shown signs of worsening. They'd been on the China shoot when a monsoon hit and in the Philippines during the tornado. Both knew what could happen in a situation like this, and neither man was foolhardy. But here he was, sitting at base camp, and there was no sign of them.

So where were they?

Stuart stared out at the trail and willed them to appear.

Lightning crashed overhead, illuminating the surrounding jungle in a flash of stark, white light. Stuart flinched. He thought he saw movement in the shadows. Then the darkness returned.

He cupped one hand around his mouth. "I think I saw something!"

Jerry, who was closest to him, mouthed, "What?"

Stuart leaned closer, shouting and enunciating each word. "I . . . think . . . I . . . saw . . . something."

Jerry frowned, and Stuart pointed out at the jungle. When the lightning flashed again, they both peered into the foliage, but there was nothing to see. Nothing moved, save for the trees and plants, bending and snapping under the shrieking wind.

"There's nothing out there," Jerry yelled. He had to repeat it twice before Stuart understood him.

Another section of the roof was sheared away. Rain poured into the shelter. Pauline screamed, loud enough to be heard over the storm. All of them moved toward Raul's corner, cowering together in the mud. The shelter's floor was turning into soup with each passing minute. Troy pulled his sodden hat from his head and wrung the water out of it. Then he put it back on and shrugged miserably. Rain dripped steadily from the tip of his crooked nose.

Stuart got settled, crouching on his haunches next to Jeff and Pauline. He slipped in the mud and almost fell over on them, but steadied himself at the last moment. He stared back out at the jungle, his thoughts returning to his missing coworkers. He felt helpless and frightened, and his panic increased with each blast of thunder. They could be hurt—or worse. Struck by lightning. Trapped under a fallen tree. Getting lost in the dark and the rain and slipping off a cliff. Swept out to sea by a storm-swollen wave. The possibilities were limitless, and his mind seemed to relish conjuring one potential catastrophe after another.

Stuart didn't have many friends. He didn't have time for them. He didn't even own a pet. His work was his social life, and as soon as one season wrapped, it was time to start another. He was always on the go, always rushing to the next location, and his small, cramped cabin aboard the network freighter felt more like home than his apartment in Binghamton or his expansive condominium in Los Angeles.

Mark and Jesse were his friends—or at least the closest thing he had to friends. Associates, certainly. He cared about them and their well-being. Right now, they were out there somewhere, lost in the storm, along with the six missing contestants—Roberta, Matthew, Sal, Richard, Ryan, and Shonette. The contestants might be lost or hurt, as well, and that was unfortunate. But Mark and Jesse were his friends. If something had happened to them, he'd never forgive himself for picking them to remain on the island with him while everyone else went back to the ship.

This was bad. Each potential *Castaways* contestant signed a mountain of legal waivers and forms, and they all knew the risks of competing in the show. But while the network couldn't legally be held responsible for their deaths, it would be a public-relations nightmare if all six were indeed injured. Something needed to be done. Someone had to look for them, and more importantly, for Mark and Jesse.

He glanced around the shelter. If any of the other contestants were worried about their fellow players, Stuart couldn't tell. They all looked scared, but he guessed they were worrying more about themselves than anyone else. This game brought out the worst in people, and after countless seasons of documenting the worst in human behavior, he'd grown quite cynical.

No. If someone was going to do something, it would have to be him.

He considered the satellite phone again, then shoved it back down inside his pocket. He stood, crouching in the shelter and waded through the mud to the entrance. The others raised their heads in surprise, watching him. Jerry and Becka started to rise but Stuart motioned at them to sit back down.

"I'll . . . be . . . back," he shouted as loudly as

possible, overenunciating the words so that they could read his lips. "Stay . . . here!"

Jerry started to protest, but Stuart cut him off with a wave of his hand. Then, bending his head against the wind, he struggled out into the storm. The wind slammed into him immediately, knocking him back a few paces. Gritting his teeth, Stuart spread his feet apart and pushed forward again. It felt like walking in quicksand. Windblown grit and debris lashed at his face, and he squinted his eyes to protect them. His nose and lips felt hot and dry, despite the downpour. Stuart looked back only once. The others were huddled together, watching him go. None of them stepped forward to go with him. Turning, he pressed slowly onward, making his way toward the trail.

Visibility was null and the terrain grew more treacherous. Much of the ground was flooded or slippery, and each step was a chore. Determined, Stuart blinked the rain from his eyes and struggled to see. When the lightning flashed again, he spied the trail. Some of it had already been eroded from the rushing waters. He memorized its location and headed for it.

Being out in the storm did nothing to ease his fears. If anything, the situation merely accentuated them. Stuart told himself that Mark and Jesse would have done the same thing for him. A nagging voice in the back of his subconscious told him that he was fooling himself, that they'd have left him to his own fate. Silencing those doubts, he thought instead of the six missing contestants. Surely, the network would approve of this search expedition. Indeed, he might be rewarded for going above and beyond the call of duty.

If he lived.

"This sucks. Fuck you, Ivan."

He slogged to the edge of the camp, found his bearings again, and shuffled into the night, hoping against hope that he wouldn't have to go too far and that he wasn't too late.

When lightning lit up the jungle again, and he saw movement in the shadows, Stuart jumped. After his initial fright passed, his spirits soared and he hoped it might be one of the missing. A second flash revealed nothing but trees and vines. He told himself that it had just been his imagination. His frayed nerves were getting the best of him. He stepped over a fallen tree blocking the path, and then cupped his hands over his mouth and shouted for Mark and Jesse. Then Stuart realized just how foolish such an attempt was. Jerry hadn't been able to hear him sitting just a few inches away. How would the two missing crew members ever hear him?

He passed the storage shed and peeked inside the wreckage, wondering if maybe someone had taken shelter inside and been injured when the tree fell on it. The collapsed structure was empty. He moved on, picking his footing carefully, and watching for any sign of the missing.

Although he didn't notice, the shadows disengaged themselves from the trees and followed along behind him, creeping steadily closer.

CHAPTER TWELVE

Roberta bit her lip as another thorn-covered vine ripped into her cheek, lacerating the skin and drawing a thin line of blood. She winced, but made no sound. She could no longer tell if the monsters—whatever they might be—were pursuing her, but she didn't want to cry out and alert them to her presence. She touched her cheek and her fingertips came away sticky. When she touched the cut again, the rain had already washed the blood away. Another jagged thorn pierced her bare ankle as she struggled on.

"Ouch!"

She paused, leaning against a broad tree trunk, and struggled to breathe. Her lungs felt like two big fists were squeezing them. Her pulse throbbed in her temples, keeping time with the thunder. She listened for sounds of pursuit, but the storm drowned out all other noise. She thought she heard one of the creatures' strange, warbling howls, but after a moment, she decided it was just the wind. Wheezing, Roberta pulled the thorn from her ankle. Then she ran on.

Her mind swam, and it was hard to focus on anything but continued flight. She considered hiding, but decided against it. The creatures were obviously familiar with the jungle—they must be native to the island, after all—and they displayed at least a rudimentary intelligence. They'd know the terrain better than she did. What were they? She'd never seen anything like them before. The savagery they'd displayed with their attack, and worse, the sheer glee they seemed to express. Roberta grew nauseous just thinking about it. The adrenaline coursing through her body didn't help matters. She collapsed to her knees and vomited in a puddle. Her stomach heaved, but there wasn't much. Her diet had consisted of small portions of fish, rice, and fruit, with the exception of one slice of pizza she'd won during a contest several days ago. Her stomach didn't seem to care. She gagged and sputtered until the muscles in her abdomen ached. Roberta waited for her dizziness to pass. Then she grasped a limb, pulled herself back to her feet, and continued fleeing through the dark. While her allergies had subsided, Roberta was feeling every bit of her fifty-four years.

Wet, cold, exhausted, and bleeding, she stumbled out onto the trail by accident. She glanced around, terrified, and tried to get her bearings. The ground was a slippery, sodden mess. Her feet sank into the mud. It took Roberta a moment to realize where she was. Between the blinding rain and her own fear, she couldn't see anything clearly. The edges of her vision were blurry, and once-familiar landmarks now seemed nonexistent or strange and permuted. The tangled hanging vines became creeping tentacles and serpents. The looming, swaying trees transformed into giant fingers, thrusting up from the earth. The howling wind mimicked a fire siren. Still struggling to breathe, Roberta closed her eyes for a moment and reminded herself that it was just her imagination.

But the hand that fell on her shoulder and squeezed was not. It was very real. Fingers pressed tightly into her flesh.

Roberta screamed, lashing out blindly and striking something solid. She heard a grunt from behind her and the grip on her shoulder slackened, then disappeared. Her attacker moaned in pain. Without glancing backward, she fled, shrieking.

"Roberta!"

She ignored the voice. It sounded familiar, but she knew that it was just more of her imagination—the storm playing auditory tricks on her.

"Roberta, come back."

"Help," she shrieked. "Somebody help me, please!"

"Roberta, it's me. It's Matthew!"

She paused, nearly tripping. Slowly, she turned around. A shadowy figure stood in the center of the path. She couldn't make out any of his features, but he certainly seemed taller and skinnier than the creatures were. She sniffed the air but did not detect the beasts' sour, musky scent. The figure carried something bulky on its shoulder. The other hand gripped a spear or walking stick.

"Roberta, what's wrong? Are you okay?"

"M-Matthew?"

"Yeah, it's me. What's going on?"

She had to strain to hear him over the howling winds. The lightning lit up the jungle and confirmed his identity. His expression was calm but concerned. She noticed his familiar bamboo spear but didn't recognize the bulkier object before the lightning vanished again. The light faded, and they were both cast back into darkness.

"Matthew! Oh m-my God . . ."

She stumbled toward him. He bent over and sat the spear and the bulky object on the ground. Then he held out his arms. She collapsed against him, burying her head in his chest. His clothing was soaked and he smelled like sweat and mildew, but Roberta didn't care. At that moment, she welcomed the odor, if only to confirm that she was still alive and—for the moment—safe. Warmth radiated from his body.

"It's terrible," she sobbed into his shirt. "They're all dead. Shonette . . . Ryan . . . those things got them. And Richard's h-hand . . . and the rest of him w-wasn't there."

Matthew's body tensed, but then she felt him relax. He stroked her wet hair. His hands felt sticky, but Roberta didn't care.

"It's okay," he whispered, trying to soothe her. "Whatever happened, it doesn't matter anymore. It's all going to be fine."

"But they're d-dead! Don't you understand that? They're *dead*."

She felt him stiffen again, and his hands returned to his sides. His chest swelled as he took a deep breath. Thunder reverberated across the sky, and nearby another tree crashed to the ground.

"*Who's* dead? Who are you talking about? Did you see something? Find someone?" He squeezed her tighter.

"I told you. Shonette and Ryan. And maybe Richard and Sal. Those things killed them. Back there." She pointed into the undergrowth. "They came out of the jungle and attacked us while we were picking fruit. Shonette found Richard's hand. At least, we think it was his. They were definitely his shorts. Those ugly shorts . . . there was blood on them and they were all ripped up."

"Slow down. You're not making any sense. Was there an accident?"

"No! I'm telling you, we were attacked."

"What are you talking about? By what?"

His arms felt like a vise now. Roberta winced in pain.

"Matthew, you're hurting me."

"What attacked you?"

"These things . . . these monsters. I didn't get a good look at them. They're sort of like a cross between a human and a chimpanzee. Haven't you seen them?"

Matthew relaxed, exhaling. His chest flattened again. Incredibly, he began to laugh. Roberta slowly pulled away from him, confused.

"Monsters? Jesus Christ, Roberta, you had me worried there for a second."

"I'm telling the truth."

"Oh, really?" His voice dripped with derision.

Frowning, Roberta touched her face. The cheek that had been resting against Matthew's chest felt slick and sticky. Then another burst of lightning lit their surroundings and she saw why. Matthew was covered in blood—his clothes, hands, arms, and face were crimson. Some of it had rubbed off on her face while he held her. Roberta gasped. Despite the amount of blood, she didn't see any injuries.

"Matthew! What happened to you? Are you okay?"

Smiling, he shrugged. "I'm fine. I have been reborn."

Roberta wondered if he'd hurt his head or was perhaps in shock. His behavior was definitely bizarre.

"We've got to go," she said.

"There's no hurry. I told you that everything was going to be okay. What's the rush?"

"Matthew, you're injured. You're not thinking clearly."

"My mind has never been clearer."

"I'm telling you the truth. We can't stay out here in the open. Those things are still out there. We've got to make it back to camp and warn the others. Can you run?"

"Of course I can run. Why wouldn't I be able to?"

"Because you're hurt!"

"No, I'm not. I told you. In fact, I've never felt better. My mind and body are liberated. I'm no longer a slave to the system. You only wish you could feel this free."

"You're not making any sense. Matthew, we're in *danger*."

He laughed again. "Well, you're partially right."

He stepped closer, and this time, the stench wafting off him was anything but comforting. Still grinning,

Matthew reached into his pocket. Still confused and in shock, Roberta took a tentative step backward and tried to return his smile. It felt more like a grimace. She glanced down at the ground and finally realized what the object he'd been carrying was—a video camera. It occurred to her that the two crew members, Mark and Jesse, weren't with him.

"Where's—"

"You asked me if I could run," Matthew interrupted. "I think the real question, Roberta, is whether *you* can run."

"Please," she begged, without knowing why. Her stomach fluttered. She suddenly felt very afraid—even more than when the creatures had attacked. "We have to get out of here, Matthew."

Lightning flashed again. Matthew brought his hand out of his pocket and Roberta saw something shiny clenched in his fist. It glinted momentarily in the temporary light. Then the lightning faded, and she couldn't see it anymore.

But she felt it.

Matthew raked the object across her throat in a wide, sweeping arc. Roberta felt no pain, but her skin suddenly felt very cold. Her fingers fluttered to her throat. It was wet and warm. Roberta's eyes widened in shock. The object glittered. A pocketknife. She wondered if that had been his luxury item. Then she realized what had just happened. The pain kicked in. Her neck burned. Matthew's smile never faded. He stabbed her, thrusting the knife into her stomach. It felt like he'd pinched her. Then he stabbed her in the side, just above her left kidney. Then just below her left breast. When he tried to pull the pocketknife out, the blade remained stuck fast. He grunted in surprise.

"Must have hit a bone."

Roberta tried to speak, but only managed to wheeze. Clamping one hand over her throat, she turned to run. Matthew pushed her down from behind. She landed in the mud and tried to scramble away from him, scuttling through the slop.

"I don't know what you were babbling about," Matthew said, staring down at her, "but if there's been an accident and Shonette and the others are hurt, then that just makes things easier. It vindicates me. I mean, it's got to be a sign, right? That somebody upstairs is looking down on my work and finds it good?"

Roberta was suddenly very sleepy. The air around her grew colder, even though she could no longer feel the rain or wind. Shivering, she rolled over onto her stomach and closed her eyes.

The last thing she felt was Matthew's foot on the back of her head, pressing her face deeper into the mud. The pressure increased. Roberta struggled to draw one last breath—

—and couldn't.

The wind howled.

Deep in the jungle, something answered it.

CHAPTER THIRTEEN

When Shonette regained consciousness, she was disappointed. She'd been dreaming about her children, Monika and Darnell. The three of them had been sitting around the little breakfast nook in her apartment's kitchenette. Alicia Keys was playing on the radio and the television blared in the background; the weatherman promised nothing but sunshine. Shonette was getting dressed for work and urging the kids to hurry up or they'd be late for school. Monika and Darnell were complaining because she'd bought generic cereal rather than Fruity Pebbles, and she'd told them that when she won a million dollars on *Castaways*, they could eat Fruity Pebbles every day for the rest of their lives, if they wanted to. When she won, there would be no more generic brands and double shifts and coupon clipping. The kids had cheered. Then they'd given her a hug and left for school. In the dream, they'd felt warm and soft, and she could smell their familiar scent. She'd sighed, feeling comforted and strong.

It had been a good dream.

Safe.

Stirring slowly, she opened her eyes, trying to remember what had happened. Rain streamed into her eyes, and her limbs felt numb. Blinking, she glanced around in confusion. The world was dark and cold—and upside down. Lightning and roiling, black clouds raced across the ground, and mud and tree roots covered the sky. She sensed that she was moving, but her legs didn't seem to be working. Indeed, something was gripping her ankles tightly, holding her feet and legs together. Before she could react, she was jostled roughly, and her head banged against something wet and furry. She tried to cry out, and then the stench hit her—a sour, musky smell, like marinated roadkill. She turned her head away and gagged.

In the darkness, something growled.

The bottom fell out of Shonette's stomach. She realized that she was being carried through the jungle, lugged over someone's—some *thing's*—hairy shoulder. She began to struggle, and her captor growled again—deep and guttural. Sharp talons dug into her leg.

Then the memories came rushing back, and Shonette screamed.

She remembered the shredded scraps of raw meat that had once belonged to Richard, and the torn and bloodied remnants of his shorts. She remembered a band of monsters erupting from the jungle and encircling them, shrieking and growling, attacking with sharp claws and tremendous blows. She recalled the stench and the sound. She remembered Ryan, screaming with only half a face left, squirming as one of the beasts straddled him and tore open his stomach with its black talons. Then it had burrowed around inside his stomach with its hairy, elongated hands, pulling his insides out of the gaping wound and devouring them with obvious relish, while poor Ryan thrashed soundlessly, his eyes rolling to white, his cries wheezing through the hole in his face while his blood bubbled out around him. The last thing she remembered was seeing Roberta fleeing into the night, swallowed up by the downpour and pursued by several of the howling, hooting creatures, even as one of them had thrown Shonette to the ground and jumped atop her. She remembered its weight, pressing against her.

Then everything had gone black and she'd been back home with her kids.

And now she wasn't.

Shonette's head bounced against a rock. She realized just how close to the ground she was, and then remembered how short the creatures had been. Her hair was muddy and covered with leaves and twigs. Apparently, it had been dragging on the ground while she'd been unconscious. She tried to twist around. Her struggles increased, and in response, the talons dug deep into her skin. Gritting her teeth, Shonette swung her head back and forth. Her hair slapped the ground with wet, smacking sounds. She beat at her captor's furry back with her fists.

"Let me go, motherfucker!"

The creature stopped, grunting at her blows.

"That's right. You don't want any of this. Let me go, you son of a bitch."

The thing's grip shifted, and Shonette felt both its hands encircle her ankles and squeeze tightly. She screamed again, so loudly that she felt something tear inside her throat. Her cry turned into a weak rasp.

Unbelievably, the abomination laughed.

She tried to break free, but before she could, the monster slung her off its shoulder and swung her through the air in a wide arc, still holding on to her ankles. Her hair fluttered out behind her and her hands flailed helplessly. Shonette's scream was cut short as her head slammed against a massive, gnarled tree trunk.

The upside-down world turned black again.

Shonette returned to her dream, but this time, she found herself alone.

In her dreams, she could still scream.

CHAPTER FOURTEEN

Muttering curses and oaths under his breath, Stuart plodded along the trail. His feet squelched in the mud, and with each step, cold water seeped into his shoes. The wind whipped at him, pushing him backward and impeding his progress. He had to keep blinking the rain away, and flicking his wet hair out of his face, but neither helped. Visibility was almost nonexistent, except during the brief flashes of lightning, and he made his way carefully, all too aware of what could happen to him if he stepped off the trail. As dangerous—and foolish (he admitted that to himself now)—as this rescue mission was, straying off into the jungle would be even worse.

"Not my finest hour. What the hell was I thinking?"

The thunder mocked him—deep, booming laughter that echoed across the island, shaking the very ground. Stuart paused and gave the sky the finger.

"Screw you, Ivan."

He trudged on. Occasionally, he cupped his hands over his mouth and called out for Mark and Jesse and the missing contestants, but he had little hope that they would actually be able to hear him. He wished for a flashlight or a bullhorn or even a flare gun—anything that would enable him to make his presence known, but all he had on him was the satellite phone. Everything else was back in his cabin aboard the freighter.

The freighter . . . He snorted, shaking his head. Why was he out here wandering around in the middle of a fucking cyclone while that pompous prick Roland and everyone else who worked for the show got to stay safe and secure onboard the ship? He had seniority, goddamn it. Somebody else should be out here—a grip or an EMT or a fucking intern. Not him. He should be sitting in the editing room right now, warm and dry, drinking endless cups of hot coffee while sorting through hours and hours of raw footage and piecing together something usable, something that would keep viewers tuned in and the ratings high. That was his job. Not *this*. This was bullshit, and when this storm was over, somebody was going to hear about it.

One thing he was glad he *hadn't* brought with him was the camera. He'd left it back at the base camp, and as far as Stuart was concerned, the damned thing could float away and out to sea.

He was still fuming when he came across the fallen tree. It had snapped in half, and the upper portion lay across the path, effectively blocking him. Rather than walking around it and wading through the tangled undergrowth, Stuart climbed over the trunk, straddling it with one leg, then the other. As he descended to the other side, he slipped and fell, sprawling on his rear. Cold water and mud rushed beneath his clothes and between his butt cheeks. Stuart groaned. It was the single most unpleasant thing he had ever felt.

"Shit." He gripped the tree and pulled himself to his feet. Then he shuffled around, lifting one leg and then the other, trying to dislodge the mud. He felt it running down his legs in thick rivulets. Something round and jagged—a pebble or shell or nut—was wedged up against his tailbone.

To his left, something snapped loudly—probably another tree.

"Hello," he shouted, not caring now if anyone could hear him or not. It felt good to shout, to rant, to unleash some of his pent up frustration. "Anybody there? Mark? Jesse? Anyone?"

The only sound was the rain, hissing as it pelted the leaves.

Ahead of him, Stuart spotted something lying in the middle of the trail. It was too small and misshapen to be a tree. When the sky lit up again, he caught a glimpse of pale skin.

"Oh, no."

Shivering, he hurried to the crumpled form and knelt beside it. Still unable to see, he fumbled out his satellite phone and flipped it open. The display screen's meager green light offered little illumination, but it was enough for him to recognize the body. Roberta, judging by her clothes and hair. She was lying on her belly, and her face was buried deep in the mud. Her side was bloody, as was the ground around her. She did not move.

"Roberta? Oh, shit. Hey, Roberta!"

He touched her cheek. It was cold.

"Roberta?"

She didn't answer, but he hadn't really expected her to. He'd hoped, certainly, but the position of her body had told him otherwise.

Carefully, Stuart rolled her over and confirmed his worst fears. Roberta wasn't breathing and her mouth and nose were filled with mud. It dripped out as he laid her back down again. He considered cleaning out the muck and administering mouth-to-mouth resuscitation, but there was no point. Her open eyes stared sightlessly, and when he felt her wrist for a pulse, he found none. Her limbs were limp, not stiff—and still compliant. That meant she hadn't been dead long. He tried to remember how long it took for rigor mortis to set in and then realized he didn't have a clue. The extent of his knowledge on such matters, like most Americans, came from watching crime dramas.

He examined her corpse more closely. She'd been stabbed, obviously. The hilt of a pocketknife still jutted from beneath her breast. Her abdomen and throat were covered with blood. It looked wet and fresh. Stuart tried to determine if that was from the rain or because it was still running. Her body moved slightly as the mud beneath her shifted, and he then noticed that her throat had actually been cut. He hadn't noticed it at first because of the shadows and the amount of blood covering her. His eyes returned to the pocketknife. He tugged experimentally on the hilt, but the blade remained embedded in her. He pulled harder, but couldn't free it. He felt something beneath the tips of his fingers. Some sort of indentation. Crouching lower, Stuart leaned close and shined his phone's display screen on the knife. A pair of initials had been engraved on the hilt—M.H.

He sat back up and sighed. M. H.—Mark Hickerson. He'd seen the cameraman use a pocketknife before, and he was pretty sure it was this one. There weren't any other M. H.'s running around on the island, and he knew for a fact that Roberta hadn't brought a pocketknife as her luxury item. She'd brought lip balm (something that Stuart had thought was pretty clever—many contestants suffered from horribly chapped lips due to the constant exposure to the elements). But if this was indeed Mark's knife, then where the hell was Mark? And more importantly, how had his knife ended up sticking out from beneath Roberta's breast? Had there been a fight? A struggle? An accident? And if Roberta was dead, what about the others? Where were Jesse, Matthew, and the rest?

He glanced back down at Roberta's still form. Raindrops beat against her open eyes, filling them with fake tears. Shivering, he reached out and closed the lids, holding them shut until they stayed that way.

"I'm sorry," Stuart whispered. "I didn't know you very well. We never get to know any of you very well. We don't want to, you see? There's no time for that. This is reality television, but reality is what we say it is. We only want to know one aspect of you. One facet that we can exploit and sell to the viewers. You are who we portray you as, rather than your real self. We don't care about your families or loved ones or what you're really like back home—not unless we can put a spin on it. So, I'm sorry that I didn't take the time to get to know the real you. I bet you were a decent person. You certainly didn't deserve this."

Raindrops rolled down his cheeks. Stuart flicked

the mud and the blood from his fingers and wiped his hands on a clean portion of Roberta's wet shirt. Then he pressed some buttons on the phone's keypad and put it to his ear.

"Come on," he sighed. "Pick up. Pick up. Pick up."

While he waited for the ship to answer, another burst of lightning raced across the sky and that was what saved his life. In the after flash, he saw the shadow rushing up behind him. The satellite phone slipped from his hands and landed in the mud. Without turning around, Stuart had time to roll aside as the figure thrust a sharpened bamboo spear into the empty space he'd occupied only seconds before.

Stuart leapt to his feet and was momentarily taken aback by the identity of his attacker.

"Matthew?"

The wild-eyed man didn't respond. He merely nodded and jabbed the spear at Stuart again, aiming for his stomach. Stuart side-stepped the attempt and balled his fists, adopting a boxer's stance.

On the ground, a tinny, static-filled voice came from the phone. *"Hello? Hello?"*

"Can I answer that?" Stuart asked. Without waiting for confirmation, he moved toward it. Matthew thrust the spear at him again, and Stuart paused, holding his hands up.

"Hello," the voice called again, almost lost in the din of the storm. *"Is there anyone there? Do you copy?"*

Matthew spat on the phone. His lips drew back in a snarl.

"I don't know what's going on here," Stuart wheezed, "but I never liked your sorry ass, anyway.

You've got to be the most fucked-up contestant we've ever had on this show. Now you can put that down and talk to me, or we can fight. Either one is fine with me. I'm sick of this storm and this island and all the fucking attention whores like you and your fellow contestants get."

Matthew didn't lower the spear, but his eyes flinched, as if surprised.

"If you feel that way," he murmured, barely audible over the storm, "then why do you participate? Why not do something else?"

"Why the hell do you care?" Stuart's caution was replaced with anger. "Why does a steel worker do what he does? Or a pizza maker or a stockbroker? This is my job, and I'm good at it, and I get paid to do it. This is how I earn my living. I won a fucking Emmy, man. What have you done?"

"Me? That's easy. I'm going to save the world."

It was the conviction in Matthew's matter-of-fact tone that chilled Stuart the most. Despite all of the network's psychological profiling and screening, the young man was obviously unbalanced and had now suffered some kind of breakdown—maybe from the rigors of the competition or the culture shock or something else. But faced with that knowledge, Stuart had more questions than ever. He still didn't know what had transpired over the last few hours, and he needed to find out before the situation spiraled even further out of control.

"Matthew." He spoke softly, trying to keep his voice calm. "Look, maybe we got off on the wrong foot. Let's both take a deep breath. Obviously, you're pretty upset about something, but we don't have to do this. Just calm down. I'm sorry I said those things to you. I didn't mean them."

Matthew laughed. His grip tightened on the bamboo shaft. Water dripped from the sharpened tip.

Stuart continued. "Bad things are happening here. Look—Roberta's dead, as you can see. Some of the others are missing. Do you know what's going on? Have you seen any of them? Shonette and Ryan. Richard and Sal. And Mark and Jesse. They went out with you, right? Do you know where they are?"

Matthew didn't respond. He stared at Stuart without blinking. Stuart was reminded of a lizard.

"Do you know who did this?" Stuart pointed at Roberta's corpse. "If so, then you need to tell me."

"Monsters."

"What?"

"Monsters," Matthew repeated, motioning at Roberta with the tip of his spear. "She called me a monster. But she was wrong. I'm not the monster. You are. You and all of the people like you."

Stuart took a step backward, preparing to run. He didn't like how this sounded. He noticed that Matthew was breathing fast.

"Hey," he said. "Don't talk like that, man. We can work this out, right? Just calm down. Nobody on this island is a monster."

"That's where you're wrong."

Matthew tensed, and Stuart saw what was coming next. For a moment, he considered making a dive for the pocketknife, still embedded in Roberta's chest, but then he remembered how impossible it had been to remove it. If he tried now, Matthew would impale him before he could free it. He took a deep breath and balled his hands into fists again, ready for the assault.

But the attack came from around them, rather than from Matthew.

All at once, the sodden greenery rustled with activity and at least a dozen—maybe more—shadowy, stunted figures leaped out onto the trail, surrounding them. Without either man realizing it, Stuart and Matthew drew close together, their backs to one another. With no lightning to illuminate the scene, neither could make out any details of the newcomers' appearances, except that they were short and bulky, and smelled terrible—like a damp basement full of dead mice and mildewed newspapers. The new arrivals closed ranks, drawing closer. They moved in silence.

"Who's that?" Stuart challenged. "Mark? Is that you, man?"

Matthew stood stiff, pressing closer against him. His breath whistled through his nose.

"Jesus," Stuart whispered. "They smell like the inside of a gorilla's stomach."

"No," Matthew muttered. "They smell like death."

"Shut up."

One of the intruders hissed, and Stuart caught a glimpse of white teeth in the darkness.

"Who are you?" he asked again. "What do you want? Are you hurt?"

Its response was guttural and totally inhuman—but it was speech nevertheless. Stuart was reminded of a monkey trying to talk.

"Jesus Christ! What is this? What are they?"

"Monsters," Matthew said. "Roberta was right, after all. But so was I. I'm not the monster. They are."

Ignoring him, Stuart's gaze flashed toward the discarded satellite phone. The display was still lit, and he wondered if someone was still on the other end, listening to this situation. If so, would they understand what was happening? At least enough to send help?

The shadowy figures crept closer, pausing to study Roberta's prone form. One of them crouched and sniffed her. The wind shifted, and Stuart winced, turning his head away from the foul stench.

"Jesus," he muttered. "What is this?"

"This is the end," Matthew said.

The stench grew stronger.

"What are they?" Stuart asked again.

A bolt of lightning crashed through the sky, momentarily shedding light on the path, and Stuart got his answer. He saw all too well, and what he saw made him scream.

Matthew began to laugh.

Howling as one, the creatures attacked.

Matthew's laughter turned into screams. Stuart's screams turned into pleas.

Then both were silenced.

On the ground, a faint voice continued to drift from the satellite phone.

"Hello? Stuart? Is anyone there? If you can hear me, the meteorologist says the worst of the storm has passed. It should all be over in the next hour or so. Then you guys will be okay. Do you copy? Hello? Goddamn it, why doesn't anybody answer?"

CHAPTER FIFTEEN

Sighing, Brett Heffron set his paper coffee cup on the console, readjusted his headset, and tried again.

"Hello? Stuart, if you can hear me, press one of the buttons on the phone. I should hear it beep, even if I can't hear you."

He waited, but there was only more static. It had been like this for the last five minutes, ever since he'd received the call from the island. For a brief moment, at the beginning of the call, he'd thought he heard Stuart's voice, but then everything turned to static. According to the controls, the connection was solid, but something—probably the storm—was interfering with the audio. He turned the speakers up and adjusted the sound, trying to diminish the background noise, but it did nothing to improve the quality. All he heard was an occasional snippet of sound—one syllable of a word, half a crash of thunder, the sputtering hiss of rain.

And then, incredibly, for an instant, something that sounded like a wild animal, which was, of course, impossible, since there were no mammals indigenous to the island. It squealed and roared. Then the static returned.

"That," he muttered to himself, "is some weird-ass feedback."

The ship rolled, and his stomach lurched. Brett wasn't given to seasickness, but the swells from the storm were bigger than anything he'd ever encountered.

"Hello? Stuart, do you copy? I say again, press the buttons on your keypad if you can hear me."

Another squeal, then more static.

Brett wore a headset with a microphone, and his ears were starting to sweat beneath the foam-covered earpieces. Despite the other technician's insistence that the equipment should be kept in a cool environment, Brett had cranked the heat up when the storm hit. Now it was hot inside the radio shack. He made a mental note to turn the heat down next time he got up.

He tried adjusting the equipment one more time, and then said, "Stuart or whoever this is, I don't know if you can hear me, but I'm not copying you. Suggest you try calling from another location. I say again, the meteorologists say that the storm is almost over. Ivan is on its way out. Just hang in there a little bit longer. Freighter out."

He flicked a switch, breaking the connection, and removed his headset. He tossed it onto the console and then dug in each ear with his pinkie finger, removing the sweat and wax buildup. The computer monitor in front of him flashed from his unfinished game of solitaire to the screen saver. He clicked the mouse, bringing the game back up again, and then took another sip of coffee.

"Ugh . . . shit."

He grimaced. The coffee had been lukewarm to begin with, but now it had turned cold and the artificial creamer he'd dumped into the cup earlier was now a partially dissolved mound of sludge.

He tried checking his e-mail, to see if there were any messages from his friends back in Los Angeles, but the wireless network was down, as well.

"No coffee. No communications. Pulling a stupid night shift. Shit, I'd be better off on the island with those other saps."

Brett was twenty-six years old, and would turn twenty-seven in another week and a half. This wasn't the first time he'd spent a birthday onboard a ship, anchored in some remote part of the world rather than at home with friends and family. Sometimes it seemed like much of his adult life had been spent at sea, rather than on land. After graduating high school, Brett had served four years in the navy as a radioman. When he got out, he'd gone to college courtesy of the G.I. Bill, but after two semesters, decided that more school wasn't for him. For a year, he'd worked for a satellite radio company, but when a corporate merger was held up by the federal government and the company started hemorrhaging money, Brett had been let go. He'd landed on his feet, responding to a note on craigslist.com, and got a job as a communications specialist on the network freighter. Until then, he'd never watched a single episode of *Castaways*, and now, after working on the show, he avoided episodes like the plague.

The hatch to the compartment opened with a metallic clang and Gina Tremblay, the other communications specialist, stepped into the room. She smiled at him, then waggled the two cups of coffee that were perched precariously in one hand. Brett's gaze drifted to her long, slender legs, but then he noticed that she'd caught him looking. Her smile faltered just a bit. Quickly, he focused instead on her face.

"Coffee for two? You read my mind, Gina."

Her smile returned. "Well, if you want a cup, how about giving me a hand with the door?"

Brett slid out of his chair and closed the hatch behind her, locking the lever in place. Then he gratefully accepted one of the two cups and turned the heat down before returning to his seat. Gina took the chair beside him.

"What are you doing up?" he asked. "You're not supposed to be on until tomorrow morning."

"I couldn't sleep. The storm is tossing the ship around so much, and I had to hang on to my rack just to keep from falling out of it. I gobbled half a dozen packs of crackers to keep from getting sick."

"Yeah," Brett agreed, "it's been bad. It's passing, though. Things should settle down soon."

"Anything from the island?"

"Yeah, actually, I received a transmission just a few minutes ago. It came from Stuart's phone."

"Duh. He's the only one on the island *with* a phone right now."

"Smart-ass."

"Is everything all right? How are they holding up?"

"I don't know. There was too much interference, and I couldn't hear shit. Just a few fragments here and there." He paused. "There was one weird thing, though."

"What?"

Brett shrugged. "I don't know. A sound. This strange growling, snuffling sort of noise. Like an animal of some kind."

"There aren't any animals on the island."

"I know. That's why it was weird. Wish I knew what it was."

Gina kicked off her shoes and propped her feet up on the console, stretching her legs. Brett tried very hard not to notice, and made a point of turning his attention back to the game of solitaire on the computer monitor.

"It was probably just a bird," Gina said. "A parrot or a cockatiel or something. My mother used to have a cockatiel. They can sound pretty strange when they get going. Maybe it was scared of the storm and was acting spastic."

"It wasn't a bird. At least, not like any I've ever heard before."

"Maybe some kind of weird feedback from the storm?"

"No. This definitely sounded more like an animal. I keep wondering if maybe it was one of those wild pigs that used to live there. You know, the ones that originally came from the shipwrecks? They were all supposed to have died off, but maybe we were wrong."

Gina grinned.

"What?" Brett asked.

"The only pig in the vicinity of this island is you—checking out my ass every time I turn around. I swear to God, Brett, you're worse than Mr. Thompson."

His ears burned, but then he realized that she was just teasing him.

"What can I say? It's a much better view than anything else on this hunk of junk."

She winked. "Damn straight it is. And I'll tell you the same thing that I told Roland last time he copped a feel—you can look, but you'd better not touch."

"Where is Mr. Thompson anyway? I haven't seen him all night."

"He's getting cozy in his cabin with one of the new interns."

"That figures. Is it a guy or girl this time?"

"I don't know and I don't care. Long as he keeps his disgusting hands off me, he can sleep with whomever he wants. It's not like there's a shortage. The network execs keep providing him with new conquests."

"Ever think about tipping off one of the gossip magazines or celebrity websites? I bet one of those places would pay good money for pictures of some of his shenanigans."

"No way," Gina said. "I need this job."

"Yeah, me too."

"Well, aren't we quite the pair?"

The ship lurched to starboard suddenly, and Brett's cup of coffee fell to the floor. Gina managed to grab hers before it fell, but the hot liquid splashed out, burning her thumb and index finger.

146

"Ouch!"

"Goddamn it." Brett picked up the crumpled paper cup and tossed it in the overflowing trash can. Then he grabbed a roll of paper towels from the supply closet and mopped up the mess.

Gina sucked her fingers. "You want what's left of mine?"

"No, that's okay. I'll go get more. We really do need a coffeepot in here, though. With the amount of money the sponsors are paying for a thirty-second spot, you'd think the network would spring for one."

The freighter rolled again, tossed by a massive swell. Brett and Gina heard something crash out in the passageway and roll down the hall.

"Whatever that was," Gina said, "they should have tied it down. Don't people read their memos?"

"I thought the worst of the storm was supposed to be over. This sure as hell doesn't feel like it."

"It is," Gina replied. "This is just the last vestiges. I stopped by the weather shack on the way up here. Ivan is supposed to pass over completely in another hour or so. We didn't even get the worst of it. The center was about one hundred miles north of our position."

"Any damage that you know of?"

"The Globe Corporation lost an oil rig about two hundred miles to the northwest. And I heard some of the others talking about a distress call from an Indonesian fishing boat. But other than that, I haven't heard anything."

"Well, I just hope the folks on the island are okay."

"Yeah." Gina nodded. "I hope so, too. Imagine—risking your life just for a chance to be on television."

"But to be fair, they didn't know there was going to be a cyclone."

"Maybe not. But they signed up, didn't they? This show has been on for enough seasons, they should know to expect anything. They give it all up—their families, their home lives, their careers—put everything on hold for a chance to win a million dollars. But it's not about the money, is it? It's about being famous. Being on television. It's the hope that they might get recognized in their hometown or get an offer to pitch cold medicine in a commercial. That's a pretty shallow worldview, if you ask me."

"Wow." Brett was stunned. "I've never heard you talk like that. I had no idea you felt this strongly."

Gina shrugged. "All I'm saying is, they signed up for the show of their own free will, so they can't complain when the island throws its worst at them. Whatever happens, it's their own fault because they're the ones who put themselves in the situation in the first place."

Nodding, Brett mulled it over. They sat in silence for a while. The freighter creaked and groaned, rocking back and forth. Gina pulled a Sherrilyn Kenyon paperback out of a desk drawer, turned to a folded-over page, and began reading. Brett returned to his game of solitaire, but he had trouble concentrating on it.

They waited for the storm to pass.

CHAPTER SIXTEEN

Jerry stared out into the darkness and said, "I think it's starting to let up."

Becka pressed closer against him. "Do you really think so?"

"Yeah, I do. It's not raining as hard anymore, and the wind seems to have died down."

As if in disagreement, they heard a loud crack from the jungle as another tree toppled over. Thunder rumbled overhead almost as an afterthought.

Jerry ran a hand over his stubbly head. "Or maybe not."

"This is just the eye passing over," Stefan said.

Jerry was surprised by the comment. Like the rest of his fellow contestants, he'd assumed that Stefan was asleep. He'd sat through most of the storm with his eyes closed, not moving or speaking, his breathing shallow.

"Take advantage of the quiet while you can," Stefan continued. "It will begin again soon enough."

"This ain't the eye," Troy said. "Hurricanes have eyes. This is a fucking cyclone."

"They are the same thing," Stefan corrected him. "And this is most certainly the eye."

"The fuck do you know?"

"Obviously, quite a bit more than you."

"Jesus fucking Christ, I need a fucking cigarette if I'm gonna be trapped in this shit with you, Stefan."

Pauline held her hands out in front of her and examined them.

"Oh," she said through chattering teeth, "my fingers look like prunes."

"All of our fingers do," Becka said. "But I don't think you'll be getting a manicure anytime soon."

Pauline rolled her eyes and looked away.

Jeff disentangled himself from the others and walked to the damaged shelter's entrance. He ran a hand through his wet, jet-black hair and peered up at the sky. Then he turned back to the group.

"You know, I think Jerry might be right. You guys can all hear me now, correct?"

They nodded.

"Yeah," Raul said. "So?"

"Earlier, we were sitting on top of each other and we couldn't hear shit. We had to shout into each other's ears."

"You're mistaken, I'm afraid." Stefan stood and stretched. "I'm quite certain this is just a temporary lull. The rest of the storm system will return soon enough."

Troy stirred. "If we're lucky, when it does, maybe it'll fucking take you with it."

Stefan grinned. "You should follow my example and reserve your energy, wrench-bender."

"Oh yeah? Why's that, asshole?"

"Because you're going to need it."

Pauline frowned. "Why don't you guys save the conflict for the cameras?"

"Maybe we're practicing," Troy said. "Or maybe I just don't like the fucker."

Raul walked over and joined Jeff at the entrance. "You're right. The rain is slowing. Look at it. It's just drizzling now. Eye of the storm or not, we should take advantage of it. Maybe we can get the fire started again."

"I doubt it," Jerry said. "Everything is soaked."

"Well," Raul insisted, "we should still do something."

"Like what?" Jeff asked.

"I don't know. Fix this leaky-ass roof, for one thing. Or go out and find the others."

"I agree," Jerry said. "I'm worried about them. Sal and Richard, especially. They were right on the beach when this thing hit. And Stuart hasn't come back yet, either."

"Maybe he found the others," Becka said, "and they're all together. They'd have been better off staying put than trying to make it back here. Especially if any of them are hurt."

"All the more reason to try and find them," Jerry said.

"I wouldn't, if I were you."

"Why not, Stefan?"

"Because when the storm returns—and it most assuredly will—then you'll be trapped out there, as well."

"Yeah," Pauline agreed. "Or what if they make it

back while you guys are gone, and then Ivan starts again? Then we'll just have to worry about you guys."

Raul glanced back out at the jungle. "Well, y'all can stay here if you want, but I'm going to make an attempt. It's the right thing to do. If it was me out there, I'd want somebody to find me. Anybody want to go along?"

"I'll go," Jeff said.

Troy stood and readjusted his cap. "Fuck it. I'll tag along. Anything beats the hell out of sitting here with Stefan."

Stefan blew him a kiss and sat down again. Troy returned the gesture by giving him the finger.

"I'll stay here," Pauline said. "I'm already wet enough."

Jerry wondered if she'd meant the statement as more of her sexual double entendres. If so, nobody took the bait. They were too preoccupied.

He nudged Becka with his arm. "Will you be okay here for a little bit?"

She smiled. "I'll be fine. Go ahead. Raul's right. It's sweet of you to ask, though. Just come back safe, okay?"

"I promise."

And then, quite unexpectedly, she leaned closer and gave him a brief kiss on the cheek. It happened so quickly that Jerry had to convince himself that it hadn't been his imagination. Her lips were soft and warm, and her breath tickled his ear. When she pulled away, he felt the kiss lingering. It was the only part of his body that felt clean.

"H-hey," he stammered.

Becka blushed, and quickly turned away.

"Just for luck," she murmured. "And to thank you."

"For what?"

She stared into his eyes. "For watching out for me—taking care of me. It means a lot. Until this morning, I thought I was strong. Then, during that challenge, I started to have doubts, and I almost gave up. It's been a long day, and I don't know how I would have gotten through it without you. You make me feel safe, and I know nothing will happen as long as you're here."

Jerry opened his mouth to respond, but a warbling, drawn-out wail cut him off.

"What the fuck was that?" Troy shouted.

"Quiet," Jeff said. "Listen."

The long howl continued and was answered by another. Then both faded and silence returned. The rain was just a quiet patter now. Even the thunder had ceased.

"What the hell was that?" Troy asked again.

"I don't know," Jeff admitted.

"It's the producers," Raul said. "They're playing some kind of joke on us. We're already spooked from the storm. They figure this is a good opportunity to fuck with us a little bit more."

"No," Jerry said, "that doesn't make sense. If they were playing a practical joke, they'd want it on film. Where are the cameras?"

"Okay," Raul said. "Then if it wasn't them, what was it?"

"I think you're right that it's somebody screwing around. I just don't think it's the crew."

Raul frowned. "Richard or Sal?"

"Maybe. Or Ryan or one of the girls. Maybe even Matthew."

Pauline laughed. "You know, until now, I'd completely forgotten about him."

"That's why he's a wily competitor," Stefan mused. "He stays in the background. Don't we all wish Troy would do the same?"

The wiry mechanic spun around and stomped toward the Welshman.

"That's it, fuck-stain. Fuck the cameras, fuck the contest, and fuck you. You and me are going a round."

Stefan climbed wearily to his feet. "I think you need a reminder."

"And I think Raul and the others need to know what you fucking said when they were gone."

Stefan arched an eyebrow. "Are you certain you want to do that?"

Raul turned. "What's he talking about, Stefan?"

Troy grinned victoriously. "This afternoon, while you guys were off getting firewood, your buddy here—"

The howl started again, closer this time. It was answered by several others.

"Okay," Becka gasped. "Maybe we should all just stay here until the others get back or help arrives."

"Look . . ."

Jeff pointed into the darkness. The others turned in that direction. A pair of yellow eyes stared back at them. The eyes blinked, and then returned. Then another pair appeared. And another. Then six more. Then a dozen.

In the murky blackness, something growled.

"What the fuck?" Troy yelled.

Pauline shrieked. Raul and Jeff backed slowly away from the opening as the eyes drew closer and the growling increased.

"What is that stench?" Stefan murmured.

Jerry dove for the back of the shelter and scrambled through their meager belongings in the darkness. Everything was wet, and it was hard to find anything. His hand closed around the familiar hard plastic casing of a flashlight. He wondered where it had come from, and then remembered that Vaughn, a contestant who had previously been exiled, had brought one as his luxury item. Apparently, he'd forgotten to take it with him, and it had lain here all this time, buried in the back of the shelter. Jerry clicked it on and shined the powerful beam into the darkness.

And froze.

A dozen figures—maybe more—filled the base camp. Most of them were short, standing around four feet in height, with a few reaching almost five feet. They were bipedal, and each was covered with thick, curly hair that varied from chestnut to black. Their heads were shaped like small melons, their ears pointed, and their furrowed brows sloped noticeably. The most prominent facial feature was their thick lower jaws, which seemed almost oversized in comparison to the rest of their face. By contrast, their feet were tiny, with fat, round heels and long toes that ended in claws. Their hands had the same characteristics, and on each, five long fingers were equipped with curved, black talons. A few of them had noticeable deformities—extra fingers, stunted limbs, or misshapen noses.

In the instant before they attacked, Jerry thought to himself that he was looking at a race of cryptids—an unidentified species of primate or maybe a missing link. The island's legends came rushing back to him, and the amateur cryptozoologist in Jerry was fascinated, even though he wanted to flee. He shined the light directly into the glaring eyes of one of the creatures, and it reared back, flashing a row of teeth that Mother Nature had clearly designed for eating meat.

"Shut it off," Jeff ordered. "Shut it off before they—"

The apelike things attacked. They sprang forward as one, charging the ruined shelter. The contestants scattered. Jeff and Raul ran out of the entrance and dodged left and right. Pauline dashed after them. Becka and Troy retreated to the rear of the shelter, cowering next to Jerry. Stefan crouched low and held his ground.

"Turn that fucking flashlight off," Troy whispered.

Jerry complied. It didn't matter anyway. At that moment, the clouds opened up in the wake of the departing storm, and thin, pale moonlight shone down upon the postcyclone devastation, and the carnage that followed.

Two of the creatures pounced on Raul, crushing him to the ground with their weight. The others glimpsed a flurry of arms and legs—both human and otherwise. Then Raul screamed, lost beneath the pile-on like a quarterback in a particularly ghoulish game of football.

Jeff's retreat was cut short as one of the monsters leaped in front of him. The thing clacked its claws together in defiance, and Jeff backed away from it—right into the arms of another. It grabbed him in a bear hug, pinning his arms to his sides. Jeff was short—almost the same height as his attacker. He slammed his head backward, smashing his captor's nose. The beast grunted, but held firm. As Jeff struggled helplessly, its companion strode forward and raked its claws across his abdomen, slicing through shirt and skin. Jeff threw his head back and cried out in agony. The veins stood out in his neck. The creature slashed again, and Jeff's eyes went wide with pain as his intestines slipped from the wound in ropey, purplish white strands and began coiling at his feet.

That's my intestines, he thought. *Oh my God, that's my fucking guts!*

He head butted his captor again, and this time, successfully broke free. He stumbled away from them with his guts unwinding behind him, as if they were a leash. The creatures seized the glistening strands and tugged. Jeff fell to the ground face-first. He squirmed in the mud, slipping from consciousness as he succumbed to shock. A second later, Raul's torso was tossed atop Jeff's limp form. Raul's head, arms, and legs were scattered across the camp. He'd been pulled apart while alive.

Shrieking, clawing at her cheeks in frenzied panic, Pauline tried to run the other way, but three of the creatures surrounded her. She screamed as they closed in, grasping and tearing at her clothing. Jerry was alarmed to see that all three were sexually aroused. They each sported bulbous, bobbing erections. Becka must have noticed it, too, because she grabbed his arm and squeezed. Her fingernails dug into his skin, drawing blood.

"Oh no," she whispered. "Oh God no, please no . . ."

Pauline's clothing was torn away, revealing her naked body. One of the things licked its lips with a black, glistening tongue. When she screamed again, it backhanded her savagely. Pauline slumped forward, and one of the other beasts caught her before she could fall. It slung her over its shoulder and bounded toward the jungle.

Jerry glanced at Stefan. The man had flattened himself out on the ground and was pulling mud overtop himself in an attempt at camouflage.

"Come on," Jerry urged the others. "Out the back. Quickly."

He turned and pushed through the leaves and branches that formed the shelter's rear wall. Troy followed him, crawling along through the mud on his hands and knees. They stopped when they got outside.

"Becka," Jerry whispered, holding out his hand. "Come on. Hurry."

She stared straight ahead. "Pauline . . ."

"Never mind her," Troy said. "Just hurry the fuck up, before they spot us."

As if he'd willed it to happen, the attackers turned their attention to the shelter. Roaring, they charged forward. Becka turned and scrambled out the exit, but then stopped, screaming.

"They've got my legs! Jerry, help me!"

Dropping the flashlight, he grabbed her hands and pulled. "Hold on."

"Don't let go," she begged. "Don't let go."

"I won't."

"They're clawing me," she sobbed. "Oh God, it hurts!"

"Troy, give me a hand! Troy?"

Jerry risked a glance over his shoulder. The mechanic had vanished.

"Troy! Goddamn you, help us."

"Don't let go," Becka pleaded again. "Not like Pauline. I don't want to be like Pauline."

Her wet, muddy hands started to slip from his grasp. Jerry dug his feet into the mud and tugged harder. He bellowed for Troy, but there was no answer.

"Jerry?"

He heard the terror in Becka's voice. Their eyes met, and then, suddenly, she was yanked from his grasp and pulled through the opening.

"*Jerrrrrrryyyyyy . . .*"

"No! Becka? I'm coming! Hang on . . ."

He scrambled forward, but a furry snout erupted from the wall and snarled at him. Jerry skittered backward. At that moment, he heard footsteps pounding behind him. Troy dashed past him and smacked the creature in the face with a thick length of wood. Blood flew from its snout, and a long, half-rotten incisor landed in the mud. Moaning, the creature retreated back into the shelter.

"How ya like that, you motherfucker? That's how we do it back in Seattle, you fuck. What you—"

159

The answering roar drowned out the rest of Troy's challenge.

Jerry scrambled to his feet. "Becka . . . they've got her. We have to—"

Still holding the makeshift club in one hand, Troy grabbed his arm. "We got to run. You ain't gonna help her by charging in. There's too many of them."

"Screw you. I'm going after her."

"You'll get yourself killed, and then she'll be fucked. If you want to save her, then listen to me. We'll come back for her, man. I promise. I ain't no asshole. We ain't leaving her and Pauline with these fucks. But we've got to get away, man. Now, come on."

Without waiting for Jerry's response, he turned and ran into the darkness. Jerry hesitated, glancing around for any sign of Becka, but she was gone. The creatures, however, were all over, and converging on him now that they knew where he was. Cursing, he ran after Troy.

"I'll be back, Becka," he shouted. "Just hang on. I'll be back!"

As he ran into the darkness, Jerry was certain that he heard the creatures laughing, mocking his promise to her. The sound was malevolent—and intelligent.

Then the jungle swallowed him whole.

CHAPTER SEVENTEEN

Stefan waited, hiding in the mud with his eyes squeezed tightly shut, not moving and barely breathing. His nose itched, but he dared not scratch it. His eyes watered. He lay there and listened to Becka's terrified screams as she was dragged away. He heard Jerry's anguished shouts over his inability to help her. He eavesdropped on Troy's insistence that they flee. He heard Jeff's final, low, drawn-out death rattle. Throughout all of this, he did not move. Stefan listened to the curious growls and snuffling sounds as the things—mutant chimpanzees were what he thought they resembled—examined their kills. He suppressed a shudder at the wet, smacking sounds and little grunts of satisfaction as they ate.

He stayed quiet, remaining motionless until long after the sounds had faded. Even then, he was cautious. He opened one eye, just a slit, and then the other, waiting for his vision to adjust again. The camp remained deathly still. Even the storm seemed muted now. When he was certain that there were no more of the creatures in his proximity, he lifted his head and peered around.

The base camp was deserted. Even the corpses were gone, apparently carried off by the attackers. All that remained of them, as far as he could tell, were scattered puddles of bloody rainwater, a few scraps of clothing, and a single shoe. He didn't know who it had belonged to.

Stefan wiped the grime and muck from his eyes, nose, and ears. Then he found a relatively clean pool of water and washed his hands, arms, hair, and face, scrubbing vigorously. Finally, he rinsed his mouth and spat. Looking around the empty camp, he realized that visibility had improved slightly. The darkness didn't seem quite as oppressive anymore. He glanced up at the sky and glimpsed a few dim stars peeking out from between the thick cloud cover. The moon, while partially concealed, was visible again.

Perhaps he'd been wrong. Perhaps the storm was indeed passing, after all. The rain had certainly lessened. It was now just a light mist, seeming to hover in the air rather than fall from the sky. If Ivan was indeed moving on, then there was a possibility that a rescue party would be arriving soon. Stefan hoped that Stuart had the presence of mind to radio the ship with his satellite phone, but even if he hadn't, the network would surely send somebody to investigate their welfare as soon as it was safe to fly again. The helicopter would have to land near the circle of protection, so Stefan decided to head there. The area would also provide a strategic bonus. It was located between the beach and a broad clearing. If he positioned himself there, he'd have a clear view of the jungle, and anything that came out of it to attack him would have to cross the open clearing to do so, giving him ample warning and time to mount a defense.

He rubbed his cold arms, trying to get the blood flowing again. Still keeping his ears attuned to the jungle in case one of the creatures returned, Stefan searched through the debris for anything useful. Anything that would help him survive the trek from here to the beach. He came up empty-handed. The concurrent assault from Tropical Cyclone Ivan and the monkey-things had turned the camp into nothing more than a jumbled pile of broken branches, downed trees, and congealing muck. The fire was extinguished, and the fire pit's stones were scattered and lost. All their gear was gone or damaged, as was their meager food stores.

"Bloody hell. Not even a grain of rice left."

He found a bloodstained scrap of Raul's shirt, and used it to wipe more dirt from his face. Then he frowned.

"Well, I suppose that wasn't very smart, now was it? Cleaning away mud with a soiled piece of linen? I need to get my wits about me."

Stefan headed for the path to the beach. He walked slowly, his senses carefully attuned to his surroundings, alert for the slightest noise or movement. He had no way of knowing how many of the creatures lived on the island, but he guessed their overall numbers must be small. Judging from what they'd done to his fellow contestants' corpses, they were carnivorous—possibly omnivorous. But if meat was a staple of their diet, Stefan doubted there was enough wild game here to allow a large number of the creatures to thrive. The ones that had attacked the camp, while fierce and strong, had looked under-fed and scraggly. Still, whether the island's population was a dozen or a hundred, Stefan intended to avoid them if at all possible. No matter how many they had in their ranks, he was still outnumbered.

In addition to the monsters, he also intended to avoid his fellow contestants, should he come across any who were still alive. Stefan calculated silently, counting them off on his fingers as he walked through the darkness, picking his way through the downed trees and flattened vegetation that covered the trail. Raul and Jeff were most obviously dead. He'd seen that for himself. Pauline and Becka had been abducted; for what purpose he couldn't be sure, but they were certainly out of the picture. Jerry and Troy had fled in the other direction. Either the creatures had caught up with them, or the two had escaped. Stefan had no way of knowing for sure, but decided to count them as living until he knew otherwise. As for the rest—Richard, Sal, Shonette, Roberta, Ryan, Matthew, and the three missing crew members—they, too, were an unknown quantity. There were too many variables to determine their fate successfully. They could have been injured in the storm or cowering in some makeshift shelter or additional victims of the marauders.

Ideally, they were all dead. That would be unfortunate, of course. He wasn't a monster, after all. He'd feel sympathetic toward their families. But if the rest of the contestants were deceased, then he would automatically win the prize. After all, he'd be the last person left on the island—alive, at least. Stefan didn't know whether there was a legal precedent for that, but once he made it back to the mainland and threatened to go to the media with everything that had happened, he was positive that the network could be convinced to accommodate him generously for everything that had occurred.

He grinned, white-capped teeth flashing in the darkness. Perhaps he'd forgo the prize payout and seek his fortune through litigation instead. After all, his pain and suffering were worth a lot more than a mere million dollars. Indeed, if he kept his head and his wits about him and made it off this island alive, he'd be wealthy beyond his wildest dreams. One million dollars would seem paltry in comparison to what he could potentially gain from the network.

In the throes of avarice, Stefan crept on, hoping with all his might that his boasts had been fruitful and that he was, in fact, the last person left on the island.

Jerry and Troy dashed through the jungle, half blind from the rain and their own fears. Troy slew another of the monsters with his club, beating its head and stomach and shoulders until it collapsed to the ground, and then hammering it until its skull caved in and its brain was wet, scattered pulp. He would have continued smashing it had Jerry not shoved him onward. As they ran, they heard the creatures crashing through the foliage behind them, but eventually, the sounds of pursuit had faded. Troy slipped in the mud and tumbled down a slope, losing his club. He frantically searched for it, but the weapon was gone. Uninjured, they ran on.

Despite their terror, the exhausted men eventually took shelter beneath the broad roots of a tree growing out of an embankment along a creek bed. Although the stream had risen higher because of the rain, the flood hadn't reached the roots. The gnarled lengths formed a sort of cave that cut deep into the soil of the bank. They crawled inside and huddled together in the darkness, waiting.

"Are they gone?"

"Fucked if I know," Troy whispered. "I ain't sticking my head out to see."

"Well, neither am I."

Troy took his hat off and wrung it out. "I don't hear anything. Maybe they gave up."

"Or maybe they're just waiting for us to come out. Besides, how can you hear anything with all this water rushing by?"

"I've got good ears."

Jerry clenched his jaws and slammed his fist into the dirt.

"Take it easy," Troy said. "We'll get out of here eventually."

"That's not soon enough. We need to get out of here *now*. Those things have got Becka. Every minute we stay here, she gets farther away. Who . . . who knows what they might be doing to her?"

"You think I'm not worried about that, too? Jesus fucking Christ, Jerry. You and her are about the only people in this goddamned show that I like. But we ain't gonna do her any good running off half-fucking-cocked. We need to be careful. We're smarter than those fucking things—whatever they are."

"Cryptids," Jerry muttered.

"Who shot who in the what?"

"They're cryptids. It's a term for unknown creatures—animals that haven't yet been discovered. Lake creatures. North American hominids. Things like that."

"Lake creatures? You talking about the Loch Ness Monster?"

"No. I'm talking about science and biology. Why is it so hard for people to accept that maybe some of the lakes in Scotland have an unknown species of giant eel or that the Pacific Northwest has an undiscovered ape of some kind?"

Troy shrugged. "Don't matter to me, man. You forget, I saw those things, too. They looked like monkeys, sure, but they weren't, were they?"

"No, they weren't. At least, not exactly. It's hard to say. Everything happened so quickly, and it was dark. I was more worried about Becka and not really paying attention. But if I had to guess, I'd say they were some sort of missing link—not really human, but not really a primate either."

"Look, Jerry, no offense—but how would you know? You're a video-store clerk."

"It's a hobby of mine."

"Okay. Everybody needs a hobby. Mine's X-box and PlayStation."

Despite his desperation, Jerry smiled. "Those are also hobbies of mine."

"I knew there was a reason I liked you."

"I've noticed something, Troy."

"What?"

"You're not cursing as much. Why is that?"

Troy glanced away, watching water drip from the tree roots.

"Because I'm fucking scared, man. I've never been so fucking scared in my life. There, you fucking happy, motherfucker?"

"I'm scared, too," Jerry admitted. "But it's nice to have the old Troy back."

"Fucking A. So you really think those things are some kind of missing link?"

"I don't know. But remember when we first got here, they told us all those legends about the island? The natives believed that it was inhabited by a race of short, hairy people who lived in the caves. Our attackers were short and hairy. We've been here how long and we never saw any of them? Not even a footprint or a tuft of hair or at least some droppings? That tells me they may have been hiding in the caves."

"Why?"

"Because the caves are the one place none of us have been to yet. I don't even know where they are. Do you?"

Troy shook his head. "Somewhere in the middle of the island. That's all I know. I've been a little too preoccupied with the fucking game to go exploring."

"Well, this whole region is full of similar stories. There are folktales on the Indonesian island of Flores about a race of shy little people. Some researchers call them South Seas leprechauns. They were supposed to live in caves, too. Up until a few years ago, most people dismissed these reports as bullshit, but all legends have some basis in fact, and some Australian and Indonesian anthropologists found proof that they were real."

"They fucking found leprechauns?" Troy leaned back and chortled with laughter.

Jerry's ears turned red. "In a cave on Flores, they discovered the fossilized remains of a tribe of tiny humans. They found seven different skeletons, ranging in height from three to four feet. The media nicknamed them Hobbits, because everybody had *Lord of the Rings* fever at the time."

"Those movies kicked fucking ass. You ever see his earlier stuff? *Dead Alive* and *Meet the Feebles*? That's some sick fucking shit, man. I loved them both. That second one was like the Muppets on goddamned crack."

"Yeah, I saw them. I work in a video store, remember? Damn kids keep stealing our copies. We can't keep them in stock."

"So these things were where Peter Jackson got the idea for the Hobbits?"

"Tolkien," Jerry corrected him, "and probably not. They weren't actually Hobbits. That was just the nickname the scientists gave them, so the media would actually pay attention to the story. What they actually were was an evolutionary offshoot of human beings."

"Those things that attacked us weren't fucking human, man."

"Don't be so sure. The fossils on Flores were shorter versions of Homo sapiens, just like the Pygmies in Africa. They existed side by side with the Neanderthals, and probably evolved from Homo erectus."

Troy snickered. "Homo erectus? You've got to be fucking kidding me."

"Settle down, Beavis. The point is, these things were hanging around on Flores while modern humans were inhabiting the mainland. You've got to wonder where they came from. These islands don't have a lot of natural wildlife, aside from all the birds and reptiles. They sprang up from volcanoes, mostly, far away from other, bigger land masses. So it's not like these things could have migrated. The only wild mammals in this region are the ones brought over by ships."

"So they've been here all along?"

"Maybe. I don't know for sure. But if they have been, then they're regressing. The ones on Flores had primitive weapons and tools. The ones that attacked us didn't use weapons. No stone-tipped spears or arrows, or flint knives. Nothing like that. You'd think, after all this time, they'd have evolved some."

"You sure about that?"

"No. Like I said, it's just a hobby. And some researchers think the fossils on Flores were just regular humans who'd suffered from dwarfism. So I might be wrong about all of this. Who knows?"

"Well, it makes sense to me. Better than thinking we got our asses kicked by a bunch of fucking monkeys."

The two fell silent for a while, listening to the churning floodwaters. The jungle was eerily quiet. Eventually, Jerry worked up enough nerve to sneak out of their hiding spot and clamber up the embankment. He peeked over the side and searched the terrain. Thin, pale moonlight illuminated the scene. Nothing moved. If the creatures were still there, then they were hidden. He ducked back down into the crevice.

"Looks like the coast is clear," he panted. "And the storm is pretty much over, too. I think we should chance it."

"Okay," Troy agreed, "but we need a fucking plan, man. We can't just go rushing off into the forest and shit."

"Think you can remember how to get back to the camp from here?"

"Maybe. I don't know. It was dark, and I wasn't paying attention to where the hell we were going, you know? Especially after I fucking fell. But I can try to find it. I remember some of the landmarks."

"I say we retrace our steps and make it back to the base camp before we go after Becka and Pauline. We don't know for sure if the others are dead or not. We may find some help."

"Raul and Jeff looked pretty fucking dead, dude."

Jerry grimaced, remembering the sounds he'd heard during the slaughter of his fellow contestants.

"Yeah," he said, "but Stefan might have made it. He was hiding when we left. And Stuart and all the others weren't in camp when we were attacked. Now that the storm is over, they may have come back. If so, Stuart can radio the ship and get help."

"And if not?"

"Then we're on our own here."

Troy sighed. "I'd kill for a fucking smoke. I wish I had one of Raul's."

"What are you talking about?"

"Stefan said Raul brought cigarettes as his luxury item."

Jerry shook his head. "Raul doesn't smoke. Stefan was just messing with you. Raul brought a tube of lip balm as his luxury item."

"That motherfucking British cocksucker."

"Welsh."

"Same fucking thing."

"Well," Jerry said, "if it's any consolation, right now I could use a smoke, too. You help me get Becka back safe and sound, man, and I'll buy you a truckload of cigarettes."

"Shit. You ain't got to do that. If we rescue them both, and Becka's hanging on you, then Pauline will have no fucking choice but to reward me for saving her. It ain't like Stefan tried to help her ass."

Jerry was stunned. "You're still playing the game?"

"I never stopped. Life's a game, Jerry. I played it before I came here, and I'll play it long after—provided we fucking live, of course."

It took them a while to find the base camp. Twice they walked in a circle, and once, their progress was cut off by a massive crevice. Eroded soil had been washed out to sea, leaving a wide trench that they had to go around. When they finally found the camp again, they almost didn't recognize it. The shelter was barely standing, and all the other crude structures had been torn down by either the storm or the creatures. The fire pit was in shambles, with most of the stones missing, and the remaining firewood was scattered and wet. The muddy ground was covered with footprints—both human and otherwise, but it was impossible to tell which way the abductors had gone. Tracks crisscrossed each other repeatedly, obscuring any real direction. There was no sign of Raul, Jeff, or Stefan. Apparently, Raul's and Jeff's bodies had been carried away, along with the missing women.

"Let's split up," Jerry said. "Look for anything we can use. Anything."

Troy knelt and crawled inside the leaning shelter while Jerry searched the outskirts of the camp. He flipped some fallen branches over with his toe and recoiled. A human finger lay in the dirt. The end was bloody and appeared gnawed on. A gold wedding band, still affixed to the finger, glinted in the moonlight.

"Raul's," he muttered, fighting down his rising bile. "Where's the rest of him?"

There was a muffled shout from the direction of the shelter. Jerry turned to see Troy emerge from the ruins, cursing. The mechanic was bent low to the ground, studying something.

"What's wrong?"

Troy pointed over his shoulder at the shelter. "Come take a look. You ain't gonna believe this fucking shit."

Curious, Jerry hurried toward him. Troy held up his hand.

"Careful," he warned. "Watch where you step."

"What is it?"

Troy led him inside the shelter and pointed to the rear corner. There, almost hidden in the shadows, was a deep, man-shaped impression in the mud where Stefan had hidden.

"Think they found him?" Jerry asked.

"Nope. There's no blood, and the impression is pretty damned clear. If that Welsh fuck had struggled, I'd think the mud would be more . . . strewn about? You know?"

Jerry nodded. "Then what were you looking at?"

"His footprints. The motherfucker got up and walked out of here. I figured that much out. But then I fucking lose them out in the camp. The ground is too torn up to follow them."

"You think there's a chance he went after the girls?" Jerry's tone was hopeful.

"Not a fucking chance. This is Stefan we're talking about. That cocksucker is only looking out for himself."

Jerry glanced around the deserted camp. "Then where is he?"

"Who knows? Probably fucking hiding somewhere. Forget about him. I hope those things ate his stupid ass. He'll give them a wicked case of indigestion."

Jerry stepped outside the shelter and cupped his hands over his mouth. He drew in a lungful of air and began yelling.

"HELLO?"

His voice echoed.

"IS THERE—"

Troy snuck up behind him and clamped a hand over Jerry's mouth, stifling his shouts. Jerry struggled, but Troy hissed in his ear. His breath reeked.

"The fuck are you doing, man? You want to tell those fucking things where we are?"

Jerry shook his head.

"Then shut the fuck up. Now."

He removed his hand. Jerry spat on the ground.

"Sorry. I'm just worried about Becka—and the others, too."

"Well then, let's quit fucking around and go find them. Sooner we do, the sooner we can get the fuck off this island."

"We need weapons," Jerry said. "Anything to defend ourselves. Maybe we can make some spears like the one Matthew had."

They searched through the wreckage. Jerry came across Becka's sodden diary, and a lump formed in his throat.

"We'll find you," he whispered.

They began gathering sturdier lengths of wood. Troy stumbled across the flashlight Jerry had cast aside. Both were relieved to discover that it still functioned.

"I wonder why Stefan didn't take this?"

"Because he's a stupid shit," Troy said.

"Or maybe he just overlooked it."

Troy shrugged. "Could be. His loss, our fucking gain."

Working quickly, they manufactured two crude spears by snapping the longer branches in half, leaving a jagged, pointed edge at one end. Troy found a rectangular, smooth-edged rock. He gripped it in his hand like a knife.

"Ain't neither one of us motherfucking MacGyver, I guess, but it will have to do."

"Let's hope so."

"Here." Troy tossed Jerry the flashlight. "You hold on to this. I'll keep the other spear and the rock. Let's go get your girl."

"You sure that rock's gonna be enough?"

"Fuck yeah. I mean, I'd prefer a fucking AK-47, but beggars can't be fucking choosers, you know? Long as I still got my hat, I'm good to fucking go."

Jerry shook his head. "You are one weird side-kick, dude."

"Damn straight. Those monkey-looking fucks don't stand a chance against us."

They searched the camp's perimeter, shining the flashlight beam along the ground, until they found a series of footprints leading away. It was impossible to tell how many of the creatures had passed in that direction, but when they examined the vegetation, they noticed it was crushed and trampled.

"The storm didn't do that," Troy said. "Looks like we found a fucking trail."

Jerry didn't respond. Gripping the flashlight in one hand and the spear in the other, he followed in their wake. Troy followed along behind him. As they walked, Jerry's thoughts turned to Becka's unexpected kiss.

You make me feel safe, she'd said, *and I know nothing will happen as long as you're here.*

"Hold on, Becka," Jerry whispered. "We're coming to get you. Just hang on."

Chapter Eighteen

Becka awoke to whimpering cries, and she wondered for a moment if they were hers. They sounded odd, garbled and muted, as if they were echoing off something. She tried to speak, but her tongue and mouth were dry. Groaning, Becka touched her face and winced. A sharp jolt of pain ran through her body. Her muscles ached, and her face felt hot and swollen. Her cheek and lips were puffy.

Memories came rushing back to her. During the trek through the darkness, she'd tried to escape several times, and their abductors had beaten her for it. She vividly remembered one of the creatures savagely backhanding her while Pauline simply watched, hanging limply over one of their shoulders. Becka had shouted at her to help—to join her and fight back, but Pauline had closed her eyes and turned her head away as Becka was pummeled into unconsciousness.

Her thoughts turned to Jerry. She hoped he was okay.

Becka lay still, closed her eyes, and waited for the pain to subside to a tolerable level again. One by one, her senses slowly returned. She was lying on her back on a hard, bumpy surface. Stone, judging by the texture. The cries—whoever they belonged to—increased in pitch and intensity. She tuned them out and listened instead to the other sounds—grunts, snuffling, growls, and a sort of rapid-fire series of rumbles that resembled a crude form of speech. She also heard the unmistakable crackle of flames and the small pops of damp wood on a fire. Beneath these were the wet, smacking sounds of feasting.

She sniffed the air and gagged. It was a heady, noxious mix of wood smoke, mildew, dampness, and the horrible, fetid stench of her captors. Their reek seemed more powerful now than it had at the camp, as if it had permeated her surroundings.

She opened her eyes carefully. Immediately, they began to water and sting. Doing her best to ignore it, she glanced around and saw that she was in a cave. It was dark, but a flickering glow chased the shadows into the nooks and crannies. As far as she could tell, none of the creatures was nearby. She carefully raised her head a bit and looked around.

She was lying in an open alcove connected to a large antechamber. Several tunnels led off from the cavernous space. Some sloped downward, twisting and coiling deeper into the earth. Others traveled upward, presumably toward the surface. Stalactites and stalagmites—she couldn't remember which one was which—dotted the underground landscape. Some of them were nothing more than broken stumps, apparently snapped off during some past struggle or upheaval. Others looked thousands of years old. A few of the walls were decorated with some kind of drawings, but she couldn't make out what they depicted. The roof of the chamber was at least twenty feet high, and at the center, it peaked into a small natural chimney. She stared at the aperture, hoping for a glimpse of the moon or the stars, but saw only blackness. Smoke drifted through the hole. She followed the smoke back down. In the center of the cavern was a large stone pit. A fire burned inside it, fed regularly from a stack of nearby firewood. Her abductors sat around the fire.

She counted thirty-two of the creatures and assumed that there were more she couldn't see, perhaps elsewhere in the caverns. Their stink was pervasive. They filled the chamber, young and old, male and female, weak and strong, participating in some sort of feast. The females sat apart from the males. One creature in particular seemed to hold a place of honor. It sat closest to the crackling blaze, and the flames cast flickering reflections off the silver fur that covered its lean body. Its chest was crisscrossed with pale, ragged scars. The rest of the tribe members deferred to the elder in their gestures and their proximity to him. They brought him his food and did not meet his eyes.

She noticed that many of the younger creatures had obvious birth defects—stunted limbs, malformed eyes or ears, bulbous snouts, or misshapen hands and heads. Becka felt a momentary pang of pity for them. The emotion vanished a moment later when she realized what they were eating. At first, Becka's mind refused to accept what she was seeing. But then she recognized the tattered scraps of clothing—and the tattered scraps of faces, and bit her lip to keep from screaming.

The remains of Ryan, Matthew, Sal, Richard, Jeff, Raul, and Stuart lay in a jumbled, bloodied heap of limbs, torsos, and innards. As she watched, the creatures reached into the pile, tearing off pieces of meat, and then squatted or sat next to their companions and began to eat. The fire was apparently just for heat or light because they consumed the flesh raw. Becka gagged. Hands and feet were gnawed like chicken legs, stripped of their meat and tossed aside. Bones were cracked open, the marrow sucked out by eager, slurping mouths. Brains were scooped like caviar, oozing from hairy fists. A sallow, deformed male licked the gooey remnants from his elongated fingers. Eyeballs were tossed into the air and caught like popcorn to the amusement of others. Hearts were eaten like apples. Floppy livers and kidneys were gobbled down with delight. A pair of young creatures fought over a length of intestines like they were links of sausages. The squabble ended only when the gory, glistening prize snapped in half, sending both of them tumbling to the floor of the cave and showering them with gore. Their mother hooted with laughter and then buried her snout into a ragged piece of flesh from someone's rump.

Blood filled Becka's mouth as her teeth clamped down harder on her bottom lip, but she barely noticed. The feasting sounds grew louder, and she could no longer hold back. The cry started deep down inside her and bubbled slowly to the surface as she backed away.

"Sshhh," a voice whispered from the darkness behind her. "Don't make a sound. Don't even breathe loud. Momma will be home soon."

"Sh-Shonette? Oh my God! Is that you? Are you okay?"

Even as she asked, Becka knew that her fellow contestant was far from okay. She could tell from the woman's voice. From the shadows came a confused sigh.

"Eat your breakfast. They've forgotten about us for the time being. D-don't remind them . . . that we're here."

"Shonette? It's me, Becka. Is that you?"

There was a pause. "Yeah, it's me. Crawl b-back here, Becka, but d-do it slow. Don't attract their . . . attention."

Becka crab-walked slowly backward, keeping her eyes fixed on the carnage in the main chamber. Her back pressed up against the cavern wall, and she turned her head to the left. There, hidden in the shadows behind a particularly large boulder, was Shonette. She was naked and bleeding from dozens of scratches. Most of the wounds were shallow, but one looked deep and ugly, and was already puffy from the first signs of infection. Shonette cowered against the wall, her hands clenching her hair tightly. She didn't even seem to notice. Her wide eyes glistened.

"Shonette . . ." Becka slid closer and put an arm around her. She noticed that Shonette's pupils were dilated. The back of her head looked swollen, and her hair was matted with blood. More blood glistened on the cavern floor between her legs. Shonette shuddered and flinched as Becka touched her, but she didn't move away.

"Are you okay?" Becka asked. "Are you hurt?"

"I . . ."

"It's okay. Just talk to me."

"My head. I hurt my head . . . somehow."

"What's going on? What did they do to you?"

Shonette nodded out at the cavern. "The . . . the same thing they're doing to Pauline right now."

"Pauline? Is she okay? Where—"

The whimpers returned, then suddenly transformed into a rising shriek. The cry was cut short by the sound of flesh striking flesh—a hard, smacking blow.

"They raped me," Shonette said quietly, as if she were discussing something as trivial as the weather or what to watch on television. Her tone became calm. Placid. "They raped me, and now they're raping her. I guess you'll be next."

Becka opened her mouth to reply, but her mounting fears had stolen away her voice. All that came out was a short, strangled sob.

"They go easier on you if you just stay quiet and don't move," Shonette said. "Ain't like the men back home. These things seem to like it when the woman just lies there like a wet dishrag. Wish I'd known before they started on me. You keep it in mind when your turn comes. Stay still, and don't fight. Oh, and hold your breath. They're pretty goddamned ripe. My guess is that they aren't big on showers or baths. That storm certainly doesn't seem to have washed them off any. Maybe we can ask

Roland to give us some soap and shampoo as a prize for the next challenge."

She giggled softly, and the sound of it terrified Becka even worse than the scenes in the cavern below.

Pauline cried out again, and Becka cringed at the sound of the blow. It was followed with a roar, and then a series of grunts and panting noises. Becka closed her eyes, took a deep breath, and thought of Jerry.

Please be okay, she prayed. *Please come get us . . .*

Groaning, Shonette stirred next to her. A thin line of drool dripped from the corner of her bruised and bloodied lips.

"Anybody else make it?" she asked.

"I don't know," Becka said. "Jerry and Troy—I think they may have gotten away."

"Good for them. Maybe they'll get help."

"Maybe," Becka agreed. She felt a sinking feeling in her stomach.

They left me, she thought. *They ran away and let these things take me back here. How would they even find us now?*

"What about Stefan? I didn't see him out there on the smorgasbord pile."

Becka frowned. She didn't remember Shonette being this callous or indifferent before. She wondered just how mentally stable her fellow contestant was after her ordeal.

"I don't know what happened to Stefan," she said. "What about Roberta? She never made it back to camp. Have you seen her?"

Still pulling her hair, Shonette shook her head. "No, she's not here. Maybe she escaped."

"Or maybe they killed her."

"If so, then she's the lucky one. She wins the contest, as far as I'm concerned. Fuck being the last one on the island."

Shonette giggled again, and Becka fought back tears.

Out of sight, the panting sounds increased. Each time Pauline cried out, it was answered with another blow. Eventually, she fell silent. The growls and grunts turned to animalistic moans of pleasure.

"Oh God," Becka whispered. "What are they doing to her?"

"I told you. You want specifics? Just use your imagination."

"Where is she? Are you sure it's Pauline? I don't see them out there."

"They're right around the corner," Shonette said. "There's another little hole in the wall, just like this one, right next to us. They've got her in there."

"Stay here."

"Where are you going?"

"I can't just sit here and listen to her being raped. We've got to do something. Just stay put."

Becka crawled forward on her hands and knees, clenching her teeth as sharp, jagged rocks pressed against her skin. Shonette reached for her, protesting, but Becka ignored her frightened pleas. She felt compelled to see, even though she didn't want to. Her stomach roiled at the very idea of witnessing what was going on in the next alcove. Still, she crept on, determined to do something about it if she could. She was damned if she was going to end up like Shonette, with her mind snapped, babbling at the cavern walls. She couldn't let Pauline end up like that either if she could help it.

She reached the end of the outcropping and flattened herself against the cave floor, hoping the creatures in the main cavern were too engrossed in their celebration to notice her. The sounds of Pauline's assault grew louder. Holding her breath, Becka peered around the corner.

And wept.

Pauline lay on her back. Her clothes had been torn off and tossed aside. One of the creatures writhed atop her, thrusting in and out and punctuating each stroke with a gasp. Its black tongue lolled from its mouth and thin strands of saliva dripped onto her breasts. Two more creatures crouched on each side of the helpless woman, holding her legs apart. Another straddled her head, forcing her shoulders to the floor. All three were erect. Becka gaped in horror at their swollen, hairy shafts. Each was covered with rugged contours and bulging black veins, and the tips glistened with slimy pre-cum. The repulsive organs bobbed and swayed in the air. The largest of the creatures grinned lasciviously as the one between Pauline's legs moaned and shuddered. Its hairy buttocks quivered as it surrendered to the throes of orgasm. It withdrew a second later, stroking its blood-slicked member, and then collapsed against Pauline and lay still.

Grunting, another of the monsters pulled its sated companion aside and took his place. The space between Pauline's legs was in ruins. In the moment before the next creature entered Pauline, Becka caught a glimpse of her face. It was expressionless. Her eyes stared at some far off point in the cavern ceiling. Pauline had left the building.

Becka began to hyperventilate. Tears streamed down her face. She scurried back to Shonette's corner and curled up tightly next to her. If Shonette noticed, she didn't acknowledge it. She mumbled something about Fruity Pebbles and seemed to be talking to someone who wasn't there. Becka turned to her and noticed that Shonette was crying, too.

Becka thought again of Jerry. She listened to the sounds of rape and feasting and tried to decide which was worse. She prayed that they would kill her. When that didn't happen, she asked God to do it first. She begged to have a heart attack, an aneurism, to slip into a sudden coma—anything that would help her escape. When those prayers also went unanswered, she cried harder. God wasn't coming to save her. Neither was Jerry. Unlike the game, there was no circle of protection she could take shelter in.

Around the corner, the noises stopped. She heard talons clicking against the stone. A shadow loomed at the entrance to their alcove. Then another. And another.

Somehow the three monsters' laughter was the worst sound of all.

Becka's sobs turned into screams as the creatures approached.

CHAPTER NINETEEN

Jerry and Troy pushed on through the forest, shoving the greenery aside and carefully following the trail left behind by the cryptids. Once they knew what to look for, it was easy to spot the signs of passage, even in the dark. Dozens of footprints were splattered through the mud, and the creatures had snapped branches and trodden on lilies and ferns during their retreat. Occasionally, they found a splash of blood, stark against a leaf, or a tuft of brown fur clinging to a vine. The two men walked single file and proceeded in silence, communicating only in gestures and grunts. Jerry shined the flashlight on the ground in front of them, occasionally probing the soil with the tip of his spear. Troy gripped his own spear and his makeshift stone knife. Both were scared and tired, but both were also experiencing a second wind, brought on by adrenaline and concern for Becka and the others. When a low-hanging branch snatched Troy's hat from his head, he didn't even bother to curse as he retrieved it.

The storm slowly abated, and now a thin layer of mist rose from the ground as the temperature started to warm again. Jerry hoped that the fog didn't grow too thick, lest they miss the trail and go in the wrong direction. Thunder rumbled occasionally, but it was distant now and fading.

Troy signaled a pause and both men leaned against a broad, gnarled tree trunk that had withstood the pummeling storm, and caught their breath.

Jerry freed a pebble from his shoe. "At least the bugs aren't back yet."

"Fucking little bloodsuckers." Troy panted. "I wonder what time it is? I'm fucking beat."

"I don't know. But it feels late. Hopefully, the sun will come up soon."

"Think that'll help our situation?"

"Not necessarily. But it will warm things up again, at least. And by then, help should arrive."

"By then, it might be too fucking late."

"You're not helping things, Troy. Talk like that—it's useless. We've got to stay positive, for Becka, at least."

"Positive? Dude, I'm the most positive son of a bitch on this island. I'm positive that everything sucks all the time. That's my motto. Hell, I've got it tattooed on my ass—*everything sucks all the time.* And let me tell you, man, I'm positive that this fucking sucks worst of all, and I'm positive we're gonna die."

"Thank you. That's very helpful. You have any more positive vibes to add to the situation?"

Troy shrugged. "It is what it fucking is."

"You were all for this a while ago!"

"What the fuck do I know? I'm just a guy who bends wrenches for a fucking living. But I've been thinking about it as we go along, and this ain't nothing but a suicide mission, man. We're better off getting the fuck out of here."

"I'm not leaving without Becka."

"And if she's dead? What then?"

Jerry didn't respond.

Troy sighed. "Look, dude, no offense, but maybe we should consider our other options while we still can. Even if she is alive, you ain't gonna do much against these things with a fucking bamboo spear."

"You did okay with your club."

"That was against one. Not an army."

"Well, like the slogan says, I'm an army of one."

Troy shook his head. "You're a goddamn fool is what you are."

Jerry started forward again. "You can run if you want, but I'm going on. You coming?"

Troy gaped, then glanced at the ground.

"Yeah," he muttered, "I guess so. I ain't fucking running around this goddamned island by myself."

"Then shut up and come on."

"I'll tell you one thing. I could—"

"Use a smoke," Jerry finished for him.

"What? You a fucking mind reader now?"

Despite his annoyance with the man, Jerry grinned. "Something like that."

"No shit? Well, if you've got any more super powers, now would be a good fucking time to use them."

They crept on in silence. All around them, the island started to come to tentative life again. A few angry birds squawked from the treetops. Troy almost stepped on a small lizard. It scampered off, hiding beneath a stone. A snake uncoiled from a nearby limb, and Jerry recoiled from it. Overhead, the leaves rustled. Although the storm had ceased, a strong breeze still cut through the foliage, swirling the mist around their feet.

They'd traveled for about fifteen minutes when Jerry stopped and held up one hand. Troy halted behind him, shuffling from foot to foot to stay warm.

"What's up?" he asked. "Why are we stopping?"

Jerry clicked off the flashlight. "I smell smoke."

"Smoke?" Troy sniffed the air and scowled. "Oh, that's just fucking great! Now the goddamned island is on fire. Fucking lightning must have hit a tree or something. That's it, man. Game over. We've got to—"

"Would you lower your voice?"

"Sorry," Troy whispered. "Where do you think it's coming from?"

"I don't know. I can't tell with all this fog and the wind. Somewhere close by, I would imagine."

"I don't hear it. Maybe it's small."

Jerry nodded in agreement.

"You think those crypt-things—whatever the fuck you called them—can start a fire?"

"Maybe," Jerry said. "I guess it's possible. They must have evolved at least that far."

"Well, maybe they're sitting around toasting marshmallows and signing Kum-ba-fucking-ya."

Jerry rolled his eyes.

"Hey," Troy said. "It fucking beats the alternative. If it's a wildfire, we're fucking toast, Jerry."

"Quiet," Jerry hushed him. Abruptly, he ducked down and peered into the dark. "Listen."

"I don't—"

"Shut up."

Somewhere in the shadows ahead of them came the sounds of rustling leaves and snapping branches, as if something was crashing through the undergrowth.

"Oh shit!" Troy tensed, gripping his weapons tighter.

"It's moving away from us," Jerry whispered. "Come on."

"Fuck that. I'm staying right here."

"Then fuck you, Troy."

"Fuck me?"

"Yeah. Fuck you."

Jerry crept forward, keeping his spear pointed ahead of him. Troy hurried along behind him.

"Wait!"

"I thought you weren't coming?"

"You've got the fucking flashlight, man. I ain't staying out here in the dark, and I can't find my way back to the path without it."

As they drew nearer to the sound, they noticed a wide swath of crushed vegetation. Something had been dragged through it, smashing the ferns and flowers to the ground, and disturbing the dirt and beds of moss. Jerry sniffed the air again. He still smelled smoke, but now, it was overpowered by another odor—the same foul stench they'd smelled back at the camp.

Troy recognized the sour reek, as well. "It's one of them, isn't it?"

Nodding, Jerry parted a thicket of vines and peered through to the other side. Troy pressed up beside him. In a moonlit clearing not twenty feet away from them was one of the hominids. This one appeared severely malnourished and weak. Huge swaths of fur were missing, and bones jutted sharply beneath its mangy hide. It moved slowly, dragging a heavy burden behind it with one arm. After a moment, they recognized it.

It was Roberta.

The creature hauled her across the ground by her hair. It was eating something from its free hand, but they couldn't tell what—a dark morsel, about the size of an apple. As they watched, Roberta's body caught on a rock, and a clump of her hair came out by the roots. Her head slumped to the ground. Yowling in frustration, the beast tossed its meal aside and kicked her limp form. Then it seized one of her arms and continued pulling her through the clearing. Roberta didn't resist.

"She's dead," Troy breathed. "She has to be."

"Or unconscious."

"No way. Did you see her fucking hair come out? That shit would wake a person up no matter how fucking out of it they were."

They remained still, watching as the thing dragged her to the end of the clearing and disappeared into the thick vegetation. The low-hanging branches closed like curtains, concealing the creature from view.

Jerry pointed, indicating they should follow. Troy shook his head. Jerry pointed again, insistent. Slowly, they crept forward, careful to stay downwind, trusting that the strong breeze would mask their scent and sound. A thin branch snapped backward, slapping Troy in the face and leaving a bright red welt across his left cheek, just below his eye. He bit his lip to keep from crying out. Jerry mouthed an apology.

The smell of smoke grew stronger as they crossed the clearing, and the mist thickened, turning into swirling clouds of fog. It swelled up around them, filling the open space and limiting their visibility. Worse, the clouds drifted across the moon, obscuring its meager light. Jerry considered turning on the flashlight but decided against it. They could still hear Roberta's body being dragged along, and the small grunts of exertion from her captor. They followed the sounds as the fog grew even denser. They both shivered—partly from nerves and partly because of the damp air.

Jerry glanced at the spot where the creature had tossed its meal, and blanched. At first he didn't recognize the object. A second later, Troy whispered confirmation.

"Fuck me running. That's a heart, bro. A human fucking heart."

Gagging, Jerry took shallow breaths until his nausea had passed. Then he motioned them onward. They reached the edge of the clearing, and abruptly the noises ceased. Troy tapped Jerry on the shoulder, and Jerry glanced at him.

What now? Troy mouthed.

Jerry didn't respond. Instead, using his spear, he pushed the tree limbs and bushes aside and peered through the greenery. Then he nodded ahead of them. Troy followed his gaze. His bushy eyebrows arched in surprise.

The open mouth of a cave stared back at them. It

was located at the bottom of a rocky hill. There was no sign of the creature or of Roberta. The area reeked of the creatures, and the smell of smoke grew overpowering, stinging their eyes. They crept forward a few steps and studied the ground. The soil around the cave entrance was obviously disturbed. Roberta had been dragged across it. Jerry spied a scrap of her clothing caught on a sharp rock.

"It's a fucking cave," Troy whispered.

"I can see that," Jerry snapped, his patience at an end. "Look up the hill."

Troy did, then shrugged. "I can't see shit. It's all covered in fog."

"That's not fog. It's smoke."

Troy's eyes grew wider. "You mean it's a fucking volcano?"

"No, you idiot. It's fucking wood smoke. Can't you smell it?"

"Dude, don't call me a fucking idiot. I'd expect that shit from Stefan, but not you."

Jerry took a deep breath. "I'm sorry, man. Seriously. I'm just scared."

"It's cool. I am, too." Troy glanced upward again. "Where's the smoke coming from? Not the caves."

"I don't know. But it looks like that thing took Roberta inside the cave, so there's a good chance that's where they took Becka and the others. We've got to go in there."

"I knew you were gonna fucking say that."

"Come on," Jerry urged quietly, moving forward.

Shoulders slumping, Troy followed.

They split up and approached the cave from both sides, alert for any signs their presence had been detected. Gravel and twigs crunched under their feet, but otherwise, the silence continued uninterrupted, as if the island itself was echoing their stealth—or perhaps waiting for something. When a bird suddenly cried out in the darkness, Troy nearly screamed.

They crouched over and peered into the dark opening.

"It looks pretty small," Troy whispered, dropping to his knees. "You sure that fucking monkey-thing could fit inside there?"

Jerry knelt beside him and poked his head inside the crevasse. Then he withdrew again.

"It could have fit through there easily," he said. "The tunnel is narrow for the first six feet, but then it opens up wide enough for us to stand. And it looks like it's been well used. The floor is smooth, and there isn't any debris."

"Okay. But we still don't know for sure that's where the motherfuckers went. What about all that smoke? Maybe they've got a camp on top of the hill."

"Trust me. They went into the cave."

"How do you know?"

"Because there's blood on the cave walls, near the floor, and more scraps of Roberta's clothing."

"Oh." Troy sighed. "Well, fuck me running, then. I guess we have to follow."

"Yeah, we do."

They stared at each other, unmoving.

"After you," Troy said, gesturing with his spear. "Like I said before, you've got the fucking flashlight, man."

Swallowing hard, Jerry turned toward the opening. He shivered and blinked the sweat from his eyes. The ground seemed to spin, and for a second, Jerry was afraid he was going to pass out. Then he thought of Becka, and the dizziness cleared.

"Okay," he whispered. "Let's do this."

The blackness inside the cave's entrance seemed like a solid thing, waiting to absorb them both. After a moment's hesitation, they stepped forward and it did just that.

CHAPTER TWENTY

Stefan hurried down the moonlit path, nearly slipping repeatedly in the mud and darting around fallen trees and other storm-tossed debris, but stopping for nothing. A thick fog surrounded him. He slowed occasionally to listen for sounds of pursuit, but even then he did not completely stop. Each time, he heard nothing. As far as he knew, he was alone on this part of the island. He assumed that the creatures had moved farther inland, returning to whatever lair they'd originally crawled from. If Jerry, Troy, or any of the others were alive and had thought to fall back to the circle of protection and landing zone as he had, they could be following him or ahead of him. But somehow Stefan doubted it. Other than the wind in the trees and the stirring wildlife, alert again now that the storm had passed, nothing moved.

Yet something had indeed passed this way since the storm ended. The path to the beach showed signs of recent disturbance, as if a heavy weight had been dragged along it. This wasn't storm damage from Ivan. This was something else—something post-storm. As he ran, he spotted the occasional claw-toed footprint. The tracks always headed in the opposite direction, away from the beach, back toward the base camp and the island's unexplored center.

Stefan rounded a curve in the path and finally halted. Ahead of him, a massive fallen tree blocked the trail. The wet bark felt rough against his hands. He clambered over the tree and cocked his head again, listening. To his surprise, this time, he heard a voice.

"Hello? Stuart, do you copy? This is Brett. Is anyone there? Mark? Jesse?"

The voice was muffled and tinny, as if coming from far away. Had the wind been blowing any harder, he might not have heard it at all. Stefan tensed, glancing about, trying to see through the fog.

"Hello? Is someone there?"

There was a brief pause, then a response.

"Stuart? If you can't talk, just press the buttons. Let me know you're receiving this."

Stefan followed the voice. Incredibly, it seemed to be coming from the ground. Specifically, from *under* the ground.

"Well," he whispered, "this is certainly odd."

"Is there anyone there? I say again, this is Brett Heffron calling. We're getting ready to send the chopper, and we need to know your status ASAP. Please respond. Stuart, do you copy?"

Stefan knelt in the middle of the path. Cold water soaked his knees and shins, but he barely noticed. His eyes widened in surprise. There was a faint red and green glow coming from beneath the mud, barely noticeable through the mist. He scooped handfuls of the muck aside and almost cheered out loud when he uncovered the satellite phone. He wiped it off on his shirt and hurriedly brought it to his ear.

"Hello! Yes, I'm here. Can you hear me?"

"Well, it's about time," the person on the other end said. "Who's this?"

"This is Stefan. Who is this?"

"Stefan? This is Brett Heffron. I'm a communications specialist assigned to the network's freighter. Is Mr. Schiff available?"

"No, he's gone. They're all gone. I found his phone lying here in the mud. Had I not had the good fortune to be walking by while you were talking, I might not have noticed it at all."

"What do you mean 'gone'?"

"I'm afraid there's been an incident."

"What's happened. Is everyone okay?"

"Sadly, I'm afraid not. There's been . . . well, we've had some trouble."

"Shit. That's what we were afraid of. Does anyone require medical assistance?"

Stefan paused. "Well, that's hard to say. I don't, personally, but I don't know about the others. My best guess is yes. There have been a few fatalities."

There was silence from the other end, and for a moment, Stefan feared the signal had been interrupted. But then Heffron spoke again.

"Stefan, hang on a minute, okay?"

"Oh, yes. Quite."

"I'll be right back. Just stand by."

He waited as told. The wind picked up, rustling

the trees. Clouds obscured the moon again, and the darkness seemed to press closer. The fog wound around the trees. Something cried out in the shadows, shrill and frenzied.

"Just a bird," he muttered. "Just a bird, expressing its contempt for this situation."

When the moon appeared again, Stefan breathed a sigh of relief. Then his attention was drawn to something on the path, glinting in the moonlight. He walked toward it. The mist parted, and he saw a big depression in the mud, as if something heavy had been lying there during the storm. He looked back the way he'd come, remembering the signs of some heavy burden being dragged along the path. Then he glanced back down at the depression. Next to it was a muddy pocketknife with the blade extended.

"Hello. What's this?"

Kneeling, he plucked the knife from the mud and wiped away the grime. The initials M. H. were engraved on the side. The stainless-steel blade was crusted with brownish red blood—sticky and congealed, but not quite dry. Before he could examine it further, Heffron came back on the line.

"Stefan? Is there anyone else with you?"

"No, I'm afraid we're scattered all over the island."

"And you don't know the current whereabouts of any of our crew members or your fellow contestants?"

"Raul and Jeff are dead."

"You're positive about that?"

"Of course I am. I don't know about anyone else. I haven't seen anyone."

"Jesus . . . Okay, can you make it to the meeting area?"

"Actually, I was already on my way there when you called."

"Good! Go there, and if you find any of the others, tell them to do the same. We're sending help right away. The EMTs should be there shortly."

"Tell them to bring along some guns."

"W-what?" Heffron sounded surprised. "Say again?"

"I said, tell them to bring guns. Lots of guns. They'll need them. It seems that we're not alone on this island."

"Are you saying the island is inhabited? That there are other people there?"

"Yes, in a manner of speaking. But they're not people. They're . . . *things*."

He heard Heffron mutter something to someone else, but the sound was too muffled to make out clearly what was said.

"Stefan, are you sure you're not injured?"

"I'm fine. I'm not hallucinating, and I'm not delusional. Just get here and you'll see for yourself."

"Okay. Just hang in there. Make your way to the landing zone. Be advised that the team is on the way."

"Tell them I'll be waiting in the circle of protection, Mr. Heffron."

"Keep the satellite phone with you, okay?"

"Will do. Shall I turn it off to conserve the battery?"

"Yeah, you might want to do that. But I'll be standing by here, and if you need to reach me, just dial one. That will put you through directly to me. Okay?"

"Dial one. Cheers."

"Just hang tight. They're on the way." Heffron terminated the connection.

Stefan stared at the phone. It felt empowering somehow, to be holding this piece of technology now, after weeks of sleeping on the ground and building fires with flint. The phone made him feel safe and filled him with renewed confidence. He briefly considered trying to call someone in the United States, but decided against it. He had no family, other than an ex-wife and two kids he hadn't seen in five years, and he didn't really have a desire to speak with any of his friends. They were more like acquaintances, really, and after what he'd just been through, their petty concerns and drama seemed more trivial than ever. Besides, they'd hear from him soon enough. They all would. He was the sole survivor, after all—the last one left on the island. He was about to be famous.

He turned off the phone and put it in his pocket. Then he wiped the blood off the blade of the pocketknife and put that in his pocket, too. As he did, he caught sight of his waistline, and it occurred to him just how much weight he'd lost during his short time here.

The reality-television diet, he thought. *That has quite the ring to it. I should write a self-help book about it. I could be rich.*

He started down the path again, his step a little

lighter and his shoulders not quite as slumped. The air seemed warmer, and the mist dissipated. Even the wildlife seemed to be affected by his mood. He heard bird calls throughout the jungle. His senses seemed hyperaware, and he was almost convinced that he could feel the sun dragging itself toward the horizon to chase the moon away.

But then again, why bother with writing a book? I'm going to be rich anyway.

Throwing aside caution, Stefan laughed out loud. The sound echoed through the darkness. He was still chuckling to himself as he rounded a turn, slipped in the mud, and fell face-first into a puddle. Cold, brackish water rushed up his nose and down his throat, choking him. Sputtering, Stefan tried to push himself up, but his hands kept skittering through the mud, and he couldn't find purchase. He rolled over instead, blinking water from his eyes, and tried to stand. Instead, he fell over again. This time, he heard a wet snap. It sounded very near. For a second, he thought it was a tree branch, but then he felt the pain.

"Oh, no. Oh Jesus bloody fucking Christ . . ."

He glanced down at his foot. His ankle was already swollen, and in the moonlight, he saw an ugly, dark purple bruise spreading beneath the skin. Stefan pulled himself up and stood on his uninjured foot. Then, carefully, he tried to put his weight on the other leg. The resulting pain made him cry out harshly. He toppled over again and lay there, writhing and moaning.

"This is not good. This is not good at all."

Deciding to call for help, Stefan reached for the

satellite phone, but it was gone. He patted his pocket frantically. The knife was still there, but the phone had slipped out during his tumble. He clawed through the mud, searching for it. The fog returned, swirling around him. His cold fingers closed over the hard plastic phone casing. Breathing a sigh of relief, Stefan called the ship.

"Are you okay?" Heffron asked when Stefan reported what had happened.

"I don't know if it's broken or just sprained, but don't you worry about that. I'll be at the landing zone. You just tell them to wait for me."

"Maybe you should just stay put until help arrives."

"Nonsense. I'll be there."

He hung up and returned the phone to his pocket. Then he began to crawl forward, pulling himself through the mud, inch by inch.

"Wait for me, mates," he whispered. "You'd just better bloody well fucking wait for me. I'll be along shortly. And then, we're bloody well going home."

CHAPTER TWENTY-ONE

Mercifully, Pauline's screams stopped once she passed out from shock.

Becka's screams, however, were just beginning.

"Get back," she shrieked as the three creatures entered the alcove and closed in on her. "Get away from me!"

If they understood her tearful pleas, they gave no indication. They filed into the alcove, one after the other, and the tight space suddenly felt even smaller. Despite their short stature, they seemed to loom like giants. Their stench filled the limestone cranny, and Pauline's blood still shined on their half-erect organs. The beasts leered at her prone form. Becka scrambled backward. The monsters' approach never slowed. The expressions on their snarling faces made their intent all too clear.

They can't rape me, she thought. *They just got done with Pauline. They can't get it up again that quickly. No male can, no matter what the species.*

Biology—or fate—proved her wrong. As if aroused by her panicked terror, all three of the beasts began to swell again. Thick ropes of drool dripped from their slavering, oversized jaws. Their hands clenched and unclenched in anticipation.

Becka backed against the cave wall and cowered in fear. She wanted to be strong, but couldn't summon the courage now that they were here. She hated them even more for that. Not only were they about to rape her, but they'd taken away her strength and dignity. Becka's mind flashed back to the last contest, the race—swimming to shore for a chance to win a place in the circle of protection, and thus, extending her stay on the island. It had only been yesterday, but it seemed like years ago. So much had happened between then and now. But the one thing she remembered clearly as the monsters closed in on her, was how she'd almost given up during the competition. She recalled the resignation that had overwhelmed her—and then, the sudden burst of resolve and competitiveness that had followed.

No, fuck this.

Once more, her depressed futility gave way to a sense of frustration and anger. She hadn't come all this way and lived through the storm and the attack just to give up now. She was in this to win. No matter how much she hurt, no matter what they did to her, there was no retreat and no surrender. Not yet. She glared at the monsters. They could rape her if they wanted, but Becka swore it would cost them.

Out of the corner of her eye, she glimpsed Shonette. The black woman had curled into a fetal ball and wedged herself as far behind the boulder as she could, almost completely hidden in the shadows. She made no movement or sound.

"Shonette," Becka shouted. "Help me! We've got to fight back."

"Be quiet," Shonette whispered. "I told you. If you don't resist, they'll go easier on you."

"Shonette!"

"Hush now. Don't fight it. Just go along. Think of another place. A happy place. I'm in my kitchen with my kids and there are Fruity Pebbles."

The creatures' shadows fell over Becka. Her tear-stained face was level with their engorged members. Their combined stench assaulted her senses. Becka gagged, and her throat burned with sour bile. Her resolve shattered with their proximity.

"Shonette," she sobbed hoarsely. "Please . . ."

"Don't ask me to watch, Becka. Please don't ask me to do that. I can't look. I can't hold your hand. See, I'm with my children and they need me right now. You have to do this by yourself."

Attracted by Shonette's ramblings, one of the creatures turned to her and grunted. Shonette immediately fell quiet. Becka saw her quivering uncontrollably. The curious monster stepped toward her.

"All the Fruity Pebbles you want, Monika," Shonette muttered. "All that you want."

The creature shook its head rapidly, like a dog, spraying spittle all over the women and the cavern walls. Then it reached into the cranny and grabbed Shonette's arm. She squealed, but put up no resistance. Slowly, it began to drag her out of the shadows. Shonette's eyes were squeezed tightly shut.

"All that you want," Shonette repeated. "Come here, Darnell. All the cereal you want. All that you want . . . all that you want . . . just let me get off this island . . . *all you want . . . please no not again no more please no no nononono nooooo . . .* "

"Leave her alone," Becka yelled. "Get your fucking hands off of her, you bast—"

With a sharp grunt, one of the creatures slapped her across the face with the back of its furred hand. Becka's head struck the stone wall, and immediately, she saw stars. Until now, she'd always assumed it was just a saying, but there they were, floating in her vision—bright pinpoints of sheer white light. The attacker struck her again, knocking her head in the opposite direction. Her cheeks felt flushed and hot, and she tasted warm blood squirting through her mouth. Becka felt something hard and sharp slide down the back of her throat and realized with alarm that it was a tooth. She coughed, but it was too late. She'd swallowed it. More blood dribbled out from between her swollen lips. She spat on the cave floor and groaned.

Rough hands seized her shoulders and pushed her to the floor. Screaming, Becka beat at the creature with flailing hands. She grabbed two fistfuls of hair and pulled, earning herself another hammering blow. She clawed its back, tugged out fistfuls of wiry hair, and yanked hard on its ears, but it pushed her away and shoved her the rest of the way down to the floor. She tried to get a knee between herself and her attacker, but the second monster grabbed her legs and pulled them apart. Becka screamed as the first held her arms against her side. She felt its slick, hot erection slide against the bare flesh of her arm. Repulsed, Becka turned her head and vomited. There wasn't much in her stomach other than acid. As she dry heaved, the creatures laughed, amused by the display.

Next to her, Shonette put up no resistance. She simply repeated her crazed mantra over and over again, shuddering as the third creature groped roughly between her legs with its long fingers.

"Shonette," Becka moaned, "you've got to fight."

If Shonette heard her, she gave no sign. Her body went limp. The only indication that she was even still conscious was her repetitive whispering. Becka's heart sank even lower.

One of the beasts clawed at Becka's top, slashing the thin material with its talons. The material fell aside, revealing her breasts. The attacker frowned, ogling them, and hooted with disappointment.

Becka's fear turned to anger. "We can't all have boob jobs, you hairy son of a bitch!"

The creature's frown deepened.

Becka spat in its face.

The monster reared back, wiped the spittle from its snout, and bared its teeth. Despite her desire to appear brave, Becka whimpered. The creature responded with a deafening roar. Its sharp white teeth flashed in the darkness. Before she could react, it lashed out, striking her twice more across the face. Its claws raked her cheek, slashing narrow, bloody furrows in her skin. Then it seized her breasts in its rough hands, squeezing them hard. Those same talons dug deep. The beast tugged and pulled. The last of Becka's resolve shattered. Screaming, she struggled to get away, but the other's hold on her legs remained unbroken. The more she fought, the tighter they gripped. The calloused palms felt like sandpaper-covered vises. They ripped away her shorts, and Becka wailed. Something inside her throat snapped, and her shrieks became whispers.

One of the creatures positioned itself between her legs and pressed against her. She felt the slick heat, felt it throbbing, and threw up again—bile, blood, another tooth. The convulsions turned into dry heaves. Then she felt it invade her slowly, just an inch at a time. Becka closed her eyes, held her breath, and tried to block out the violation with the only weapon she had left—her mind. She thought of her parents, of her cat, of college and friends and the first boy she'd ever kissed. When none of that worked, she thought of Jerry. The creature thrust deeper, and she prayed again, this time for death.

When she heard the deep, rumbling grunt, she assumed it was just one of her attackers. She didn't realize that another one of the creatures had entered the alcove until she felt her rapist suddenly withdraw. Even Shonette fell silent. Wincing in pain and shuddering with revulsion, Becka opened her eyes. The creature that had been menacing Shonette and the two monsters that had been savaging her were standing up and had their backs to the women. Becka peered between them and saw why. The silver-haired elder stood in the opening, silhouetted in the firelight. It snarled at the three younger creatures in their weird, hooting language, and though Becka couldn't understand the words, she had no problem discerning their meaning. The old one's penis, while withered, was visibly aroused, as well, and he wanted to have a turn. The other three were clearly displeased with the turn of events, and refused to step aside. The chieftain's growls took on a menacing tone, and even though he hadn't raised his voice or made any threatening movements, the three younger creatures were suddenly cowed. They bowed and scraped and whined apologetically. Then they scrambled out of the way and shuffled past their leader with their heads lowered, obviously unwilling to meet his gaze. They returned to the main chamber without glancing back.

When they were gone, the elder turned that same malevolent glare on the two women. He gave Shonette only a cursory glance before focusing his full attention on Becka. Then, without preamble, it came for her.

Crawling on all fours, Becka managed to skitter into Shonette's former hiding place. She'd almost wedged herself into the crack when the chieftain grabbed her ankles and pulled. Becka grasped at the rock walls and one of her fingernails peeled back, bringing a fresh burst of agony. Screaming, she clutched at the floor, searching for a handhold, a purchase, anything that would stop her from being dragged back out and raped. Her fingers closed over a softball-sized rock, and she seized it without really thinking about it. The old creature pulled her completely out of the crevice. Without bothering to flip her over, it tried to take her from behind. It pressed against her back and she felt the thin member—much smaller than those of the younger creatures'—creep between her buttocks. Enraged, Becka lashed out blindly with the rock. There was a sickening crunch, and it felt like the rock had hit something soft. Wetness splattered her face. She struck two more times, and then, the monster's crushing weight was suddenly gone. She heard it slump to the floor behind her.

Coughing, Becka whirled around and gaped. The silver-haired creature lay crumpled before her. Its rheumy, heavy-lidded eyes were open, but stared sightlessly. Its gray, lifeless tongue lolled from its mouth. There was a large indentation on the side of its head, right above the left temple. Given the poor lighting, she couldn't tell how deep the wound was, but blood matted the fur and pooled on the stones where it lay.

Still gripping the rock, Becka prodded the creature with her foot. It didn't move. Cautiously, she knelt, staring closely at its chest. Then she held her fingers under its nose. It wasn't breathing.

"Holy shit."

Becka sat down and began to shake. Her entire body trembled, and the rock slipped from her fingers. Her vision grew blurry and the cave seemed to dim.

Shock, she thought. *I'm going into shock. Some kind of delayed reaction to . . . to what happened.*

Apparently, the rest of the tribe was oblivious to what had occurred. The sounds of the feast continued to echo from the main cavern. She didn't know how long her crime would go undiscovered, though. Gritting her teeth, she drew her knees up to her chest and stuck her head between them. Then she took deep, measured breaths until the nausea, dizziness, and shaking had subsided.

When she felt better, Becka crawled over to Shonette and gently shook her. The black woman's eyes were closed, but her chest rose and fell slightly.

"Shonette. Wake up. We're getting out of here."

"I'll be home soon, baby. You and your brother just hang tight."

"Come on, Shonette," Becka whispered louder. "It's me—Becka. Wake up."

"Becka?" Shonette's eyes fluttered open. "I told you not to piss them off. Now it will be worse. Why couldn't you just let me stay home with my kids?"

"Listen to me." Becka shook her harder, squeezing her arm firmly. "Snap out of it. I killed the leader, Shonette. He's dead. The others are gone."

Shonette bolted upright and glanced around. When she saw the chieftain's corpse, she moaned.

"Oh, no you didn't!" Shonette's voice cracked. "What the hell were you thinking? Why did you do that, Becka? Why couldn't you just go along? Do you know what they'll do to us when they find out?"

"They're not going to find out because we're getting the hell out of here."

"We can't. They'll make it worse."

"Make it worse? How can it be any worse? They *raped* us, Shonette. They raped Pauline. It doesn't get any worse than that."

"They'll kill us."

"So?"

Shonette uttered a choked sob.

"Look," Becka said, stroking the frightened woman's arm, "this is our chance. We have to take it.

I'm not just going to sit around here, waiting to be a victim again. I'm going, and if Pauline is still alive, I'm taking her with me. You have to come, too."

"I can't." Shonette's upper lip quivered. "Just leave me alone. I can't go out there."

"Why not?"

"Because I'm afraid."

Becka sighed. "So am I. But if you give into that fear now, then you've let them win. And I'll be damned if I'm going to allow that to happen. Now, let's go. Can you stand?"

Wiping her eyes, Shonette nodded. "I-I think so."

"Good. That's a start."

"My head hurts *really* bad, Becka. Makes it hard to think. And I'm so thirsty."

"You might have a concussion. Just hang in there. We'll get out of here and then find you some help."

Shonette's eyes filled with fresh tears. "I don't want to die. Please tell me we're not gonna die?"

"We're not going to die."

"Bullshit."

"Well, if we stay here, that's exactly what's going to happen, Shonette. Now get up!"

Shonette tottered to her feet, swaying slightly. She touched the wound on her head with one hand and winced, hissing in pain.

"Damn. They really messed me up good."

"It'll be okay. Let's get dressed."

They collected the tattered remnants of their clothes and attempted to fashion some crude covering by tying the rags together, but ultimately, the cloth was too damaged.

Becka sighed in frustration. Not only had they

been beaten and raped, but now they had to suffer this additional indignity. It seemed to weaken them somehow. Not only would they have to escape naked, but now she felt exposed—more vulnerable.

Shonette stared at the elder's corpse. "Is that thing really dead?"

"I think so." Becka nodded. "He wasn't breathing."

"So what now?"

"You stay here and rest. I'm going to sneak next door and check on Pauline. Then the three of us will get out of here."

"But *how*?"

"I don't know," Becka admitted. "At least, not yet. Let's just take it one step at a time."

"Hell," Shonette snorted. "Why not? Taking things one step at a time has kept us in the contest this long. Why not a little longer?"

"Exactly."

"What if they posted a guard?"

"I'm pretty sure they didn't. If there were more of those things standing outside the entrance, they'd have rushed in here as soon as I conked their leader on the head."

"Be careful," Shonette whispered.

Turning away, Becka bit her lip and prayed that she was right about the guards. She crawled into the darkness on her hands and knees, ignoring the sharp rocks that dug into her already sore skin. When she reached the opening, she dropped to the floor. The smell of wood smoke grew stronger, as did the tribe's stench. She crept to the ledge and peered over the lip. Below her, the feast continued.

None of the creatures showed any signs of interrupting their leader's attempts at mating. Becka breathed a sigh of relief. She had no doubt that if his murder was discovered, the rest of the tribe would tear her limb from limb and eat her just as they had the others.

Her stomach cramped as she thought about her fellow contestants. Sweet little Ryan. Richard and Sal. Jeff and Raul. She hadn't known any of them well, and indeed, she'd disliked the last two because of their affiliation with Stefan, but that didn't change the fact that she felt sorrow for their fate. Nobody deserved that. They'd come here to play a game, to be on television. They'd had families. Loved ones. Even that creepy Matthew must have had someone waiting for him back home.

Vowing that the same thing wouldn't happen to her, Shonette, or Pauline, Becka inched out onto the ledge and carefully crawled toward Pauline's alcove. The ledge was about eight feet wide and twelve feet above the main cavern floor. As long as she stayed low, Becka was sure she could navigate its length without being seen by the preoccupied creatures.

"Pauline?"

Becka's voice was barely a whisper, and she wasn't surprised when the other woman didn't answer her. She wriggled closer, dislodging a loose stone with her foot. It tumbled over the side of the ledge, clattering below. Becka's breath caught in her throat. She froze, pulse pounding, waiting to see if the disturbance had been noticed. When the sounds below didn't cease and there was no great outcry, she continued.

The next cave over was smaller than the one she and Shonette had been held captive in, and its interior was much darker. It sat farther back in the wall and the firelight from below didn't penetrate the cranny. Becka peered inside. All she saw of Pauline was one bare foot, the flesh stark white against the blackness.

"Pauline? It's me, Becka."

The foot twitched.

Becka hurried inside and rushed to Pauline's side, and nearly cried out when she saw the injured woman's condition. The creatures had beaten Pauline even worse than they had Shonette. Like the other women, she'd been stripped and mauled. Her expensive, once-perfect, artificial breasts were covered with deep cuts and scratches that would leave behind scars no plastic surgeon could heal. Her abdomen and thighs were similarly mutilated. Her lips were cracked and some of her fingernails were missing, most likely broken off on the rocks. A section of her hair had been torn from her scalp, leaving a pink, oozing sore. One of her eyes was swollen shut. The other was encircled with bruises. Her arms and legs were also bruised—a horrific rainbow of sickly yellow, red, black, and purple. Worst of all was the damage between her legs. When Becka saw it, she shuddered and began to weep.

"Oh . . . Pauline, can you hear me?"

She stroked Pauline's hair, and the woman stirred, blinking her eyes.

"B-Becka?"

"Yeah, it's me. Don't try to talk, okay? We have to be quiet."

Pauline nodded in understanding. The movement made her groan softly. She closed her eyes again.

"How bad does it hurt?" Becka asked.

"Pretty . . . pretty bad. They . . ."

"I know. You don't have to say it. I know what happened. They did the same thing with Shonette and me."

"Shonette's alive?"

"Yeah. She's right next door. We're going to get out of here and get some help. Everything's going to be okay now."

Despite the obvious pain it caused her, Pauline shook her head. "No, it isn't. Nothing's ever going to be okay again."

"Yes, it will. We'll get through this. You'll see."

"No, Becka. Y-you don't understand." She licked her cracked and bleeding lips and then continued. "When I was a senior in high school, the guy I went to homecoming with . . . he raped me. I swore to myself it would never happen again, but now it has. And as bad as it was back then? This is much worse. They aren't . . . *human.*"

She sobbed quietly and laid her head in Becka's lap. Becka held her, whispering consoling words and trying to soothe both her physical and emotional pains, even though she could do nothing for either. Becka closed her eyes and leaned back against the wall. She suddenly felt exhausted. They stayed that way for a long time, while the animalistic sounds of the feast continued to drift up from below.

"Did you see the statue?" Pauline asked.

Becka opened her eyes. "What statue?"

"Over there, in the corner. It's a little statue of one of those things, carved out of rock. I found a piece of one earlier, too. It had a squid head but a human body. It was all broken up."

Becka looked where Pauline pointed. Sure enough, there was a small stone effigy of one of their captors. It was about twelve inches high, and though crude, it displayed clear attention to detail and craftsmanship. The rock had been cut in such a way as to depict fur, and even the prominent lower jaw was noticeable. Could one of the tribe members have carved it? That didn't seem possible. The creatures that had attacked them, while intelligent, had seemed bestial.

She leaned back and closed her eyes again, considering the statue's origins. Maybe an earlier generation of creatures had carved the effigy, and maybe that skill was lost on the current tribe members. Maybe they were regressing, rather than evolving.

"Pssst."

Becka's eyes snapped open and Pauline stirred slowly. Both of them looked at the entrance. Shonette stared back at them.

"What the hell is taking you so long?"

"Sorry," Becka apologized. "Pauline's in pretty bad shape. She's been through a lot."

"We all have," Shonette said, sounding more like her old self again. "But like you said, unless we want to be victims, we've got to get going."

"Come on," Becka urged, "try to stand up."

"I can't," Pauline whispered.

"Is anything broken?"

"No."

"Then you have to try. Shonette's right."

"No." Pauline suddenly seemed to find some inner

reserve of strength and conviction. Her tone became adamant. "You two go ahead. I'm just going to close my eyes and wait."

"For what?" Shonette asked.

"To die."

"Bullshit," Shonette said. "We're not leaving here without you, and we're not waiting behind just to pacify your self-pitying ass."

Becka flinched. "Shonette . . ."

"Hell, no." Shonette held up her palm, interrupting. "I'm not sitting around here and waiting for those things to come back and discover what you did to their fearless leader. You were the one who wanted to escape in the first place. You gave me a little pep talk back there and got me all gung-ho. Now I'm doing the same for her. That's all. She's wanted to prance around this island and get the boys to do everything for her. Now she's gonna have to do it for herself—and for us."

"You make it sound like—"

"I don't care how it sounds, Becka. I'm sick of this place, and I'm sick of this TV show, and I'm sick of these fucking *things*. I want to see my kids again. I want to live, and goddamn it, more than anything, I want to leave this fucking island. Right now, Pauline is delaying that. She needs to suck it the fuck up."

Becka was too stunned to respond.

"You sound like Troy," Pauline murmured, and then began to giggle. "But you smell better than he does."

After a moment, Becka and Shonette joined her.

The three women hugged each other and chuckled quietly, their bodies shaking with laughter.

"*Hey, you hairy motherfucking cocksuckers! Come out and play.*"

"Wow," Pauline gasped. You really did sound like Troy that time."

"That wasn't me," Shonette said. "Listen!"

The voice sounded muffled, as if echoing from a great distance.

"Come on, you retarded fucking monkeys. What are you—pussies? Come and get some of this, you mongoloid douche bags! Let me show you how we do it in Seattle."

"Oh my God," Becka whispered. "That *is* Troy."

A tremendous disturbance shook the cavern as below them the tribe of creatures roared as one.

CHAPTER TWENTY-TWO

"Troy," Jerry whispered. "Can I ask you something?"

"What?"

"Do you really have 'everything sucks all the time' tattooed on your ass?"

"Fuck, yeah."

"You weren't bullshitting me?"

"Nope. I really do have it, man."

Jerry stopped. Troy halted behind him.

"What's up?"

"The tunnel is starting to slope downward. Let's keep going."

Jerry estimated that they'd traveled about thirty or forty yards. Despite Troy's vehement protests, Jerry had turned off the flashlight once they'd entered the confines of the cave. He'd been worried that the creatures would see the beam. Now it was off again. Although he didn't admit it out loud, he wished that he could turn it back on. The air inside the tunnel was fetid and cloying, and the darkness seemed to press at them. Jerry had never been claustrophobic, but in those few minutes, he could easily see how other people became afflicted with it. He fought to keep his breathing under control. Even though the temperature had dropped again, he was bathed in sweat. In one hand, he clutched his makeshift spear. He let his other hand trail along the rock wall to his right. The cold, damp stone was his only comfort, and a small one at that.

Sounds echoed down the tunnel toward them, bouncing off the rough walls—grunts and hooting, punctuated with the occasional growl, or worse, a horrid, garbled version of laughter.

"Jesus," Troy whispered. "Listen to that shit. What do you think they're doing?"

"I don't know," Jerry said. "Celebrating, maybe? Feasting? Mating? Doing some kind of war dance to their island gods? How should I know, dude?"

"Because you're the fucking expert and shit."

"I'm not an expert. I told you—it's just a hobby of mine."

"Well, you fucking know more than I do."

"All I know is that they've got Becka, and thinking about it makes me sick to my stomach."

"We'll find her, man."

Jerry didn't respond. He was afraid that if he did, his voice might crack.

They tiptoed on, heading deeper into the earth. A faint hint of wood smoke hung in the tunnel, but not as much as either of them had imagined there would be. The bumpy terrain rose and fell, and they had to feel their way along, arms outstretched. At times, the roof stretched high above their heads. In other sections, they had to duck down to make it through. They didn't find any branching passages

223

until they came to a sudden sharp turn in the path. At that point, Jerry's hand left the wall and dangled into open space. He leaned forward, feeling around, but the sides of the tunnel were gone.

"I'm going to click the light on for a second," he whispered. "Watch your eyes. I don't want to mess up your night vision."

"What night vision? I can't see shit."

"Even so, look away."

Jerry turned on the flashlight, carefully keeping the beam pointed at the ground. Then he trailed it up and over the walls. He paused when he saw some dark lines that didn't appear to be natural. Moving closer, he focused the light on them, revealing a primitive cave drawing. The lines formed a sort of crude maze. At the center of the labyrinth was a dark, squiggly mass with two oval-shaped eyes peering out of it. The drawing made him feel uneasy, but he didn't know why.

"What the fuck is that?"

"I don't know," Jerry whispered. "I mean, obviously, it's cave art, but I don't know what it's supposed to represent."

There were more pictures. One showed a group of cryptids fighting what looked like a tribe of Neanderthals. Another showed several creatures that had heads like swine but bodies like humans. They seemed to be coming out of an underground tunnel similar to the one he and Troy were standing in now.

Jerry continued examining the cave. Sure enough, the tunnel branched off at this section. A second, narrower path led away from them, apparently heading back up toward the surface. Troy ventured into the split, looked around, then ducked back out again.

"It's a dead fucking end," he reported, removing his hat and smoothing his hair. "Goes up about twelve feet and then ends in a tiny little fissure. Not big enough for those fucking things to squeeze through. Might have been an exit at some point, but not anymore. Looks like it caved in. There's boulders and shit blocking it."

"So if we can't go that way, then neither did Becka."

"Looks that way." Troy put his hat on again.

Jerry turned the light off once more and they stood silently, waiting for their eyes to readjust. The muffled sounds continued drifting toward them, seeming to pour from the rock itself. It was hard to determine how close they were. The creatures could be right around the corner or a mile away. Jerry's pulse sped up when he heard harsh, ragged breathing. He tensed, preparing to run, but then he realized that it was his own. In that moment, he felt exhausted and weak, and thought he might pass out. The flashlight seemed to weigh a hundred pounds, and it was all he could do just to remain upright.

"You okay?"

"Yeah," Jerry whispered. "I'm just a little freaked out. Need to catch my breath."

"What's the plan?" Troy asked.

"I don't know, other than to just keep going on and try to find the girls."

"I've been thinking about that," Troy said. "Sounds to me like there's an awful fucking lot of those things between us and the girls. I mean, maybe the cave fucks with the sounds and all, but if that noise is any indication, there's a lot more than we thought. Maybe more than we can fucking handle. We're a couple of fucking badasses and all, but I don't know about this."

Jerry sighed. "Listen, Troy. I'm exhausted and cold and feel like I've just gone twelve rounds with Mike Tyson. And more importantly, I'm fucking worried sick about Becka. My stomach hurts, I'm so scared. I don't have a plan. I'm not the kind of guy who comes up with plans."

"You had a plan to outwit Stefan."

"That's different. This isn't reality television anymore. This is real life. So, if you've got a suggestion, feel free to jump in anytime. Can you think of something else?"

"Actually, yeah. I can."

"Well, then I would love to hear it."

Troy put his hands on Jerry's shoulders and turned him toward the side tunnel. Then he pushed him forward into the darkness.

"Hey!"

"Listen," Troy whispered. "Go hide in that fissure. Squeeze yourself as far back in there as you can—just don't get fucking stuck."

"Why?"

"Just fucking trust me, okay? I've got a plan."

"Okay." Although he was secretly doubtful, Jerry was too tired to argue about it or question the mechanic any further. "Watch your eyes. I'm turning on the light again."

Using the flashlight, he made his way into the

branching tunnel and crawled over a mound of loose rubble and debris until he'd reached the top. Sure enough, there was a narrow fissure at the end, barely wide enough for him to stick an arm through, let alone crawl through. He turned the flashlight off again and got positioned.

"You good?" Troy called. "All settled in and shit?"

"I'm all set. And we've wasted enough time. Whatever you're going to do, do it already."

"Okay."

Troy was silent for a moment, and Jerry wondered if he'd left. Maybe he'd been waiting to abandon Jerry and had just needed the opportunity. After all, Troy had no loyalties to Jerry or Becka or anyone else. They weren't lifelong friends. They were contestants on a television show. They barely knew each other. Jerry shook his head. What did he really know about Troy? That his brother had been involved in a bank robbery. That he cursed more than any human being Jerry had ever met. That was all. How could he really trust him? Jerry was about to turn the flashlight on and make sure he was there, when suddenly, Troy shouted at the top of his lungs.

"Hey, you hairy motherfucking cocksuckers! Come out and play."

Jerry nearly toppled out of the nook. Gasping, he clutched at the rocks and screamed at Troy.

"What the hell are you doing? You'll have every one of them on us in a second!"

"I know. That's my fucking plan."

Even though he couldn't see him, Jerry could tell by his tone that Troy was grinning.

"That's your plan? That's your fucking plan? Are you insane?"

"Didn't you ever see *The Warriors*? 'Warriors, come out and playyyyyy'?"

"What the hell are you talking about?"

Ignoring him, Troy yelled again. His cries echoed down the tunnel, reverberating off the walls.

"Come on, you retarded fucking monkeys. What are you—pussies? Come and get some of this, you mongoloid douche bags! Let me show you how we do it in Seattle."

He tapped his spear on the floor and banged his stone knife against the wall, creating more noise.

"Oh, goddamn it." Jerry scrambled down from his perch, using his spear for balance and dislodging debris as he did so. Pebbles and stones clattered down the pile.

"Stay the fuck there," Troy warned him. "Just stay put, goddamn it. I'm gonna lead the fuckers outside and away from here. When I do, you sneak in and find the girls and get them out of here. I'll get these things to chase me toward the other end of the island, and then I'll circle around. We'll meet up at the circle of protection. That's where the chopper always lands. Hopefully, it'll fucking be there by the time we arrive."

"That's the stupidest thing I've ever heard! Are you crazy? What makes you think all of those things are going to come rushing out after you?"

"Because I'm gonna be a pain in their ass long enough that they'll fucking *have* to send everybody after me."

"Troy, this isn't going to work."

"You asked if I had a fucking plan. I said I did. I didn't say it was a good fucking plan. And I didn't exactly hear you making fucking decisions, Jerry. You want to save Becka? You said it yourself—we couldn't fight our way through all of them. I'm evening the fucking odds."

"Oh, you idiot. You goddamn unbelievable idiot."

Troy's tone turned dejected. "I'm tired, too, man. And it's too late now, in any fucking case. So, please, Jerry. Get the fuck back up there and hide!"

"Troy—"

"Goddamn it, I said please, motherfucker. Don't make me say it again."

Part of Jerry wanted to curl into a ball and cry. The other half wanted to slide down the rock pile and punch Troy in the face. He ignored both urges and scrambled back to the top, clinging to the rocks as a sick, emotional mix of fear and revulsion swept over him.

The roar that blasted up from below was deafening. It sounded like someone had bottled up all the thunder from the storm and set it off underground. Trembling, Jerry ducked his head and tried to block the noise by pushing his shoulders up over his ears. It didn't work. The roars continued, followed by the sound of pounding. He tried to figure out what it was, and after a second, it came to him.

Running footsteps.

Lots of them. It sounded like an army.

"Damn," Troy muttered. "Sounds like I fucking pissed them off good."

Jerry shook his head and closed his eyes. "Jesus Christ . . . oh, Jesus fucking Christ, this is not happening. This is not happening at all. I'm sorry, Becka . . ."

"Come on, you stinky bastards," Troy called. "I can smell you coming. You all need a fucking shower."

"Stop it, Troy," Jerry pleaded. "Please stop. We can still get away."

"Come and get it! Step right up and don't be shy. I got something for you. The golden goddamn goose is on the motherfucking loose and never out of season. It's two minutes to midnight, bitches, so die with your boots on. Bring your daughters to the fucking slaughter, motherfuckers! Up the irons!"

He's snapped, Jerry thought. *I mean, for God's sake—he's shouting Iron Maiden slogans at them now. What the hell is that about? His mind is gone. I shouldn't have pushed him so hard to come with me. It was obvious that he was terrified. Now he's over the edge and we're all screwed.*

The clamor of onrushing feet grew louder.

"Jerry?"

"What?"

"Make sure you stay there until there's no more of those things in the tunnel, man. Hopefully, there won't be many left behind at wherever they're holding Becka."

"Shut up, Troy. Just shut the hell up. Oh, Jesus . . ."

"And, Jerry? Good luck, man. You're an okay dude, as far as I'm concerned. You're both good people. Best I've met in a long fucking while. Just make sure you fucking save her."

Jerry's response was drowned out by a deafening, angry roar.

"Here we go," Troy shouted. "Fuck me running."

Jerry could only listen in horror, cowering against the wall and praying that he wouldn't be discovered, while what sounded like a veritable mob of cryptids bore down on his friend. Talons clicked on stone. Growls split the darkness. Teeth gnashed audibly.

Then a series of unexpected sounds echoed down the corridor. Troy grunted in exertion. Jerry heard a wet thud, and then something howled in pain. Then, instead of the cryptids, it was Troy who was growling.

"One down," Troy taunted. "Who's next, motherfuckers?"

One of the creatures yelped, and then shrieked. The cry ended abruptly. Several more of the cryptids roared again. The sound was loud enough to shake the debris Jerry was crouched among. Beneath the cacophony, he heard Troy laughing.

Then silence.

From the darkness, Troy muttered, "Oh shit."

Jerry heard the unmistakable sounds of Troy running away. His echoing footsteps raced back up the tunnel, heading toward the surface. The creatures rushed after him, screaming with rage. Jerry glimpsed their shadowed forms, black shapes that were darker than the darkness around them. Worse than that, he smelled them. Their stench filled the tunnel, making his eyes water and burning his nose. He held his breath as they dashed past his hiding place. Luckily for him, none of them paused long enough to investigate. They were too enraged, too focused on their fleeing quarry to notice him. Jerry feared that they might catch his scent as they filed past, but if they did, they must have assumed it was Troy's. Perhaps they had trouble distinguishing the two. Maybe all humans smelled alike to them, or maybe their noses were no better than a person's nose. After all, they weren't evolutionary offshoots of dogs or cats.

Jerry wondered how far Troy could get before they inevitably caught him. He was vastly outnumbered, and his pursuers had the advantage of knowing the terrain. Plus, Jerry still had the flashlight, so Troy was running in the dark. Running blind. He didn't know for sure, but he suspected that the creatures had much better night vision than their human prey. There was nothing he could do. He wanted to help Troy, but if he revealed himself now, he'd be killed. If that happened, Troy's brave—if foolhardy—sacrifice would be in vain, and Becka would surely die.

If she wasn't dead already.

The sweat on Jerry's back suddenly felt like ice water. Until now, he hadn't even considered the possibility that Becka and Pauline might be dead. Now that the thought had occurred to him, he couldn't put it from his mind. Crippled with indecision and fear, he remained where he was and listened to the echoes fade.

When the cavern was silent again, Jerry took a deep breath and carefully maneuvered his way back to the bottom of the rock pile. He crept back out into the main tunnel and paused, listening. If any of the creatures had remained behind and were lurking in the darkness, he couldn't hear them. He tiptoed forward and his foot collided with something soft but solid. Startled, he almost tripped. He struggled to keep his balance and bit down on his tongue. His spear slipped from his hand and clattered onto the stone floor. Wincing, Jerry knelt and patted the ground, searching for it. His fingers brushed up against fur, and he yanked his hand away, nearly crying out. The cave remained silent. Cautiously, he stretched his hands out and explored again. The fur was sticky and wet, and the body was still warm. His hands roamed over its face, and his finger slipped into a gaping hole. At first, he assumed it was a mouth or nostril, but with dawning horror, Jerry realized it was an empty eye-socket. Troy had put the creature's eye out—either with his spear or the jagged stone.

Jerry recoiled in disgust. His hands came away slick.

He fumbled with the flashlight and clicked it on, shining it over the floor. Jerry gasped. Somehow, Troy had managed to kill two of the creatures before he fled. Obviously, their murder had further enraged the rest of the tribe. No wonder they'd gone after him in such numbers. The second cryptid had been impaled through the throat. He noticed that this one had a genetic mutation—a webbed left hand. Pink flaps of membranous skin connected its fingers. Small red veins ran through the webs.

Jerry's dropped spear lay next to the corpse. After retrieving it, he turned the flashlight off again and immediately regretted it. The darkness seemed to loom before his tired eyes, pressing in on him more than ever.

He proceeded, listening cautiously, ready to flee or fight at a moment's notice if he heard more of the tribe coming toward him. Despite his fears, there didn't seem to be. The tunnel was deserted—if not soundless. He still heard some of the creatures, but now the noise was muted. Gone were the shrieking howls and ferocious roars. They'd been replaced with meek, frightened mewling and hushed cries.

Jerry paused, readjusting his grip on the spear. A blister popped on his palm and he grimaced as he felt warmth gush between his fingers.

Damn it, Troy, he thought. *What the hell were you thinking?*

Still, he had to admit, as bizarre as the mechanic's plan had been—it had apparently worked. Jerry didn't know how to explain it, but the cavern *felt* emptier. His frayed nerves calmed somewhat, and he began to hope again. Despite the confusing, echo effect the stones had on sound, the noises seemed to be stationary. Even so, Jerry moved carefully. He took his time and was mindful of not stumbling or making any sound. The smell of wood smoke grew stronger and the noises grew progressively louder.

He rounded a slight curve and saw a yellow-orange glow ahead of him. It took a moment for his eyes to adjust. The light flickered and danced.

Fire. That explains the smoke. It must be going out another exit, though. Otherwise, there would be more of it in this passageway.

As he drew closer, Jerry hunched over and stuck closer to the wall. The tunnel ended abruptly, opening into a huge cavern with a high ceiling. He inched forward until he could see inside it. A large fire blazed in the center of the cave. The smoke from the fire drifted slowly toward a natural rock chimney located in the center of the roof. He spotted more cave art on the walls. The crude illustrations depicted several different scenes and figures. Some of them were simple caricatures of birds, lizards, and fish. Others were more complex. There was a group of spear-carrying tribe members hunting something that looked like a pig (a normal pig, rather than the swine-headed figures he'd seen in the previous artwork). Another picture portrayed the cryptids standing on the beach and greeting a group of humans in a boat. A third seemed indecipherable at first. It was just a series of dots and orbs. After a moment, Jerry realized that it was the night sky, as seen from the island. The final painting showed a towering figure that looked like a cross between a gorilla and a cat. It loomed menacingly over three prostate cryptids. Jerry was left with the impression that the figures were praying to it.

Clearly, the tribe was regressing. Their own artwork showed them using tools and weapons, and possibly represented a deity of some kind, and a form of worship, but the creatures they'd encountered so far didn't seem capable of such things.

Jerry's attention returned to the task at hand. The remaining tribe members were in various places throughout the warren. Most of them wore expressions of obvious distress and worry. As far as he could tell, most of the tribe's males had run off after Troy, leaving behind the females and the children. A few toothless old males remained, but not many. Most of the young had mutations and deformities. One of them, barely a toddler, was gnawing on something. Alarmed, he realized it was a human leg bone. The flesh had been stripped from it, and the salivating child was sucking out the marrow. Roberta's corpse lay next to it. Jerry turned his head away and took deep breaths.

When he looked back again, he saw another young one crawling across the floor. Instead of legs, the poor creature had two short stubs. It bawled hungrily and was picked up and comforted by a young female with three breasts—two of them full and ponderous, while the third was stunted and shriveled. The child nuzzled at all three. Jerry's initial disgust was forgotten, and he almost felt sorry for their plight. Then he saw a bloodied scalp with blond-brown hair lying near the fire and recognized it as Ryan's; his pity vanished.

How many years have they been inbreeding? he thought. *That's why they took the girls alive. They need to increase the gene pool.*

He wondered if such interspecies crossbreeding would actually work. Then he thought of Becka again and his fears returned, stronger than before. He had to find her before it was too late.

Jerry scanned the rest of the cave. About twelve feet up the far side of the cavern was a rock ledge, running along the wall's length like a catwalk. It was dotted with several smaller caverns and grottoes. There was no sign of Becka or Pauline, and he saw no other tunnels exiting the main hall. If they were indeed still alive and being held captive, his best bet was to look for them on the ledge above. But how could he get up there? At the rear of the cavern, he noticed a large pile of boulders and debris about eight feet high. Positioned on top of this mound was a crude ladder, fashioned from bamboo and lashed together with vines. He saw no other way of attaining the ledge. Apparently, this was the only means of getting to the upper level.

Sure. All I have to do is stroll through the fucking enclave there and avoid getting ripped to tiny little bite-sized pieces by a bunch of angry mothers trying to protect their young, then scale that ladder without breaking my fucking neck, then find Becka—if she's even up there.

No, she's up there. She has *to be. Because if she isn't . . .*

If she wasn't, then Jerry wondered if he could even go on. To have survived the storm and the subsequent massacre of his fellow contestants, to see Becka taken from him and to feel the helpless, futile desperation that followed her capture, to have ventured this far into the tribe's warren, and to witness Troy's maniacal sacrifice—if Becka wasn't there, or worse, if she was there but dead—then there was really no point anymore. He'd be better off just walking into the cave, laying down his spear, and letting the remaining tribe members do to him what they'd done to the others.

Then he thought of her smile and the trusting expression on her face—and the kiss.

Troy's voice ran through his mind. *Just make sure you fucking save her.*

Okay, Troy, he thought. *If you were here, you'd*

probably say something profound like, "Fuck it."
So, fuck it. Fuck them all.

He peered into the cavern. The closest of the creatures were about ten feet away—a young mother, almost a child herself, judging by her height and weight, and two small children who were presumably hers. One of them was an infant, surprisingly free of physical deformities, as far as he could see. The other was maybe two or three years old, and blind. Its eyes were milky white, with no cornea or pupils. Yellow pus leaked from the corners of both useless orbs, drying and matting in the fur on its face. It stared sightlessly, and its bulbous, misshapen head lolled back and forth, barely supported by its thin neck.

Fuck it, he repeated to himself.

Jerry stood and shoved the flashlight into his pocket. Then, gripping his spear in both hands, he belted out a scream and charged into the cave. The startled creatures leapt to their feet and scattered, frightened by the outburst. Their hooting shrieks filled the air. Mothers clung to their infants and swept the older children behind them. They bared their teeth, snarling at him. Taking advantage of the chaos and uncertainty that his entrance had caused, Jerry grabbed the blind child and yanked it away from its clinging, three-breasted mother. The creature held on to her spawn, tugging on its arm. Jerry pulled harder. The young cryptid bawled and screamed, terrified at being used as a tug-of-war piece. Its sightless eyes jiggled frantically. Jerry thrust his spear at the older creature and she shrank away, releasing the child. He spun the toddler around, putting its back to him. Then, with one arm coiled tightly around its scrawny neck, he held the tip of his spear to his throat and faced the tribe.

They circled him slowly, clearly enraged by this violent intrusion. While not as physically large as their male counterparts, the females possessed many of the same dangerous attributes, including the long, curved talons and razor-sharp teeth. They displayed both to him, promising of what was to come. As one, they drew closer.

"Back off," he shouted. "Back up right now, or the kid gets it."

To accentuate his threat, Jerry pressed the spear into the youngster's throat. The child quivered. Hot urine trickled down its leg, pooling around Jerry's foot. The ammonia-like stench was almost overpowering. Jerry coughed and his eyes watered. Mistaking it for a sign of weakness or doubt, the females inched closer. His hostage's mother bellowed her fury.

"I mean it," he continued, trying not to choke. "Get the fuck back!"

Jerry was certain that they didn't recognize his words, but they clearly understood his intent. Growling, the adults backed off, retreating to a safer distance. Their eyes, however, never left him. The very atmosphere felt malevolent. Could he really blame them? After all, he was the intruder here. He was the one who'd entered their home and was menacing one of their children.

No, screw that. They started this.

But for what reasons? To feed, certainly. It was obvious to Jerry that the island's ecosystem could no longer support a tribe of this size. Most of the creatures showed signs of being malnourished. And perhaps, to expand their breeding stock and end the mutations that were plaguing their community. Were their methods evil? No. They were primitive and savage and animalistic, but the same could be said of some of mankind's transgressions from its less-than-proud past.

He pushed the blind creature forward, and it stumbled. Jerry felt a momentary pang of guilt, but he forced the emotion back down and clenched his jaw. He kept the spear point against the child's throat, making an indentation but not piercing the skin.

"It's going to be okay," Jerry murmured, and then wondered who he was trying to convince—himself or his captive. "Everybody just stay back. I don't want to do this, but you've left me no choice."

"Jerry?"

He paused, shocked at hearing another human voice. All around him, the tribe growled softly.

"Becka?" He risked a glance upward at the ledge, searching for her.

"I'm here. So are Pauline and Shonette. Jerry, what's happening?"

"Oh my God! Becka . . . are you okay? What did they—"

"Never mind that now. What's going on?"

"You're rescued."

The tribe's agitation increased as Jerry and Becka shouted back and forth. A few of the braver ones began to edge closer again. Jerry jerked the sagging hostage upright again and renewed his pressure on the spear point. The child's breathing turned into a harsh wheezing, but Jerry didn't release his hold.

"Get back, goddamn it!"

"Jerry, what's happening?"

"There's no time to explain. Just listen to me. Can you guys walk?"

There was a pause, and then Becka yelled, "I think so."

"Then get down here. And hurry! I don't know how long I can hold them off. They're pretty angry with me right now."

Jerry felt himself starting to panic again. He took a deep breath and watched the circling females carefully.

"This is what we call a Mexican standoff." His voice cracked.

As if sensing his fear, the tribe grew braver again. They slashed at the air with their claws and gestured menacingly. The mother of his captive snapped her slavering jaws, and stretched an arm toward her child. The mewling toddler reached for her, but Jerry pulled him back.

"Stay still. It will all be over soon. Hurry up, Becka!"

If she heard him, she didn't respond.

"Becka?"

His shout boomed across the cavern. The only response was from the creatures. They began to creep forward again, and this time, when Jerry hollered at them to stop, they ignored him.

* * *

"Is it really him?" Shonette asked.

Becka nodded and tried to get Pauline to sit up. "Shonette, help me get her on her feet."

"Come on, Pauline. The cavalry is here. It's time to go."

Pauline opened her eyes again, looked at them, then shook her head. She tried to lie down again, but Becka pulled her back up.

"Pauline," Becka urged. "We have to go. You can't stay here."

"Yes, I can," she slurred. "You two go ahead. I'm just going to close my eyes and go to sleep for a long time."

"The hell you are," Shonette said. "Get up. Now!"

Pauline ignored them both. "When I sleep, I can't feel anything. I don't think. I don't feel. It's nice."

Jerry's voice echoed up from below, urging Becka to hurry up.

Becka put Pauline's left arm over her shoulder, and nodded at Shonette to do the same with her right. Shonette did, and together, they lifted the protesting woman up off the floor. They had to support her between them. Pauline was dead weight in their arms. She hung limply, refusing to use her legs.

Jerry hollered again. "Becka?"

"Pauline," Becka pleaded, "you have to help us. Jerry can't stay down there forever. We have to get moving. Please?"

"Will you both leave me alone if I do?"

"Yes," Shonette snapped. "Hell, yes. If it will get your ass in gear, then I'll promise to never speak to you again. Now let's go."

They shuffled toward the edge of the stone ledge,

still supporting most of Pauline's weight. She limped along between them, her head hung low, her chin brushing against her bloodied chest.

A tumultuous cry rang out from below. It sounded like the creatures were growing more agitated. Becka heard Jerry's voice beneath their growls and snarls. It had gone up several octaves. He sounded terrified.

"Jerry! We're coming."

"Hurry. They're getting worked up again."

They hurried to the edge of the ledge and peered over the side. Jerry was near the main tunnel. He held a young creature in front of him as a hostage. Most of the tribe was gone, leaving only the females, children, and a few of the infirm behind. The angry mothers had closed ranks around him on three sides, and were inching closer.

"Over there." Shonette pointed to a rickety-looking ladder poking up over the lip of the ledge.

They hurried over to it. The ladder's base was positioned in a pile of rocks.

"That doesn't look very sturdy," Shonette said.

"It's either that or jump," Becka pointed out. "But how are we going to get through them all? Jerry's on the other side."

Shonette let go of Pauline, and she sagged lower.

"Stand up," Shonette told her. "You've got to do your part now."

"What are you doing?" Becka asked.

"Just hang on."

She ran back across the ledge and disappeared into the alcove. When she returned, Shonette was dragging the body of the chieftain.

"We put him between us, just like we did with Pauline. If they think he's our hostage, they'll let us pass."

"That will never work," Becka said. "One look, and they'll see that I bashed his head in."

"That doesn't prove he's dead. And if we get Pauline to walk directly in front of us, that will help block the view."

Realizing that she didn't have any better ideas and that there was no time to argue in any case, Becka nodded her head in agreement and then started down the ladder. When she reached the rock pile, she glanced over at the tribe. They hadn't noticed her descent—they were all preoccupied with Jerry and his captive. She motioned at Shonette to hurry.

Grunting, Shonette grabbed the corpse by its ankles and lowered it over the side. Becka almost toppled over, but managed to secure it. Then Shonette clambered down to the floor as well. They readjusted the dead creature between them, then motioned at Pauline to come down. Pauline shook her head.

"Pauline," Becka pleaded. "Come on!"

Whimpering, she eased out over the ledge and lowered herself over the side. Then, moving slowly, she began her descent. When she'd joined the others, they made her stand in front of them.

"Okay," Shonette whispered. "Just stay right in front of us and don't panic. We stick to this wall here and put our backs to it. Go straight toward Jerry and don't stop for anything. If it looks like they've caught on that their fearless leader is dead, then toss him to the side and run. Everybody understand?"

Becka nodded. Pauline just blinked sleepily.

"Pauline, do you understand?"

"Yeah. Walk in front. Stick to the wall."

"Right," Shonette said. "Let's go."

They started forward. The corpse weighed a lot more than Pauline had, and Becka and Shonette struggled in exertion. The leader stank, and they breathed through their mouths to avoid coughing. They'd managed to traverse half the cavern's length before the tribe noticed them. The outcry became even more frenzied when they saw their elder slumped over between the women. Becka snuck a glance at Jerry. His eyes were wide, and his expression was shocked. But beneath that, he seemed relieved to see her. His gaze strayed to her nudity. Then he quickly looked away.

"What are you doing?" he called.

"Stay there," Becka yelled. "Keep them off us just a few seconds more."

Half the tribe turned and came toward them. The other half remained where they were, creeping up on Jerry and his hostage.

"We're doing good," Shonette muttered. "Just a little bit more to go. Just a—"

With a sudden cry, Pauline bolted for the open tunnel, abandoning them. She cut right through the middle of the startled creatures.

"Oh shit." Shonette slipped out from underneath the corpse. "Run, Becka! Run."

Jerry echoed her sentiments and began backing toward the exit. Shonette and Becka dashed toward him, trying to keep the wall to their backs. Several of the creatures rushed to their fallen leader and wailed over his corpse. More of them raced after the fleeing culprits. A bloated, pregnant female with one good eye, who stood near the sputtering fire, snatched a rock from the ground and flung it at Pauline. It struck her in the back of the head and she stumbled. Another creature flung itself onto her back, crushing her to the floor.

In an instant, a dozen females and children had joined the fray, biting and slashing and pulling. Pauline's screams reached a frenzied peak, and then became one long, drawn-out moan. They tore her limb from limb, pulling her arms from their sockets and tossing severed fingers and her internal organs into the air with savage abandon. Her blood coated their fur, and their claws dripped with gore.

Becka and Shonette reached Jerry's side, but six more creatures were right behind them. Jerry spun the blind child around and shoved him forward. Crying out, the toddler tumbled to the cavern's floor. Jerry, Shonette, and Becka raced for the exit.

"Here!" Jerry handed Becka the flashlight.

"What are you—"

"Run, goddamn it! Don't worry about me. I'm right behind you. But I'm the only one with a weapon."

They fled down the tunnel. The flashlight beam bounced off the walls. Becka was in the lead, followed by Shonette. Jerry brought up the rear.

Howling furiously, the tribe members plunged into the darkness after them.

CHAPTER
TWENTY-THREE

Troy exploded from the jungle and ran out onto a high cliff. Panting, he took shelter behind a large boulder near the edge of the precipice and paused to catch his breath. His chest heaved. The sea sprawled below him like a black velvety blanket. The rippling water had a soothing effect. Far out on the horizon, he saw the blinking lights of the freighter. Closer to shore, the moon reflected off the waves. Then he realized that it wasn't moonlight, but lights of a different kind. He turned his attention upward, and spotted the chopper bulleting toward the beach. Spotlights swiveled, pouring over the land and sea below.

"Shit! It's about fucking time. Now all I gotta do is make it down there."

Behind him, the sounds of pursuit had finally faded. Troy had led the cryptids on a frantic chase across the island, killing three more of them in the process and injuring several others. He hadn't come out of the running battle unscathed. There were four deep gashes on his back where one of the creatures had raked him with its talons, and a matching set on the calf of his left leg. He'd been poked by branches and jabbed with thorns, had tumbled down a hillside and fallen into a ravine, gashed his knee open on a sharp fragment of volcanic rock, gotten jabbed in the cheek by something in the dark, and wrenched his back (which had pained him intermittently since he'd originally injured it in an auto shop three years earlier). Both of his ears still rang from the constant barrage of roaring cries he'd been subjected to for the last half hour. The wounds on his back and leg cut swaths through his tattoos, and that hurt him in ways the pain couldn't.

Through it all, he'd somehow managed to hold on to his hat.

Troy listened to the waves crashing below and the birds shrieking at one another above, and beneath it all, the rhythmic thrum of the helicopter's rotors. Exhausted as he was, he could have happily stayed there, hunched behind the boulder and clinging to the cliff's edge all night long. Instead, he grabbed some broad leaves from a nearby bush and dabbed at his wounds. His blood hadn't clotted yet, but at least the flow had turned into a trickle. He turned his head, trying to peer over his shoulder at the gashes in his back, but the movement brought a fresh burst of agony. Moaning, Troy gritted his teeth and closed his eyes until the pain had passed. He wondered how he'd ever get the tattoos fixed. Could an artist put fresh ink over scar tissue?

He struggled to his feet again and studied the tree line. Nothing moved. Either the creatures were hiding, waiting for him to come out, or they'd given up the chase and returned to their den. He sniffed the air and found no trace of their repugnant stench. Chances were good that they'd gone back to the cave. If so, he hoped that he'd bought Jerry enough time to rescue the others and get the hell out of there.

Wincing, Troy limped along the edge of the cliff and searched for a way down to the beach. The helicopter had passed from sight, and although he could still hear the rumbling of the rotors and the high-pitched whine of the hydraulics, it sounded like the craft was powering down, which probably meant that it had landed. All he had to do was get there before they left again.

Or before the cryptids got them, too.

He readjusted his grip on the spear and sighed. His rock knife had been lost during the chase, after he'd used it to knock out the teeth of an attacking monster.

"All in all," he groaned, "I wish I were back in fucking Seattle. A million dollars ain't worth this shit. Hope you got your girl, Jerry."

He threaded his way carefully along the edge, sticking close to cover in case any of the beasts emerged from the jungle. He still wasn't entirely convinced that they'd given up the hunt altogether.

Troy's stomach grumbled. Clutching it, he tried to remember how long it had been since he'd eaten. Well before the storm, at least. Breakfast had been rice and a few scraps of dried fish, washed down with flat-tasting boiled water. He'd had nothing since then. Upon realizing that, he suddenly felt famished. Dawn was just a few hours away. All he had to do was make it to the landing zone, get on board the helicopter and in a few hours, he could be eating blueberry pancakes with maple syrup and big, long strips of crispy fucking bacon on board the network's freighter.

And then top it off with a cigarette.

He reached a section of cliff where the sheer drop faded. The ground sloped gradually downward. It looked like water had rushed through here at some point, piling debris along the cliff side. Large boulders, dirt, dead trees and other flotsam and jetsam provided a definitive, if treacherous, path down to the beach. Troy studied it carefully. The landslide was his quickest bet. He didn't know how much farther he'd have to walk to find an easier descent—if one even existed. His thoughts turned again to Jerry and Becka. He hoped that they were okay.

Moving carefully, he started down the slope. Soil and pebbles slid out from beneath his feet and rustled in the darkness. The angle hurt his back, but Troy kept going. Better a bad back than ending up as dinner for one of those things. A steady breeze battered him. He looked down once and felt the bottom drop out of his stomach. Growing dizzy, he leaned backward and grabbed onto a jutting rock.

"Jesus fucking Christ, that's a long way to fucking fall."

He navigated around deadfalls and jumbled boulders, slipping several times in the loose dirt but maintaining his balance. Each time he did, Troy bit his lip to keep from crying out. He grabbed a jutting branch to support himself, and invoked the wrath of a mother seabird protecting her nest. She darted forward, angrily pecking at his hand.

"Knock it off, goddamn it! I ain't gonna hurt you or your babies."

Squawking, the bird jabbed at him again. This time, she drew blood. Troy yanked his hand away and dropped his spear. It tumbled down the slope, crashing far below. The bird shrieked louder.

"Oww, bitch! Stop it. Get the fuck off of me."

His curses were answered by a low growl from above. With one mournful cry, the frantic bird took flight, abandoning her eggs. On top of the cliff, the growl changed to a yipping bark. Slowly, Troy looked up. There, at the top of the slope, silhouetted in the moonlight, was a lone cryptid. Grinning, it started down the hill and stalked toward him in broad, loping strides. Troy backed away as the beast crept forward. It stepped into the light again, and he could see that it was a mutant. A pale, pronged penis dangled between its legs. Troy guessed the organ was probably useless. The moonlight cast a sickly pallor over it. The thing's dark hair was matted with dirt and insects, but there were also patches on its body where the hair had fallen out. In the bare spots, misshapen lumps pushed out from beneath its skin. Tumors of some kind, Troy guessed.

"Your prick looks like one of those split sausages you get at the fucking diner for breakfast. I bet you have trouble keeping your old lady around, huh? How the fuck do you even get it up?"

The beast stopped, snarling at him in confusion— and perhaps, just a twinge of fear. Troy had learned quickly enough that if he hid his apprehension and confronted them directly, the creatures were slow to act. Years of being the biggest predator on the island had left them ill equipped to confront prey who talked back. Still growling, the cryptid raised its snout and sniffed the air.

"The fuck are you looking at, you broke-dick motherfucker? Get the fuck back up that hill before I do to you what I did to your fucking buddies."

The thing hooted in response.

A mosquito buzzed in Troy's ear, but he ignored it, refusing to turn his gaze away from his antagonist. They stared at each other, neither one of them blinking, engaged in a primal game of chicken. The creature's chest heaved. Troy's back ached. Dislodged gravel and debris continued to slide past them both. Troy took another step backward, and his foe matched him with one simultaneous step forward. They repeated the process again and again. The wind increased, howling up the cliff side, ruffling the beast's fur, and battering against Troy's back. He weaved unsteadily and then, before he could act, the wind tore his hat from his head and sent it hurtling back up the mound.

"Shit."

The hat landed a few feet away from the cryptid, who finally broke eye contact with Troy and stared at it curiously.

"Hey," Troy warned. "You just stay the fuck away from that. It doesn't fucking concern you."

The creature glanced at him, then back down at the hat again. Its expression was one of curiosity. Snuffling, it bent over and reached for it with one clawed hand.

"I'm fucking warning you, cocksucker. Get the fuck away from my hat."

Its rheumy eyes flicked up at him again, then back to the cap. The cryptid snatched the hat and smelled it. Its nose crinkled. Troy quaked with anger as he saw it leave a glistening trail of snot on the brim. Then followed the ultimate insult—the creature stretched out its black tongue and licked the garment. It hooted softly to itself and then glanced at Troy.

"That's it, goddamn you. You are fucking dead. Nobody—and I mean nobody—fucks with my hat, especially a fucking monkey-man like you."

Troy ducked down and picked up a football-sized chunk of volcanic rock. Then he stood again and faced the creature. With a rough, throaty chuckle, it stepped toward him again, still clutching the hat in one paw. Hefting the rock over his shoulder, Troy charged. The beast roared in challenge. Troy swung the rock, aiming for its face. He missed as his opponent sprang backward. It swiped at him with its free hand, but Troy managed to dodge the eviscerating blow. They squared off, facing each other again.

"You know how much pussy that hat's gotten me over the years? Now you want to do the same thing, huh? It ain't gonna work for you, though, shithead. You ain't had pussy since pussy had you."

The cryptid growled.

Troy gave it the finger. "Christ, you fucking stink. And you've got more back hair than a fur fucking coat. You got hair everywhere. I mean, just fucking look at you."

The creature narrowed it eyes and snarled. Troy winced at its breath.

"Don't get pissy with me, motherfucker. It's true.

You've even got hair on your fucking dick. My brother had a name for that. He called it 'carpet dick.' That's what the fuck you have."

The thing lowered its head and sprang. Troy had been hoping for just such a move. He'd goaded the creature in anticipation of it. As it closed in on him, he darted to the side and stuck out his foot. Momentum and gravity caught up with his opponent. The cryptid stumbled past him, arms windmilling. Troy slammed the rock into its back, and the monster fell. Troy snatched at his hat, but it was too late. With a cry, the cryptid rolled down the hill, arms and legs flopping helplessly as it crashed into rocks and bounced off them again like a pinball. His hat fluttered along in its wake. It took a very long time for the thing to reach the bottom, where it lay still.

Troy took his time descending the rest of the way to the beach choosing his footing carefully. When, at last, he reached the bottom and stepped out onto the white sand, shells crunched under his feet. He barely felt them. He approached the crumpled form. The creature had broken its neck in the fall, but he wasn't sure if that was before or after it had split its head open on the rocks. Blood and brains cooled in the sand. His hat lay a few inches away. He snatched it up before the gore could reach it. He brushed the sand from the brim and gave the hat a cursory check. It seemed no worse for the wear.

Troy put it back on his head and then spat in the corpse's glassy eye.

"I fucking warned you. Nobody messes with my fucking hat. No one."

Turning, he hurried down the beach toward the landing zone, muttering to himself as he limped through the sand.

Stefan crawled on determinedly, dragging himself hand over fist through the mud. His nails were cracked, and his fingertips were bleeding from dozens of small cuts. When he heard the helicopter's tumultuous approach, he almost wept with relief. Each time his ankle brushed against a branch or stone, he was overcome with white-hot agony. His vision kept blurring from the pain, and his face and forehead were bathed in sweat. Despite that, he couldn't stop shivering.

"Stupid bloody program . . . pack of wankers."

He slid to a halt and collapsed facedown in the muck. Then he raised his head and fumbled for the satellite phone, intent on calling Heffron and advising him that he was on the way. But his hand stopped halfway to his pocket, and despite the haze of pain that he was in, Stefan became suddenly alert.

He smelled the creatures before he heard them—a sour musk floating heavy and sluggish on the night's breeze. He rolled himself off the path and into the underbrush, biting his bottom lip until it bled, to keep from crying out at the torture to his ankle. Then he lay totally still, trying to control his trembling.

Two of the hairy things shuffled by, muttering to each other in a series of garbled grunts and snorts. Their attention was focused on the path, and for one alarming moment, Stefan thought that they might be tracking him. But no, they were going the wrong way, heading farther into the jungle. Perhaps they were hunting someone else, or maybe they'd been positioned as sentries on the beach and were rushing off to report the arrival of the helicopter.

After he was sure they were gone, Stefan exhaled a rush of breath and moaned softly. He thought again to call the ship, but decided to wait a few moments until the pain had settled down again to a more manageable level.

Stefan closed his eyes and waited, while all around him, the jungle began to rustle with life.

CHAPTER TWENTY-FOUR

Becka, Shonette, and Jerry bolted from the cave into the forest. Shonette had developed a limp during their race through the tunnel. Jerry was ready to drop from exhaustion. Becka still had the flashlight, but in her panic, she'd forgotten that she was holding it, and the beam uselessly bounced off the treetops.

"Which way?" she shouted.

Jerry pointed, gasping for breath. "Straight ahead. Don't stop for anything. Just follow me and stick close."

Behind them, the sounds of pursuit echoed from the tunnel mouth. The creatures were close behind. There weren't as many now as there had been at the beginning of the chase. Many of the females had lagged behind or returned to the warren, presumably to guard the young and the frail. But at least a dozen still gave chase, and it sounded as if they would emerge from the cave at any moment.

The three of them dashed into the tree line and crashed through the undergrowth. Now that the storm was over, the mosquitoes had returned in force, but they barely noticed them. Jerry took the lead, snatching the flashlight from Becka's hand, and directing them back toward the base camp. He made an effort not to stare at either woman's breasts, but it was hard to do, even while being chased by marauding humanoids.

Jesus, he thought. *Here I am on a tropical island with two naked women. That's every heterosexual man's dream. Too bad I'm running for my life.*

As they fled, he looked for familiar landmarks and signs of his and Troy's earlier passage through the area. Each time he found one, his confidence and hope grew. Maybe, just maybe, they'd escape. If they could reach the camp, they'd be able to increase their speed on the trail, rather than bounding through the thick vegetation as they were now.

"So Troy is alive?" Becka asked. "And Stefan, too?"

Jerry nodded. "As far as I know, they were before. I don't know about now, though."

"I hope Troy's okay."

"Me too."

"I . . . I've got to rest," Shonette panted. Her limp had grown more pronounced, and she was slowing down. "Please, y'all. I can't . . . catch my breath."

"Just a little farther," Jerry urged.

"I can't . . . make it any farther . . ."

Jerry grabbed her arm and helped her along. Becka took her other arm and assisted. Although they could no longer see the cave, they heard the creatures emerge from it. Their howls and shrieks filled the night.

And then those terrifying cries were answered.

From straight ahead of Jerry, Becka, and Shonette's position.

"Oh shit," Jerry whispered.

Becka halted. "How did they get in front of us?"

Moving quickly, Jerry directed Shonette and Becka into a thick cluster of leafy bushes that were slowly being choked by ivy and overgrown vines. They crawled on their hands and knees to the center of the cluster, and the foliage closed behind them, concealing their location. They peered between the branches and vines, holding their breath and waiting. Seconds later, the now-familiar stench hit them.

A group of male tribe members emerged from the greenery. They appeared tired and haggard. Their shoulders slumped dejectedly, and their heads lolled. When they heard their females' cries, they became alert again and ran to the cave.

Shonette shifted from one knee to the other. She started to whisper something, but Jerry put a finger to his lips. She fell silent again.

When the creatures had passed from sight, Jerry hurried the girls out of their hiding place, still insisting on silence. They crept on, mindful of where they stepped, lest a branch or twig snap under their feet and alert the tribe to their presence. They could hear the things conversing in their guttural language. They sounded pissed off. Jerry couldn't blame them.

Although he didn't speak of it, Jerry was more concerned about Troy now. The mechanic had led the males of the tribe away with his crazed stunt. He'd begun to believe that Troy might possibly survive the chase. That some of the creatures had now returned did not bode well for his friend, though.

They reached the clearing that he and Troy had passed through earlier, when they were tracking the cryptid that had been dragging Roberta's corpse. They increased their pace again. Shonette kept up with them, but she was dragging one leg behind her now. As they crossed through it, they heard a familiar sound—the staccato beat of a helicopter overhead. Their spirits soared and they quickened their pace.

"They're here," Becka said. "Will they land in the usual spot?"

Jerry nodded. "Troy and I thought so. That's where we'd planned to meet up. If he or Stefan are still alive, I'm sure they'll make for it."

Shonette rubbed her arms and shivered. "I hope they've got some clothes for us. Or at least a frigging blanket."

"I'm not looking." Jerry's cheeks turned red. "Just so you know."

Shonette waved her hand dismissively. "Right now, Jerry, I don't really give a shit. Help yourself to an eyeful if it will get us to the helicopter."

The roars of the tribe grew louder. They were clearly upset by the helicopter's arrival. As the three of them reached the far end of the clearing, they heard crashing sounds from behind them, as the creatures gave chase again.

"Go," Jerry shouted. "They're coming back."

Jerry turned the flashlight off so that the monsters wouldn't see it, trusting his instincts and night vision to get them safely back to camp and from there, onto the path to the beach. He grabbed

Becka's hand and pulled her along. Shonette struggled to keep pace beside them. Jerry ducked under a branch, and it snapped back, catching Becka across the chin. She cried out in pain, and their pursuers presumably heard the noise, because, with a triumphant shout, they charged into the clearing.

"Are you okay?" Jerry stared in concern at the red welt on Becka's chin.

Wincing, Becka nodded. "I'm fine. Just go!"

"After everything we've been through tonight," Shonette gasped, "that little knock on the chin is the least of her worries."

Jerry frowned. What, exactly, had the creatures done to them during their captivity? Had his worst fears been realized? Had Becka been raped? He opened his mouth to ask, but then decided against it.

"What?" Becka noticed his expression.

"Nothing," he said. "I'm just glad you're alive."

Despite their situation, she smiled. "Me too."

Jerry's heart beat faster. Then he noticed that Shonette was starting to lag behind.

"Is it broken or sprained?"

"I don't know," she said. "It just hurts like a son of a bitch. Maybe it's just a charley horse. Don't worry about me."

"Do you want me to carry you?"

"No," she insisted. "That will just slow us down more. I'll be okay."

They kept running. Behind them, the sounds of pursuit drew closer. Jerry thought about making a stand, fending off the marauding creatures while the girls got away. But he knew just how foolish that would be. He wasn't Troy. Yes, he might kill a few of them, but there was only one way the battle would end—with him being torn to bits like Pauline, and the rest of the tribe hunting down Becka and Shonette.

The steady thrum of the helicopter's rotors faded, and Jerry felt his spirits sink. Surely they couldn't be leaving already?

"Sounds like they landed," Becka gasped. Her voice was hoarse.

"I hope so," Shonette said. "Otherwise, we're in a lot of trouble."

Jerry leaped over a fallen tree. "You mean more than we are now?"

"Hell," Shonette replied. "I'm just pretending that this is another exile challenge."

The suffocating darkness started to lessen. The sky was slowly turning from black to blue. The moon and stars looked faded. Washed out. Jerry pushed past a tangle of vines, and they emerged suddenly into the ruins of the base camp. Becka and Shonette's eyes widened as they took in the destruction. Jerry, already familiar with the magnitude of the devastation, didn't pause. He snatched up two more splintered lengths of bamboo, and handed one to each of the girls.

"Here. The ends are pointy, so jab or poke with them."

Becka eyed the spear dubiously.

"It's better than nothing," Jerry said. "Let's go."

Becka paused, remembering her diary. There was no telling where it was amidst the wreckage, but a part of her regretted leaving it behind. Then the pursuing creatures hooted and she decided there were no memories of the island that she wanted to take home with her. Better to leave them buried with the diary.

Jerry and Becka sprinted for the path to the beach. Groaning, Shonette limped along behind them, dragging her injured leg through the mud. She halted, leaning against a tree trunk with one hand, and rubbed her thigh with the other. Jerry and Becka stopped and turned. The sounds of the tribe drew closer.

"I'm okay," Shonette said. "Don't stop for me. Get going."

"Come on," Jerry whispered.

Shonette waved him away. "I told you, I'm fi—"

A scrawny cryptid leaped from the greenery on the other side of the tree Shonette was leaning against and slammed into her. They both tumbled to the ground. Shonette sprawled on her back, and the creature straddled her chest. Before she could even muster a scream, it slashed her face with its talons, clawing out her eyes. With its other hand, it plunged its fingers into her mouth and seized her tongue.

Becka started to run to Shonette's aid, but Jerry grabbed her arm and pulled her back. He shook his head and put a finger to his lips.

"B-but . . ."

He shook his head again, more insistent.

"We can't help her," he whispered. "And if we don't take advantage of the distraction, we're dead, too. Here come the others."

As if on cue, the rest of the tribe erupted from the vegetation on the far side of the camp. Shonette uttered a strangled cry, and then her attacker ripped her tongue out by the roots. Dark blood welled up from her ruined mouth. The creature shoved her tongue into its mouth and chewed thoughtfully. Almost as an afterthought, it raked one curved talon across her throat.

Jerry and Becka fled down the path, not waiting to see her die.

Both of them wept.

The first few rays of light were just cresting the horizon when Troy spotted the helicopter. He waved his arms over his head.

"Hey! Over here!"

The powerful spotlight swiveled toward him, and Troy flinched, blinded by the beam. He flung his hands in front of his eyes and cursed. The beam turned away, and he gave the helicopter the finger. Then he limped toward the landing zone. Two shadowed figures ran toward him. A third figure remained at the helicopter, peering out at the jungle through a pair of binoculars. As they approached, Troy got a glimpse of their faces. He didn't know either of their names, but he recognized one as the pilot. He'd seen him before, ferrying Roland Thompson back and forth from the island to the freighter. The other man carried a plastic case with a big red cross on it. Troy guessed that he was an EMT. They rushed to his side.

"I'm Kerry," the medic said, "and this is Quinn, our pilot. Gerling, our other EMT, is up there by the chopper."

"Good day," the pilot said, nodding.

Troy spat blood onto the sand. "What's so fucking good about it?"

Kerry gently put his arms on Troy's shoulders. "Quinn is Canadian. Don't hold it against him."

"Ain't nothing wrong with that," Troy said. "Fucking Canada gave us Rush, after all. But then, on second thought, you gave us Celine fucking Dion, too."

Ignoring the comment, the medic focused on Troy's body. "Are you injured?"

"See this fucking blood? What do you think?"

"I'd say you're hurt."

"Ding, ding, ding! You get the fucking prize."

Kerry shined a small flashlight into Troy's eyes and frowned in concern.

"Get that fucking light out of my eyes, goddamn it."

"Troy, maybe you'd better lie down until I've finished examining you. You might have a concussion."

"I don't need to fucking lie down," Troy said. "What I need is a motherfucking M-16 or a goddamn Uzi. And then I need to get the fuck off this island and call in a tactical nuke strike."

"We'll leave soon enough," Quinn told him. "I was just getting ready to head back for more people. Our initial load was just me, Gerling and Kerry here, in case we needed to immediately transport anyone back to the ship. I'm bringing more crew members with the next run. Where's your friends?"

Troy waved at the jungle. "Out there."

"Do you know their status?"

He shrugged. "I don't know dick. All I know is that we're in a world of fucking shit here, man. But Jerry and Becka will fucking be here. You can trust me on that."

Quinn turned to Kerry. "Get him stabilized. I'll be back in fifteen minutes with more help."

Troy shoved Kerry aside and grabbed the pilot's arm. "You ain't fucking going anywhere, flyboy."

"I beg your pardon?"

"You're not leaving. Jerry and Becka will be here. I promised them we'd fucking wait. So sit your ass down."

Quinn yanked his arm free. "Now look here, buddy. I understand that you people have been through a lot, but you can't just—"

In the darkness, something howled. Quinn and Kerry jumped, startled. At the helicopter, Gerling turned the spotlight toward the jungle. The howl was answered by another, then three more.

"What the hell is that?" Kerry whispered.

"That," Troy said, "is why I want the fucking M-16 and a nuke strike. But never mind that. I've got a very important question for you both."

"What?"

"Either of you guys got a fucking cigarette I can bum?"

"I don't smoke," Kerry said.

Troy turned to the pilot hopefully. Quinn shook his head.

"I quit six months ago."

Troy kicked the sand and sighed. "Just my fucking luck. I'll tell ya, man, just when I think this night can't get any worse . . ."

The howls continued from the jungle, growing louder and closer.

* * *

"She had kids," Becka muttered.

"What?"

"Shonette. She had two kids. We shouldn't have left her."

Jerry's lungs and throat burned, and the muscles in his legs ached. His feet felt like balls of flame, and a blister popped on his heel.

"Just keep running," he panted. "Conserve . . . your breath."

"I can't help it," Becka sobbed. "It isn't right. She was our friend, and we just left her there. After everything she's been through. It's not right."

Jerry started to reply, but suddenly, Becka went limp and collapsed in the middle of the trail. Her eyes fluttered twice, then closed.

"Becka!"

He ran to her side and knelt, relieved to see that she was still breathing—if shallowly. He checked her pulse and found it was steady. When he shook her gently, Becka moaned in response, and lay still.

Snapping twigs and padding footfalls alerted him that their pursuers were catching up again. Jerry tossed his spear aside, picked Becka up and slung her over his shoulders. Then, clenching his jaw, he plodded on. The added weight combined with his weariness slowed him down, and he struggled to find his footing on the slippery terrain. Taking a risk, Jerry darted off the muddy path and into the jungle, still heading for the beach. He heard creatures all around them. The tribe had spread out, trying to flank him.

Becka stirred, muttering something unintelligible.

"I told you we had an alliance," Jerry whispered.

"Me and you all the way to the end. Wasn't that the deal?"

She murmured a response.

"You awake?"

"Mmm-hmm."

"Hang on. We're almost there."

The jungle suddenly gave way to sun-bleached sand. Beyond it, the ocean spread out in both directions, swallowing the world. The sun was just starting to climb over the horizon, and the black sky was streaked with orange, red, and yellow slashes. Jerry spied the network ship, stark against the kaleidoscope of colors.

Holding Becka tightly, he summoned his last bit of strength and ran. He ignored his screaming muscles and joints, ignored the raw feeling on burning heels, ignored the pain in his lungs and throat and how hard his heart was beating. He spotted the stage, and beyond it, the helicopter, sitting in the field. The craft's spotlights bathed the beach in an eerie false dawn. The whirling blades kicked up a swirling cloud of sand.

"Over here," an amplified voice called to them over a bullhorn. "This way!"

Jerry didn't recognize it, but he didn't care. He did as commanded, running for all that he was worth.

"Hang on, Becka. We're going to make it. We're going to—"

The tribe leapt from the jungle on both sides of him and dashed across the sand, seeking to cut him off. Screaming, Jerry lowered his head and barreled through them, shoving them aside with his shoulders. One of the cryptids snatched at Becka's flowing hair, but Jerry jerked her away, leaving the creature clutching loose strands.

Another amplified voice shouted to them. This time, Jerry recognized it.

"Run, you bald fuck! Run your fucking ass off, goddamn it!"

That's Troy, he thought. *That crazy son of a bitch actually did it. He's alive!*

Grinning, Jerry found his second wind. He reached the helicopter, ducking low to avoid the spinning rotors. The hydraulics whined as the pilot powered up. Troy jumped from the chopper, head low, brandishing a battery-powered, handheld bullhorn. He was bare-chested, except for bandages that had been wrapped around him. Blood seeped through them from a dozen wounds. Several of his tattoos were missing sections of flesh.

"Glad you guys could fucking make it," Troy yelled.

They climbed aboard the chopper, and Troy shouted at the pilot to take off. The hydraulics grew louder. Jerry glanced around the interior as he lay Becka on the floor. In addition to Troy and the pilot, there were two EMTs. One of them stared out at the cryptids in shocked disbelief. The other one, keeping his wits about him, bent over Becka and examined her.

"You okay?" Jerry asked Troy.

"I'll live. You look like shit, though."

"I'll be fine."

Troy nodded at Becka. "How is she?"

"Alive."

"What's happening?" the medic examining Becka

asked as the helicopter lifted off the ground. "Where are the others?"

"They're dead," Jerry gasped. "Those things got them."

"Things? What things? What are you talking about?"

"I think they mean those things, Kerry," the pilot hollered, pointing toward the beach.

An army of beasts flooded out of the jungle and dashed across the beach and field. The chopper rose higher. Enraged, the monsters howled at the sky, gnashing their teeth and furiously shaking their fists. One wielded a human arm, waving it like a club. With a pang of guilt, Jerry realized that the arm was Shonette's.

He pulled Becka to him, buried his face in her hair, and cried.

"Everybody strap in," the pilot hollered.

"My God." Kerry stared at the scene below. "If the media gets hold of this before the network has had a chance to put a spin on it—we're screwed."

"Fuck that," Troy shouted. "Put a spin on it? What kind of yuppie corporate bullshit is that? People are fucking dead, man! I ought to toss your ass out the fucking door."

"Are you sure they're all dead?"

Troy glanced at Jerry and Becka, but neither of them were paying attention. He turned back to Kerry and nodded.

"I'm fucking positive, man."

"Our communications technician was in touch with another survivor—Stefan. He was supposed to meet us at the landing zone."

"He's dead, too."

"How do you know?"

"Because I just fucking do, goddamn it. Stefan's dead. So are the others. We go back now, and we'll be fucking dead, too."

"Well, even still, I've got some calls to make. The network executives will need to be advised right away. I'm calling my supervisor. We'll check on Stefan, too."

He fumbled in his jacket pocket and pulled out a satellite phone. Troy sprang forward, grabbed it from him, and flung it out the open door. It plummeted into the midst of the rampaging creatures.

"Hey," Kerry yelled, "what are you doing?"

"Game fucking over, man. Game fucking over."

"You asshole."

Grinning, Troy shrugged. He leaned back against the seat and sighed. He glanced over at Jerry and Becka, but they were sharing a private moment. Troy decided not to interrupt. He'd noticed when they arrived that Becka was naked. It was kind of hard to miss. His gaze strayed to the curve of her lower back, but then he turned his eyes away.

They better send me a fucking wedding invitation. Shit, I'd better be the best man.

Troy patted his head, reassuring himself that his beloved hat was still there, safe and sound. Then he turned his attention back to the medic.

"Hey, Kerry? Let me ask you something."

"What?"

"Is there anybody on board the fucking ship who can give me a fucking cigarette?"

The helicopter soared into the dawn, leaving the island in darkness.

CHAPTER TWENTY-FIVE

Stefan awoke to the sounds of birds. He felt warmth on his face and wondered if it was sunlight. Groaning, he opened his eyes, squinting. The small bird that had been perched on his cheek squawked and took flight. Stefan struggled to sit up.

At first, he didn't know where he was or why. Then his ankle throbbed, and it all came back to him—his injury, crawling along the path, and taking cover here in the thicket. The last thing he remembered was wanting to call the ship. He must have passed out from the pain and exhaustion.

He smacked his lips together. His tongue felt like sandpaper, and his head throbbed in time with his swollen ankle. Cautiously, he rolled his pant leg up, hissing in pain as he did. He blanched when he saw his injury. His ankle was swollen to twice its size, and the flesh around it was black and purple. It felt hot, and the skin turned white when he touched it.

"Not bloody good," he whispered. "Not bloody good at all."

He glanced up at the sky and was surprised to see

daylight. Through the treetops, he saw gulls circling. They seemed to hover in place, floating on the breeze. Their incessant cries set his teeth on edge.

He sniffed the air and noticed a faint but unpleasant odor. Before he could consider it further, he heard something else, in the distance. The sound was lower and deeper than the squawking birds. It took him a moment to recognize the sound. It was the helicopter, but to his bewilderment, it sounded like it was flying away, rather than coming closer. His stomach lurched in panic, and his heart hammered in his chest. Could the bastards really be leaving without him?

Moaning in fear, Stefan fumbled for the satellite phone. He pulled it free and flipped it open. It took a moment for the unit to power up.

"Mr. Heffron had better answer if he knows what is good for him. I demand an explanation for this."

Before he could dial, two things happened.

The phone rang in his hand, and all around him, the bushes rustled.

Stefan was overwhelmed with the now-familiar scent of the creatures. He took a breath and held it.

The phone rang again. The bushes rustled more violently. Twigs snapped. Something growled, low and menacing.

Exhaling, Stefan answered the phone. "Yes?"

"Stefan? It's Brett Heffron. They said you weren't at the landing zone."

"No, I wasn't."

"Well, are you okay? What's happening? What's that noise in the background?"

"Apparently, I'm not alone."

"What? Stefan, I don't understand. What's going on?"

"It's quite simple, really." Stefan cackled as the stench grew overpowering. Despite his laughter, tears coursed down his muddy cheeks. "I win, Mr. Heffron. I win! I'm the last one left on the island."

"Ste—"

"I've got to go now. I have company."

"What are you—"

"Good-bye, Mr. Heffron."

He turned off the phone, tossed it into the underbrush, and hobbled to his feet. It felt like somebody was jabbing knives through his swollen ankle, but he welcomed the pain, because it meant that he was still alive—even if it was the last sensation he'd feel.

The growls increased.

"I win," he said. "I'm the last one left on the island. I'm the last man standing."

The bushes parted, and Stefan's laughter turned to screams.

The creatures fell upon him, crushing him to the ground.

EPILOGUE

Jerry awoke in a panic and bolted upright in bed. He clenched the satin sheets in his fists and gasped for breath. He heard the distant drone of traffic. Somewhere a dog barked.

Once again, he'd dreamed that he was back on the island. In the dream, he and Troy were creeping through the tunnel, but when he turned around, Troy was gone. Then he heard the cryptids racing toward him. Their cries and footfalls echoed off the walls. Unlike in real life, the creatures spoke English, and they shouted threats and promises of all the things they'd do to him when they finally caught him. Jerry crawled into a side tunnel and was confronted by a squiggly, black, cloud-shaped mass with malevolent red eyes glowing at its center. A furry hand fell on his shoulder. Talons dug into his flesh. That was when he'd woken up.

He took a few deep breaths and rubbed his face, waiting for the last vestiges of the nightmare to dissipate. He dreamed about the island at least once a week, but this had been the worst one in at least six months. He hadn't confided in anyone about the nightmares, except for his psychiatrist. She said that he suffered from post-traumatic stress disorder, but that in time, it might pass. Jerry wasn't so sure about that. His grandfather had served in Vietnam, and the old man had suffered from PTSD until the day he died after complications from early-onset Alzheimer's disease.

Until applying for *Castaways*, Jerry had thought that was the most horrible way to die imaginable.

He knew better now.

And he now understood how his grandfather had felt.

Sometimes, when he was at his lowest, Jerry wondered if maybe Richard, Sal, Ryan, Shonette, and all the others weren't the lucky ones. After all, it was over for them. They didn't have to live with the aftermath. They didn't have to experience things like guilt and depression and anger. They didn't have to suffer panic attacks every time they saw the ocean or turned on the television.

When his pulse was back to normal and the dream was safely banished, he slid out of bed and put on his robe and slippers. The soft material felt luxuriant against his skin. The smell of fresh-cut flowers filled the room. He glanced at the clock and saw that it was six in the morning. The first few rays of sunlight crept through the drapes. He considered going out onto the patio and having his morning coffee. Maybe make some mimosas and start the day right.

Becka stirred beneath the sheets and opened her eyes. Blinking, she glanced around the bedroom. She seemed stiff. Tense. Jerry smiled at her, and she visibly relaxed. His smile grew bigger. When she returned the gesture, he forgot all about his bad dream. Even after all this time, she still made him feel giddy when she smiled. He hoped that feeling would never fade.

"Good morning, sunshine."

"Good morning yourself." Yawning, she stretched her arms over her head. The sheet slipped down, revealing her breasts. "How did you sleep?"

"Okay," he lied. "How about you?"

"Pretty good."

Jerry knew that Becka was lying, as well. A few hours before, he'd heard her moaning in her sleep, whimpering and crying out. He'd gently shaken her and whispered in her ear until she'd stopped.

"Troy's private jet lands at eleven this morning," Jerry said. "I'll send the car to pick him up."

"Isn't it funny?"

"What?"

"Troy, with his private jet and everything."

"No funnier than us, living in Beverly Hills and owning a line of successful, upscale graphic novel boutiques. You can't say we didn't put that money to good use. I just thought it was funny that the first thing Troy wanted to buy was a million-dollar mobile home."

"How about wanting to get a glass display case for his hat?"

Jerry snickered. "He's a weird dude, but I love him."

Becka stretched again. "Everyone must think the three of us are eccentric."

"Why?"

"Pick a reason. Maybe because we all refuse to own televisions."

"Screw 'em. Who cares what they think?"

A few days after their rescue, while they were still recovering in the freighter's sick bay, the network officials met with Jerry, Becka, and Troy. A videotape had been found on the island, the contents of which revealed that Matthew had been a member of the Sons of the Constitution and had killed Jesse in cold blood. It was assumed that he'd done the same to Mark. They showed the tape to the three of them and suggested that their fellow contestants might have met the same fate. Then they told Becka, Jerry, and Troy how financially lucrative it would be for them if they agreed. The executives had contracts with them, drawn up by lawyers just hours after the massacre's discovery. The offered amount was for a lot more than they'd have won by participating in the show. They held out for more—and got it. They also insisted that the other contestants' families be compensated, as well.

Federal investigators had echoed the terrorism angle. The three of them had often wondered just how the network had managed to get investigators to go along with it, but they never found out for sure. Had they sent somebody in to clean up the evidence before investigators arrived? Or were they in on the cover-up as well? He'd seen a few conspiracy theories floated online—how the government had actually killed all the contestants in a bungled operation to get Matthew, how the government had killed everyone so they could blame it on the Sons of the Constitution, how the island had really been an alien base, how something or someone called Black Lodge had accidentally exterminated everyone on the island with some kind of top-secret weapons test. Each crackpot theory was more laughable than the next. None of it was close to the truth, although the truth was just as bizarre.

"I still think we should move somewhere in the Midwest," Becka said. "Someplace where we can't see the ocean. I could go the rest of my life without seeing it again."

"We can if you want to," Jerry agreed. "We can certainly afford it."

She smiled slyly. "We could move to Montana and hunt Bigfoots."

"Bigfeet," he corrected her. "And no thanks. You've had enough of the ocean. I've had enough of cryptozoology for a while."

"As long as we're together, Jerry, I don't care what we do. We've got a pretty strong alliance, after all."

He smiled, but didn't reply.

Becka frowned slightly. "What's wrong?"

"I keep asking myself if we did the right thing. Taking the money in exchange for our silence. Don't the other families have a right to know what happened to their loved ones? Did we do the right thing, Becka?"

"We did the human thing. I don't know if it was right or wrong, but I don't care. Anybody else in our situation would have done the same thing."

"Maybe you're right."

"You're a good man, Jerry. You deserve a little happiness. We both do."

He leaned over the bed and kissed her. Becka's lips were soft and warm. She sighed, nuzzling his ear. Then she threw back the sheets, took his hand, and pulled him to her. They made love, and neither of them thought about the island.

Later, they sat on the patio and drank mimosas and watched the sun rise.

They felt like winners.

AUTHOR'S NOTE

In late 2001, I was asked to contribute a story to an anthology called *In Laymon's Terms*. The book, published by the venerable Cemetery Dance Publications and edited by Kelly Laymon, Richard Chizmar, and Steve Gerlach, was to be a tribute to Richard Laymon, who had passed away earlier that year. Dick Laymon was not only one of my all-time favorite writers, he was also a friend and mentor. So I was very honored to participate.

If, like me, you are a big fan of Laymon's work, then you are probably familiar with the *Beast House* series, which consists of three novels and one novella: *The Cellar*, *Beast House*, *The Midnight Tour*, and *Friday Night in Beast House*. The central plot of this series involves a roadside attraction in the fictional town of Malcasa Point, California. This attraction, the Beast House, is inhabited by a repugnant, savage race of beings known only as "beasts" (thus, the rather apt name for the place). In one of the books, Dick offers a brief origin for the beasts—they are a race of subhuman creatures, brought to our shores from an island off the coast of Australia by an old sea captain. The beasts then slaughter pretty much everyone they come into contact with. They are some real mean bastards. They like to fuck and kill, and fuck what they kill.

When I was asked to contribute a story for *In Laymon's Terms*, I remembered the beasts' origin. The reality television show *Survivor* was very popular at the time, and I was a big fan of the program. (I still am, although I loathe most of the rest of the reality-television genre.) I wondered what would happen if a reality show was filmed on the island where Laymon's beasts had originated—and there were still beasts lurking there. I thought it would be a pretty cool story. Most of my ideas start that way. "Wouldn't it be cool if . . . ?"

So I wrote it.

In the original draft of the story, I used both the beasts and a minor character from *Friday Night in Beast House* named Broadway Joe. At the request of the Laymon estate, I changed the monsters to something of my own creation and dropped the character of Broadway Joe, replacing him with Troy. The result was a short story called "Castaways."

The story was accepted for *In Laymon's Terms*, and also appeared in my own short-story collection, *Fear of Gravity*. A few years after its appearance in *Fear of Gravity*, it was also adapted into a graphic novel, written by Nate Southard, called *Brian Keene's Fear*. Readers have often asked me to consider turning the short story into a full-length novel. Well, your wish is my command. You hold your request in your hands. Never let it be said that I'm not open to feedback from my readers. (If this were the Internet, I'd post a smiley face icon right here, but since it's not the Internet, feel free to pencil one in yourself if you want.)

I decided that in order to novelize the story, I should remove it even further from the *Beast House* mythos, firmly setting it in my own ever-expanding multi-verse. So after talking about it with Kelly Laymon and Don D'Auria, my editor at Leisure, that's what I did. Eagle-eyed, longtime readers will probably notice some subtle links that firmly ground this novel in my own mythos (including ties to *Dead Sea*, *The Conqueror Worms* and *Terminal*).

One other note. The idea of a race of sub-beings using human females to propagate their species is one I've used before (in the novel *Ghoul*). I generally try not to repeat themes, but in the context of this tale, it seemed appropriate. I'm also not a big fan of using rape to convey a sense of horror in a novel. That's a tired trope, and many times, instead of experiencing horror, the reader is left with nothing but literary misogyny. I debated it for a while. But to have not used rape here would have been a cheat. It would have lessened the realism of the book. Let's be honest—the tribe is slowly dying off, and more and more young are being born with serious birth defects. Given those constraints, their actions were in line with the plot.

Anyway, as I said before, I consider the short story to be a tribute to Richard Laymon, and thus, the novel is too, by extension. As you probably noticed, the book is dedicated to him. (It's also dedicated to Bruce "Boo" Smith and Dan "UK" Thomas, both of whom were big fans of my work, ardent supporters of the genre, and guys who always brightened everyone's day on the BrianKeene .com message boards. Both Bruce and Dan passed away before this book was published.)

The idea for both versions of *Castaways* was 100 percent inspired by Richard Laymon and his wonderful *Beast House* stories, and I'd like to think he would have dug this. Dick Laymon was a lot of things to a lot of people. Look at his incredibly prolific body of work and you'll understand how he influenced an entire generation of horror writers. He was always very gracious with his time and assistance. Anytime you read a novel by myself, Edward Lee, J. F. Gonzalez, Tom Piccirilli, Brett McBean, Steve Gerlach, Geoff Cooper, Mike Oliveri, Weston Ochse, or many other authors from our generation, keep in mind that it was Richard Laymon (among others) who had a hand in our development—be it a kind word or an introduction to an editor or just sharing a beer and a laugh. He is missed by many, but he is certainly not forgotten. And he will be remembered for a long time to come through his many works.

As always, thanks for buying this book and my other books, and for taking the time to drop by my website and tell me what you thought of them. I wish I could return the favor and buy each and every one of you a beer (or a coffee, if you prefer), but that would get pretty expensive, and I'm fairly sure my wife wouldn't let all of us hang out in my backyard. Just know that I really appreciate your continued support. You keep reading them, and I'll keep writing them.

Brian Keene
Heart of Darkness, Pennsylvania
March 2008

Turn the page for an advance look at Brian
Keene's next terrifying novel . . .

URBAN GOTHIC
Coming in August 2009

"Shit happens," Javier grumbled from the backseat.

A car rolled slowly past, its underside almost scraping against the road. The windows were tinted, and they couldn't see the driver, but the vehicle's stereo was turned up loud enough to rattle their teeth.

Brett sighed in frustration. "Now's not the time, Javier."

But he's right, Kerri thought, gazing out the passenger window. Javier is right. There's no rhyme or reason to it. Sometimes, events just spin out beyond our control. Sometimes, no matter how careful we are, no matter how much we try sticking to the script or routine, our day gets off track, and nothing we say or do will fix it before night comes around. Shit happens—and when it does, things get fucked up.

Like now.

However, while the situation they currently found themselves in was indeed fucked up, it wasn't just a simple case of "shit happens"—at least, not entirely. Perhaps some of it could be blamed on fate, but the rest of it was purely Tyler's fault.

Kerri wondered how it was possible to simultaneously love and hate her boyfriend—because that was how she felt.

They'd driven in from the suburbs in East Petersburg to attend the Monsters of Hip Hop show at the sprawling Electric Factory club in downtown Philadelphia. While the venue wasn't in the best part of the city, the show had definitely been worth it. Headliner Proper Johnson and the Gangsta Disciples had gathered some of the biggest names in hardcore, gritty hip hop for a nationwide benefit tour—Lil' Wyte, Frayser Boy, T-Pain, Lil' Wayne, Tech N9ne, The Roots, Mr. Hyde, Project: Deadman, Bizarre, Dilated Peoples, and Philadelphia's own Jedi Mind Tricks. The girls preferred hip pop, rather than hip hop, but they tagged along anyway because it was an excuse for all of them to hang out together and get out of East Petersburg for a night. They were in Philadelphia, after all. It sure beat the hell out of hanging around Gargano's Pizzeria for another evening.

Kerri and Tyler.

Stephanie and Brett.

Javier and Heather.

They'd been friends since elementary school—long before they'd actually started dating and paired off into couples. Now things were changing. Graduation was over. College loomed. Adulthood. The real world. Although none of them verbalized it, they all knew that this could very well be the last time they'd all be together like this. Most of them were going their own ways in a few months, so they were determined to live it up.

When the concert was over, all six of them had shuffled out to the parking lot with the rest of the crowd. They piled into the old station wagon that Tyler had inherited from his brother Dustin, after Dustin went off to Afghanistan. Dustin had always kept the car running like it was fresh off the factory floor. Once, when they were all at the lake, he'd stood a quarter on its edge on the hood of the car and cranked the engine. The quarter stayed where he put it, because the engine in that Ford Woody had been tuned to purr when it idled. He'd also tuned it to roar when he stomped the accelerator. When he'd first gotten the car, Tyler had made an effort to keep it in perfect shape. But eventually, he ran it ragged, just like everything else in his life. When Kerri asked him about it, Tyler's excuse was that he wasn't as good with his hands as his brother had been. He'd never been mechanically inclined. Tyler's talents lay elsewhere—scoring a bag of weed or six third-row tickets for this concert. He liked to call these things "acquisitions." He was the closest thing to street smart they had in East Petersburg, and he knew it, too.

Half deaf from the concert and adrenalized by the late hour, they'd driven out of the parking lot with the windows down, laughing and shouting at one another. It was summer, and they were young. Happy. Immortal. And all the bad things out there in the world?

Those bad things were supposed to happen to someone else.

Until they'd happened to them.

It started five minutes after pulling out of the lot

when Tyler decided to visit a friend of his on the other side of the river, in Camden. No one in their right mind went into Camden, New Jersey, after dark, but Tyler swore he knew what he was doing. He'd promised them this friend had great weed.

Tyler had navigated the station wagon through a bewildering maze of city streets, insisting that he knew where he was going. He got flustered when the road he needed was under construction and closed. Orange-and-white oil drums topped with flashing yellow lights barred their passage.

"What the fuck is this all about?" Frowning, Tyler had pointed at the large, dented ROAD CLOSED sign.

"It's blocked off," Brett told him.

"I know it's blocked off, shithead. Thanks for your help."

"You need a GPS," Stephanie said. "My parents bought me one for my car. I never get lost."

Tyler's frown deepened. "Your parents buy you everything, princess."

Stephanie shrugged. "Well, if you had one, we wouldn't be sitting here now, would we?"

"I'm surprised you know how to program the fucking thing."

Sensing his growing agitation, Kerri had tried to calm her boyfriend. "Tyler, why don't we just turn around and go home. We don't need weed that bad."

Tyler's handsome features pinched together for a second, and she could almost see him trying to control his temper. In private, when it was just the two of them, Tyler could be really sweet, but he also had anger issues. When his temper got the better of him, things usually ended badly. He'd never hit her or anything like that. But he said things—words more hurtful than any blow.

He shook his head. "It's all good. I can get around this. I just have to go down one block and then backtrack."

The detour ended up taking them in the opposite direction of the Ben Franklin Bridge. Tyler's calm demeanor cracked when they'd found themselves driving on a meandering stretch of the Lower Carlysle Thruway, which went through some of the worst parts of the city. The road was rutted and cracked. The car bounced over a gaping pothole, thumping and rattling in ways that would have surely sent Dustin after his little brother with an assault rifle. Something scraped along the underside of the vehicle.

"Fuck me," Tyler whispered under his breath.

"You wish," Kerri replied.

They'd continued down the street, slowing to a crawl. The landscape grew steadily bleaker.

"Jesus," Brett gasped. "Look at these houses. How can anybody live like this?"

They'd stopped at a red light. Thumping bass from the car next to them rattled their windows. A large group of black youths stood on the street corner, peering in at them. When one of the teens sidled up to the station wagon, Tyler had gunned it, racing through the light. A car horn blared behind them.

"Lock the doors," Heather urged, staring wide-eyed.

Tyler had ignored her. "Where the fuck is the turn?"

From the back of the station wagon, Javier said, "Dude, there's a sign for Route 30. Doesn't that take us back to Lititz?"

"I don't want to go back to Lititz. I want to go to Camden."

"Fuck Camden," Javier shouted. "Have you looked outside? You're gonna get us carjacked!"

Tyler stared straight ahead. "You guys worry too much. For fuck's sake, we just came from a rap concert. Now ya'll are worried about driving through the city? Bunch of white-bread motherfuckers."

"In case you haven't noticed," Brett said, "you're white too, Tyler."

"I'm not white. I'm Italian."

Javier sighed.

"Everybody just calm the fuck down," Tyler continued. "We'll be fine. Long as you don't fuck with anybody, they won't fuck with you."

He'd kept his voice calm, but Kerri could tell his anger was building inside.

The last of his facade had shattered when the engine light came on and steam began billowing out from under the hood, blanketing the windshield.

"Shit!"

The engine sputtered, then died. The radio and headlights died with it. Their speed decreased from forty miles an hour to five. They'd rolled a few more yards and came to a halt. Another car horn blared behind them, the driver impatient. Tyler had tried turning on the emergency blinkers, but they didn't work.

"Motherfucker." He opened the door, got out, and waved the other car around them. Then he ducked back into the station wagon and pulled the hood latch.

"Stay in here," he said, and then he'd stomped off to the front of the car.

And now, here they were—broken down in the middle of the hood.

Tyler's fault.

Kerri shook her head, done with her ruminations.

"Shit happens," Javier grumbled again.

Heather nodded in agreement. "He just had to go to Camden tonight. If he'd listened to us, we'd be on the turnpike by now."

"Maybe we should go out and help him," Brett suggested. "I mean, Tyler doesn't know shit about cars. What's he gonna do out there?"

Kerri frowned. "Tyler said to stay in the car."

"Screw that," Brett said. "It's hot in here, and there's no way I'm rolling the windows down."

He opened the door and got out. Sighing, Javier and Heather followed him. Stephanie remained seated, rummaging through her purse. She pulled out a pink cell phone and flipped it open. The display glowed in the darkness.

"Who are you calling?" Kerri asked.

"My parents. They've got Triple A. They can send a tow truck for us."

"Hold off on that. Let's just wait a minute and see what's wrong with the car first."

"Screw that," Stephanie said. "I'm not sitting around here waiting to get mugged. Have you taken a look outside? It's like Baghdad out there."

Kerri rubbed her temples. A headache was forming behind her eyes.

"Please, Steph? Let's just wait a few minutes. If you call them now, you're just going to piss Tyler off even more."

"I don't care."

"I know you don't, but you're not the one who has to deal with him when he's angry. Please? Do it for me?"

Stephanie shook her head. "I don't know why you put up with that shit."

"I won't have to for much longer. Once I'm at Rutgers, things will be different. We'll drift apart."

"Why not just break up with him now?"

Kerri paused before answering. "Because I care about him, and I don't want to hurt him. I'm afraid of what he might do."

"To you?"

"No. To himself."

Stephanie didn't respond. She quietly closed her cell phone and stuffed it back into her purse.

Kerri murmured, "I don't think Tyler likes himself very much."

"You think?" Stephanie's tone was sarcastic. "What was your first clue?"

Scowling, Kerri opened the passenger door and stepped out into the street. Stephanie quickly followed, mouthing apologies. They joined the others, huddled around the open hood. They guys were peering down at the engine. Heather was smoking a cigarette. Kerri bummed one from her. Stephanie made a disgusted sound when she lit up.

Tyler raised his head and looked at them. "I thought I told you guys to stay in the car."

"It's hot in there." Stephanie tossed her head.

"Want me to call my parents? They've got Triple A."

"No." Tyler returned his attention to the engine. "We can figure this out."

"You're doing a great job so far."

Tyler's knuckles curled around the car's front grille, clenching tightly. Kerri motioned at Stephanie to be quiet.

Even though the sun had gone down, it was still excruciatingly hot outside. The heat seemed to radiate off the sidewalks and the pitted blacktop in waves. The air was a sticky, damp miasma. Kerri tugged at her blouse. The sheer cloth stuck to her sweaty skin. She took another drag off the cigarette, but with the extreme humidity, it was like inhaling soup. She smelled food cooking. Gasoline. Piss. Booze. Burned rubber. Hot asphalt. Stephanie's perfume. The mix was nauseating.

Coughing, Kerri breathed through her mouth and looked around, nervously studying their surroundings. She'd heard the term urban blight before, but had never really understood it until now.

They were surrounded by decrepit row homes, none of which looked hospitable. In the darkness, the houses seemed like monoliths, endless black walls with deteriorating features. Dim lights burned behind dirty curtains or through broken windows—some of which were covered with clear plastic or stuffed with soiled rags. Many of the buildings were missing roof tiles, and the outside walls had gaps where bricks or boards had crumbled away. None of the homes had a yard, unless you counted the broken sidewalks, split by the roots of long-dead trees and cracked by blistering summers and frigid winters. Cockroaches and ants scuttled on the sunken concrete amidst crack vials, cigarette butts, and glittering shards of broken glass. Ruptured garbage bags sat on the curbs, spewing their rotten contents into the street.

The sidewalks and stoops were deserted, except for a surly-looking gang of youths lurking on the street corner about a block away. Kerri's gaze lingered on them for a moment before moving on. The only businesses on the street were a pawn shop, a liquor store, and a newsstand. All three were closed for the night and shuttered with heavy steel security gates. Many of the buildings had graffiti painted on them. So did some of the junk cars sitting along the curb. A few of the vehicles looked abandoned—shattered windshields, missing tires replaced with cement blocks, bodies rusted out and dented.

She turned in the opposite direction and looked farther down the street. It seemed to terminate in a dead end. Beyond the row homes was a large swath of debris-covered pavement, as if all the buildings in that section had been knocked down. Chunks of concrete and twisted metal girders jutted from the devastation. Beyond that was a single house, much larger than the rest of the row homes. Kerri thought it must be at least a hundred years old, judging by the architecture. She supposed at one time it had been very pretty. Now it was a desolate ruin—in even worse condition than the other row homes. It seemed to squat at the end of the street, looming over the block. Beyond it was a vacant lot, over-grown with weeds and brambles. Behind that was a tall, rusted chain-link fence.

Kerri stared at the house. She shivered, despite the heat. She had the uncanny impression that the abandoned building was somehow watching them.

Tyler cursed, rapping his knuckles against the car, and Kerri's attention returned to her friends.

"Maybe we should call Steph's parents," Brett suggested. "It's pretty late, and we're in a bad neighborhood, dog."

Tyler glanced up at him, opened his mouth to respond, and then stared over Brett's shoulder. Kerri saw his face twitch. She and the others turned around to see what had attracted his attention.

The group of black men that she'd noticed a moment before were now slowly approaching them. The group appeared to be about the same age as they were. Most of the youths were dressed in either athletic jerseys or white tank tops. Their pants sagged almost to their kneecaps, held up only by tightly cinched belts and the tongues of their high-topped sneakers, exposing their boxer shorts. Gold rings and necklaces completed the adornment. A few of them wore backward ball caps on their heads. The one in the lead wore a black do-rag. Gold hoops glittered from each of his ears. He reminded Kerri of a pirate.

"Oh shit," Brett whispered. "What the hell do they want?"

Stephanie whimpered. "We're going to get mugged."

Brett nodded. "This is bad. This is really fucking bad."

"Calm the hell down," Javier said. "You guys automatically assume that just because they're black, they're gonna mug us?"

"Look at them," Brett insisted. "They sure as hell don't look like they're here to sell us fucking Girl Scout Cookies."

Javier glared at him, speechless.

The group shuffled closer. All of them walked with a sort of lazy, loping gait. Kerri's nervousness increased. She wanted to agree with Javier, but then she considered their situation and their surroundings. Panic overwhelmed her. She reached for Tyler's hand, but he was stiff as stone.

"Shit," Brett moaned. "Fucking do something, you guys!"

Javier shoved him. "Dude, chill out. You're acting like an asshole."

When the group was about ten feet away, they stopped. The leader stepped forward and glared at them suspiciously.

"The fuck ya'll doing around here?"

His voice was deep and surly. He stood tensed, as if ready to spring at them.

Stephanie and Heather clasped hands and took a simultaneous step backward. Brett slipped in behind them. Javier stepped out from behind the car and faced the group. Tyler slowly slammed the hood, and then joined him. Kerri stayed where she was. Her feet felt rooted to the spot. Her heart pounded beneath her breast.

Another of the black youths spoke up. "Man asked you a question."

"We don't want any trouble," Tyler said.

Kerri cringed at the plaintive, pleading tone in his voice.

"Then you in the wrong place," the leader said, grinning.

His friends chuckled among themselves in response. He held up a hand, and they immediately fell silent.

"Come into this neighborhood after dark," he continued, "then you must be looking for trouble. Or dope. So which one is it?"

"Neither," Javier challenged. "We had a little car trouble. That's all. Just called for a tow truck and they're on the way." He paused. "Should be here any minute now."

The leader elbowed the gangly kid next to him. "You hear that shit, Markus? He said a tow truck is on the way."

Markus smiled and nodded. "I heard that, Leo. What you think?"

The leader—Leo—stared at Javier as he responded. "I think this esse be bullshitting, ya'll. Ain't no tow trucks come down here after dark. Not to this street."

Javier and Tyler glanced at each other. Kerri saw Tyler's Adam's apple bobbing up and down in his throat.

"Now for real," Leo said. "What ya'll doing down here? You looking to score?"

"M-maybe," Tyler said. "What you got?"

Leo stepped closer. "The question is, what you got? How much money you carrying?"

Oh shit, Kerri thought. Here it comes. Next, they'll pull out a knife or a gun.

"W-we came from the M-monsters of H-hip Hop," Brett stammered, hidden behind the girls. "We're j-just trying to g-get home."

The group broke into raucous laughter. Kerri couldn't tell if it was over the all too apparent fear in Brett's voice, or the fact that a bunch of white, obviously suburbanite kids had been at a hardcore rap concert.

Leo glanced at the car, then at each of them. Kerri felt his eyes lingering on her. She shuddered. Then his gaze flicked back to the car again.

"Alright," he said, "let's handle this shit nice and easy. Ya'll give us—"

"Fuck you, nigger!"

Kerri was just as surprised as Leo and his cronies. She heard feet pounding on the pavement and turned to see Brett running away, racing toward the large abandoned house at the end of the block. A second later, Stephanie and Heather dashed off after him. Stephanie's cell phone slipped from her grasp as she fled and clattered onto the pavement. She didn't stop to retrieve it. Tyler chased after them, shouting. Javier and Kerri stared at each other for the beat of one heart, and then he grabbed her arm and pulled her along.

"Come on!"

"Hey," Leo shouted. "The fuck did you just call me?"

"Oh Jesus," Kerri gasped. "Oh my God . . ."

"What the hell is wrong with you guys?" Javier called after their fleeing friends. "You assholes are gonna get us killed."

"Shut the fuck up and run," Tyler answered, not bothering to look over his shoulder and see if Kerri was okay.

"Yo," Leo yelled, "get back here. Hey, mother-fuckers. I'm talking to you!"

Kerri screamed as she heard them give chase. Leo had stopped shouting. Their pursuers moved in silence, save for grunts, gasps, and the sound of their feet slapping the sidewalk.

"Go," Javier said, shoving her forward. He kept up the pace behind her, putting himself between Kerri and their pursuers.

The chase continued down the street—Brett in the lead, followed by Stephanie and Heather, then Tyler, with Kerri and Javier bringing up the rear. The strap on one of Heather's sandals broke, and the shoe flew off her foot. She slowed for a second, and Tyler shot past her, not stopping. Crying, Heather kicked off her other shoe and sped up again, running barefoot. Kerri noticed in horror that her friend was leaving bloody footprints. Heather must have cut her foot on some of the broken glass littering the sidewalk. Kerri wondered if the girl even realized it, or if adrenaline and instinct had overridden the pain.

They fled past the row homes and entered the wasteland of jumbled debris. The streetlights in this section weren't functioning, and the shadows deepened around them. Kerri heard something scurrying behind a pile of crumbled masonry and nearly shrieked. Behind them, the sound of pursuit halted.

"Yo," Leo bellowed, "get the fuck back here. You asking for trouble you keep going."

Ignoring him, they made a beeline for the abandoned house. It loomed before them in the darkness. Heather stumbled and fell behind, but Kerri and Javier helped her. Even though the pursuit had stopped, they didn't slow. Kerri's breathing became jagged, more frantic. She tried to calm herself by looking at her friends. Stephanie was mouthing the Lord's Prayer. Brett's face was set in a worried scowl, his steps drunken and dazed. Tyler's eyes were wide and panicked, and beads of sweat dotted his forehead.

Kerri glanced back and saw Leo and the rest of his gang lurking at the edge of the wasteland, slowly milling back and forth. He shouted something, but they were too far away to hear him. Probably another threat. Kerri wondered why they'd given up chasing them so easily. Maybe they were content to busy themselves with Tyler's car. She felt a pang of sorrow. Poor Tyler—Dustin would be livid when he found out.

Javier urged them on faster, careful to step over the worst holes, guiding them around piles of debris. Brett mumbled something, his voice low and on the edge of hysteria.

"Shut the fuck up," Javier spat. "It's your stupid ass that got us into this mess. What the hell were you thinking?"

Instead of responding, Brett quietly sobbed.

"What now?" Tyler asked, conceding to Javier.

"In there." He nodded at the abandoned home. "We hole up inside and call the cops."

"But they'll see us go inside," Heather whispered.

"I don't think so," Javier said. "We can see them back there because of the streetlights. But here, it's dark. I noticed as we were running up—you can't see shit from back there. Just shadows. Long as we're quick and quiet, we should be okay."

Stephanie eyed the house warily. "What if somebody lives here?"

"Look at it," Javier said. "Who's gonna live inside a shithole like this?"

"Crackheads," Kerri answered. "Homeless people. Rats."

Instead of replying, Javier pushed forward, plodding up the sagging porch steps. They groaned under his weight but held. The handrail wobbled when he grasped it for support, and small flakes of rust and paint rained down onto the pavement. The others followed behind him. Kerri studied the rough brick and mortar of the exterior wall. It was covered with sickly, whitish green moss. The windows were all boarded over with moisture-stained plywood sheets. Curiously, unlike the occupied row homes, this abandoned house was free of graffiti.

When they were all on the porch, Javier explored the pitted wooden door. It was misshapen and water-warped, and several coats of paint peeled off it, revealing a variety of faded colors. He found the doorknob, an old cut-crystal affair, and turned it. The door opened with a grating squeal. Dirt and paint flecks fell onto his forearm and dusted his hair. Standing back, Javier brushed the debris away.

"Hello?" Brett's voice was a hoarse whisper. "Anybody home?"

There was no answer.

They peered inside, but the interior was hidden in a deep, oppressive darkness. Kerri had the impression that if she reached her hand out, the darkness would be a tangible thing, capable of sticking to her fingers like tar.

Javier pushed forward, stepping into the gloom. Kerri followed him. Stephanie and Heather hesitated for a moment before proceeding. Brett trailed along behind them, followed by Tyler, who slammed the door shut once he'd stepped through it. The sound echoed throughout the structure. The others glared at him in annoyance.

"We need some light," Kerri whispered.

She pulled out her cigarette lighter and flicked it. The shadows seemed to converge around the flame. Tyler opened his lighter and did the same. Heather, Javier, and Stephanie flipped open their cell phones, adding the weak, green illumination from the display screens.

Kerri turned in a circle, sweeping the lighter around. A cobweb brushed against her cheek. She shuddered, brushing it away. They were standing in a dank, mildewed foyer. A hallway stretched into the darkness. Several closed doors led from it into other parts of the house. Yellow wallpaper peeled away from the dingy walls in large sheets, revealing cracked bare plaster splattered with black splotches of mildew. There were holes in the baseboards where rats and insects had chewed their way through over time.

Something scurried in the shadows—a dry, rustling sound. Heather stifled a shriek.

"Hear anything?" Javier asked Tyler, nodding toward the door.

Tyler leaned close and listened. Then he shook his head and shrugged. "Nothing."

"Maybe they're gone," Brett suggested. "Maybe they gave up."

"And maybe," Tyler said, "they're fucking up Dustin's car while we're standing here. Fuck this shit."

He reached for the doorknob.

"What are you doing?" Kerri whispered.

"Taking a peek outside. I'm just gonna open it a crack."

His hand turned. The knob didn't move. He jiggled it, but it remained motionless. Frozen.

Stephanie squeezed closer to Brett and peered over his shoulder, watching Tyler. "What's wrong?"

"It's stuck or something. Fucking thing won't open."

Javier groaned. "Did it lock behind you?"

"How the hell should I know?"

"Chill, bro. Keep your voice down. We don't want them to hear us."

"Fuck that. I ain't staying in this shithole all night. My fucking brother's car is out there."

"You should have thought of that before."

Tyler wheeled around, facing him. He jabbed a finger into Javier's chest.

"This shit isn't my fault. Brett's the one who called them niggers."

Javier stiffened. His jaw clenched. For a moment,

When she was twelve years old, Kerri's older brother had managed to get some M-80 firecrackers. They were as big as the palm of her hand and made her nervous when she held them. Her brother and his college buddies had shoved the explosive deep inside a watermelon just to see what would happen. When they lit the fuse, there was a titanic clap of thunder followed by a massive spray of seeds and pink pulp and rind.

That was what happened to Tyler's head. Only it wasn't seeds and rind, it was bone and hair and brains. Warm wetness splashed across Kerri's face and soaked through her shirt and bra. She tasted it in the back of her throat. Felt it running down her head and inside her ears. Something hot and vile and solid trickled over her lips. She gagged.

Tyler stood there for a moment, jittering. Then he toppled over with a thud.

Kerri opened her mouth to scream, but Brett beat her to it.

The giant figure lunged toward them.

Kerri thought he was going to punch Tyler, but then he relaxed. He held his hands up in surrender.

"Okay," he whispered. "Okay. Relax. But we can't go breaking that door down, man. If they're still out there, they'll hear us. Our best bet is to go into one of these rooms, find some windows, and see if we can peer through the cracks in the boards. Maybe we can figure out where they are."

Tyler nodded, slumping his shoulders.

"You're right."

He strode forward and opened the first door on his left. The rusty hinges creaked as it swung slowly, revealing more darkness. Kerri stepped up behind him, holding her lighter over his head to illuminate the room beyond the open door.

Tyler hesitated.

And in his hesitation, everything changed.

Shit happened.

Kerri saw the looming, shadowy figure standing on the other side of the doorway. She knew that Tyler saw it, too, because his entire body stiffened. He made no sound. Kerri tried to speak, tried to warn the others, but her mouth suddenly went dry and her tongue felt like sandpaper. Her breath hitched in her chest.

The person inside the room was impossibly large. She couldn't make out any features, but its head must have nearly been touching the ceiling. The figure's shoulders were broad, and its torso was thick as an oil drum. There was something in the figure's hand. It looked like a giant hammer.

Tyler moaned.

There was a flash of movement.

GET FREE BOOKS!

You can have the best fiction delivered to your door for less than what you'd pay in a bookstore or online. Sign up for one of our book clubs today, and we'll send you *FREE* BOOKS* just for trying it out... **with no obligation to buy, ever!**

As a member of the Leisure Horror Book Club, you'll receive books by authors such as **RICHARD LAYMON, JACK KETCHUM, JOHN SKIPP, BRIAN KEENE** and many more.

As a book club member you also receive the following special benefits:

- **30% off all orders!**
- **Exclusive access to special discounts!**
- **Convenient home delivery and 10 days to return any books you don't want to keep.**

Visit www.dorchesterpub.com or call 1-800-481-9191

There is no minimum number of books to buy, and you may cancel membership at any time.

*Please include $2.00 for shipping and handling.